DOWN FOR THE COUNT

KARLEY BRENNA

*For the girls who love a man on his knees—mentally and physically.
Let the begging commence.*

IMPORTANT NOTE

Dear Reader,

If you know Beckham, you know he was going through some things throughout the previous book. That being said, those things will be described in great detail within these pages. Your mental health is important, so please take care when reading these subjects. If at any point Beckham's experience becomes too much, don't hesitate to put yourself first.

This book includes the following: grief, depression, anxiety, discussion of past instances of over-indulging in alcohol, conversation of alcoholism, discussion of sobriety, brief conversation of a sibling fight, toxic parents, neglecting a child, insinuation of suicidal thoughts, brief mention of Alzheimer's, endangerment of a pregnant person (no harm comes to the baby), mention of a c-section, mention of a toxic ex, on page gun use, and kidnapping.

"A cowboy never says goodbye, it's not in his nature."
- Kurt Philip Behm

1

BECKHAM

I *killed him.*

That's what ran through my mind as I stared at the coffin sitting at the head of the aisle.

My best friend died because of me. And because of me, he wouldn't live to see his thirtieth birthday. Hell, he wouldn't even live to see his twenty-eighth birthday— the one he was supposed to be celebrating in four and a half months. Instead, *I* would be there on that date. Living. Breathing. Doing everything he should've been doing.

What a selfish fucking thing it was to die.

Grieving was cruel. I was happy before all of this, laughing at Garrett's jokes over the stupidest shit, watching him eat dirt every time he got bucked off the back of a bronc. He was the whole reason I got more serious with saddle bronc riding to begin with. The reason I packed a duffel bag full of clothes and hit the road and had the best fucking time of my life.

And now he was dead.

And I got to keep the memories.

Like I said—cruel. Selfish. Horrible.

Now, I sat in the back row at yet another funeral, remembering all of it.

But Garrett's burial wasn't today.

It was months ago.

Not an ounce of guilt had lifted off my shoulders since then, cinderblocks of regret holding them so far down I might as well be six feet under right next to him.

But rather than it being my body in that casket reflecting the cloudy sky above, it was another man.

The man who I wasn't even sure deserved a funeral to begin with.

Parker Summerhill's father.

Parker, the girl I spent the first eighteen years of my life loving, and the last ten years of my life missing.

I hadn't seen her here yet, and I was half convinced she wouldn't even show. I wouldn't blame her if she didn't.

The man was a piece of shit—always drinking instead of doing what any father should: taking care of his family. Her mom wasn't the best either, though I spared her a little more credit. She'd fight and yell with Parker's dad day in and day out, telling him he needed to do better, but then she'd turn around and be just as big of a failure.

But the day after Parker turned eighteen, her mom died.

Her death was both sides of the coin. It ended her

suffering of lung cancer from years of smoking in their little singlewide, but in turn, left Parker with her dad.

Three days after her mom passed, before the funeral was even held, Parker left town.

And I hadn't seen her since. Hadn't heard from her. Hadn't stopped thinking of her. Hadn't stopped hating myself for letting her go, but fuck—I left, too. I said goodbye to her, looked her right in the fucking eyes as I did, and said I couldn't go with her because I wanted to get more involved in rodeo. To ride broncs for money. To enjoy my twenties with my friends. Hell, I *invited* her. But she said no. She wanted to travel to ranches around the country and learn all she could about cattle ranching. I told her I'd take her anywhere she wanted once I struck gold, but that wasn't enough. She wanted out of this town. Wanted to live her life the way she always should have. Really, I think she only wanted to get the fuck away from her dad.

I didn't blame her.

Parker and I, we both had our flaws. Mine was how I set my sights on something, and I got it, no matter the sacrifices. Hers? Wanting to run.

"She's still such a sweet girl, just like when she was growin' up," said some lady with a scratchy, shaky voice from next to me in the back row.

I didn't look up from the photo of Parker's dad's face printed on the thick cardstock in my hand, knowing the lady was talking to her friend on the other side of her.

"Too bad she left like that," the other woman noted, her voice like nails on a chalkboard.

"Wonder where the dad is," the first one added, straightening in her chair to look up the rows of seats.

In the casket, I wanted to say, but kept my mouth shut. Did they even know whose funeral they were attending?

Despite my knowledge of who was about to be placed six feet under for the rest of forever, I wasn't really here for him. No, that bastard didn't deserve an ounce of anyone's attention.

I was here for Parker.

I wasn't afraid to admit I was selfish when it came to that woman. Though I'd had Parker before, I still *wanted* her.

I attributed my bouncing leg and chewed lower lip to grief. The seven stages and all that. And I knew, as much as any, that getting into a relationship so soon after a big loss was probably not the right thing to do.

I was kidding myself, though. Overthinking the possibility of her like I always did. Like when I walked into a gas station store and expected to see her at the soda machine, filling her cup to the brim with Dr. Pepper. Or when I'd show up to a vet office and hope that fate had led her to the same one, on the same day, in the same hour.

Parker likely wanted nothing to do with me. Ten years without talking, and I seriously thought I had a shot? At her dad's funeral, for crying out loud?

And even if I saw her, what was my plan? Go up there and kiss her? Hug her? Share my condolences when we all knew the type of man Clarence Summerhill was?

As if my dreams were coming to fruition at that moment, a woman stepped in front of the casket. Her shoulders were back, black dress hugging her torso while the bottom fanned out in a loose skirt, all the way to her ankles. Her blonde hair was loose, a familiar wild wave to it.

Even though I could only see her back, I knew.

That was my Parker.

Everyone else quieted as she stood there, her head slightly angled to indicate she was staring at the closed casket. Did she see her reflection? Could she see me in it? Did she know I was here?

As fast as she appeared, she began to turn, and I flicked my eyes to my lap. I didn't want her to catch me staring, but in my defense, it was a fucking funeral. Of course I'd be looking at the damn casket.

As the funeral went on, Parker was nowhere to be seen. She didn't reappear until we were all standing, and I found her once again staring—this time at a massive bouquet.

I wondered who cared enough about her father to send a man-sized display of flowers. Kinda morbid, if you ask me. They were going to die, just like him. At least they provided a bit of beauty before they did, though. Her father never extended the same pleasure.

Slowly, Parker turned, and rather than only her back this time, I caught a glimpse of the side of her face. My breath hitched, chilled air swirling in my lungs with the hurricane of emotions that stirred at the sight of her again.

The last ten years had turned her from a teen into a woman, and holy fuck.

Parker was goddamn devastating.

As soon as she turned fully, my eyes fell to her slightly enlarged belly. It was disproportionate to the rest of her body, and the reason for it was clear.

My Parker was...pregnant?

I didn't have time to dwell on that fact as her eyes locked with mine and shock settled into her features. It was as if she'd seen a ghost. Like the man who used to hold her close on those nights when her parents did nothing but fight couldn't really be standing in front of her.

We stared at each other from across the lawn, chairs upon chairs separating us as others snacked, viewed the casket, or reminisced.

Parker and I, we didn't have to voice our past. Those memories flashed in our eyes, electrifying the air that sat heavy between us. Every laugh, every smile, every goddamn tear that ever rolled down her beautiful freckled cheeks—I remembered them.

Maybe this was too much. Too soon after Garrett's passing to be attending a funeral. To be seeing Parker in the flesh. Should I talk to her? Say hi? Run away and pretend I never showed?

Who even sent me the damn invite, anyway?

Could it really have been her? Did she really want me here? I mean, she was pregnant. She probably had a boyfriend, or fuck, a *husband*, and wanted nothing to do with me. Or she wanted me to be her getaway driver from this place. And I'd do it. No question about that. I'd give her twelve more babies if she asked, too.

Fuck, what was wrong with me?

Beckham Bronson, get your shit together.

I forced my feet to move, my boots stamping down the grass as I went. I didn't take my eyes off her, not even as some old man got in my way. I walked around him, stuck in the pull that was Parker's orbit. She seemed hung up in it, too, those big hazel eyes sucking me in like they always did.

I came to a stop in front of her. Every time I blinked, I worried she'd disappear into thin air.

"Hey." I mentally kicked myself. *That* was my greeting after ten years of not seeing her?

"Hey," she repeated softly, her shoulders falling the slightest bit, like simply being in my presence eased some of the tension. She'd done the same thing when we were growing up.

I gestured to the casket before stuffing my hands into the pockets of my brown jacket. "I'm sorry about your dad."

She looked a little awestruck before giving a tiny shake of her head. "Don't be." Her lips pressed into a flat line before she added, "He was an asshole."

I let out a half-assed chuckle. "Yeah. That he was."

She just kept *staring*, ripping me to bits under her penetrating gaze. I was sure I looked about the same right now. I rocked back on my heels, feeling even more anxious than before.

"You look good." Her gaze darted to my felt cowboy

hat before finding my eyes again. "I mean, you've always looked good. You just look…"

"Older," I offered.

"More mature."

The corner of my mouth ticked up. "Was I too childish for you before?"

Her mouth popped open like a fish out of water. "No. No! I didn't mean it like that. I mean"—she waved her hands around—"you used to have chubbier cheeks and not much facial hair and now you have a mustache and a jawline and—" She let out a small laugh that was more air than anything. "Sorry. I guess seeing you after all these years has me tongue-tied."

That, or the pregnancy I was neglecting to bring up. I had to keep reminding myself it wasn't my business. To be fair, her bump was small enough that it still seemed early on, but what did I know about those kinds of timelines?

"I get it. A decade changed you, too. You look beautiful, Parker." I wanted to say so much more, but I held my tongue.

The corner of her mouth raised, her cheeks turning a light pink. Was she blushing over such a simple compliment?

Her hand came up to land on her belly. "Thank you."

I dipped my chin in a nod before tearing my gaze away from hers. I didn't want to, but I had to stop looking at her eventually. I wished I didn't, but it'd be weird if I kept staring. She'd probably think I was having a stroke or something.

"And thank you for coming," she added, pulling my focus back to her. Hell, it hadn't left to begin with.

"Yeah, of course. I mean, I came to support you. I know he was a dick, but he was still your dad."

Her head fell before she forced a small smile. I hated when she did that. "I hadn't seen him in so long. I didn't really want to. Never thought about it, if I'm being honest." She glanced at the casket. "For me, he died the day I left."

"I think he died for a lot of people a long time ago," I admitted. I was one of them. "Where are you staying in town? Didn't they sell your childhood home years ago?"

I caught the way her thumb ran circles over her belly. "Yeah, so I was told. I didn't want it anyway." She dropped her hand. "I'm staying at the motel in town."

I took note of the way she phrased it. She made it sound like she was staying alone. My eyes darted to her left hand, noting she didn't wear a ring. "Boyfriend not come with?"

Her head tilted slightly, like she knew I was skirting the obvious here. "No. I'm single."

She said it so confidently, I nearly started peppering her with questions. But instead, I settled on, "That where you're heading after this?"

"Yeah. Well, I have to take care of some things here first, but after that, I don't really have any plans..."

Her voice became drowned out as my gaze caught on a red Chevy truck in the parking lot behind her. It wasn't exactly identical to his, with its stock tires and no tint on the windows, but it was enough to have my heart rate picking up a notch. I still expected to see him sometimes, even though I was well aware he was never coming back, and when I saw glimpses of who he used to be—whether that was the vehicle he drove or his favorite food on a menu—it'd catch me off guard.

"Right. I should get going." I didn't know if I cut her off. Didn't know if she was waiting for me to reply or excusing herself or what. But I knew I didn't want to leave her. I'd stand here in silence with her all day if she'd let me, but I refused to break down in front of her.

Your childhood crush comes back after years of being gone and her first impression is you having a panic attack in front of her?

Not cute, if you asked me.

It also wasn't cute that I didn't so much as glance her way as I brushed past her and headed toward my truck parked on the street. The oak branches lining the cemetery swayed in the wind, but I didn't so much as hear the leaves rustling as I trudged through dewy grass, my pace a little too fast to not look suspicious.

Hold it together until you get to the damn truck. Then you can yell, cry, punch something—but don't let anyone see. You're better than that.

It felt like forever until my fingers closed around the handle and yanked. I threw myself onto the seat with the grace of a fucking foal, slammed the door, clicked the locks, and pressed my forehead to the cool leather of the steering wheel. My eyes squeezed shut so hard, I thought my eyelids might fuse into one and never open again. But even shutting out the world didn't stop the images of

Garrett's truck wrapped around a tree from flashing in my mind.

The skid marks on the pavement. The lone branch that had fallen, but the tree was still standing. I'd cursed the bird that dropped a seed in that very spot for being the reason that damn tree grew. For being the reason my friend died.

I had attributed his death to the other driver on the road. To the weather. The wind. The goddamn universe.

There were so many people and things to blame.

His mom for inviting him home. His cousin for calling and delaying his departure by five minutes. The gas station pump that hadn't worked, causing him to drive to the one in front of it. And I only knew that because we were such good fucking friends that he'd updated me before I got on the bronc that night.

Garrett: My luck ran out on diesel tonight, brother. Pulled up to the one damn pump that doesn't work

Me: Your luck ran out years ago when I stayed on Ass Pulverizer *longer than you*

Garrett: That's not his real name

Me: Should've been. Drive safe, G. Text me when you get there. Tell your mom I said hi

Garrett: If you love her so much, tell her yourself

And I did. At the same fucking time we told her son goodbye.

My fist slammed into the wheel as a bead of sweat dripped down my temple despite the cold temperature of the cab.

My breath came in short pants, my heart threatening

to burst out of my chest as my fingers dug into my clammy palms.

Think of three things, my therapist used to tell me.

It wasn't fucking helpful. Three things could be anything, and when I was panicking, my mind always reverted to the worst.

I stopped going to therapy after that.

I tried counting to regulate my breathing—in through the nose and out through the mouth for however many fucking seconds—but that didn't shut my mind off. Drinking had, temporarily, but my brother Reed had given me a wake-up call on that, so I quit overindulging in alcohol.

Now I just overindulged in overthinking.

I needed to text Lennon, my oldest brother, and clear my head before I lost myself to the grief.

I lifted my head from the steering wheel, prying my eyes open to take in the trunk of the car in front of me. I forced every ounce of control I had into regulating my breathing. Then I pulled my phone from my jacket pocket and clicked my text thread with Lennon. My fingers were shaking as I typed.

> Me: That motel in town still have no heat?

My gaze stayed fixed to the spot where that little bubble would pop up if he was typing. I sent up a silent thanks when it did.

Lennon: Hasn't for a few weeks, I think. Why?

Me: All I needed to know. Thanks

Lennon: Don't go playing pretend HVAC repairman, Beck. I can give you a job

Me: Busy

Lennon: Of course you are. Let me know how being electrocuted feels

Oh, I knew how it felt. Seeing Parker today was like nothing short of electricity coursing through every nerve in my body. But seeing Parker tonight? Well, that might be the death of me. So long as I could get myself under control enough not to be on the brink of another fucking panic attack in her presence.

2

PARKER

I thought having both of my parents buried six feet under would hurt more than it did. But instead, staring at the popcorn ceiling of my motel room, lying on my back atop the scratchy comforter for a blissful minute before I had to remind myself to shift, I felt nothing but numb.

If I was being honest with myself, not much in my life would change with them gone. My mom had been dead for ten years, and the only shocking thing about my father's death was that I'd figured it would have happened sooner. He never took care of himself, much like how he treated his family. Three years ago, I was almost convinced he'd already passed and I simply wasn't told. Bouncing around the United States from ranch to ranch left me no time to come back to Bell Buckle. Not that I really wanted to, anyway. I'd stayed away so long, I'd convinced myself I had no ties back here. Besides...

Beckham Bronson.

Merely seeing him today stirred up a whole plethora of things I didn't want to be thinking about right now. I had to figure out my next destination, find yet another doctor, remember to take my prenatal vitamins and drink more water and eat healthy and not eat cold sandwiches or sushi or ride a horse.

That last one hurt the most.

But fuck, I had so many things to learn and remember. I didn't have time for distractions. I was doing this on my own, which meant I had to store every little crumb of information in my hormone-crazed brain.

The only thing about today that really tugged at my heartstrings while I stared down at that coffin was the fact that my baby wouldn't have grandparents. Even if my parents hadn't died, I wouldn't have wanted them in my child's life. But on Daniel's side? My child could've had a chance at relatives. But he'd wanted nothing to do with this baby from the moment I told him, so I did what I do best.

I ran.

I just didn't think it'd land me back in my hometown in Idaho.

I glanced at the red digital clock on the nightstand beside the bed, heaving a sigh that my time of resting on my back was over.

My belly wasn't even necessarily big yet, being that I was only four and a half months pregnant, but fuck, my lower back constantly ached. I was dreading the last half of this pregnancy solely for that reason.

I rolled onto my side before shoving to an upright position, but when I got halfway up, a knock sounded on the door. I froze, homing in on that sound like I might've imagined it. It had to have been twenty seconds before a fist rapped against the door again.

I'd paid for the room, and housekeeping wasn't supposed to be in until tomorrow morning, so my only guess was either the motel manager was kicking me out for a declined card, or someone had the wrong door.

I pushed to a stand and padded in bare feet across the uncomfortably itchy carpet before stopping in front of the door and peeking through the little hole. I wasn't exactly short, so thankfully I didn't have to arch my sore feet too much to look out the dirty glass.

The man who stood there with his hands tucked in his jacket pockets made my heart rate spike, which probably wasn't good. Or maybe it didn't matter. God, I needed to stop overthinking everything. My baby was fine.

With one hand wrapped around the cold metal doorknob, I unlocked the dead bolt with the other. As I opened the door, Beckham lifted his head, hazel eyes meeting mine from under the brim of his cowboy hat.

Before I could even get a word out, he was talking. "A motel, Parker?"

My forehead creased, my mouth opening and closing twice before I could speak. "Yeah? I told you that at the— How did you find me?"

He flapped his jacket open as some kind of half-assed shrug. "I followed you."

My brows shot up to my hairline. "You *what*?" I shook my head. "You left before me."

"I didn't leave. I sat in my truck. I saw you leave before anyone else had cleared out."

My lips rolled together as I turned my gaze to the gray sky above him. I needed all the patience I could muster right now.

"Why aren't you wearing socks?"

My eyes darted back to him. "Because I don't want to? Why are you standing out front of my motel room?"

"The heater doesn't work." He said it like that was answer enough.

I closed my eyes for a brief moment as I processed what in the world that could even mean. "The owner said it'll be fixed in a few days, and I'm not—"

"Days?"

My eyes opened to find him looking at me like *I* was the crazy one here. "Yes. Days. I have heat packs, and a heated blanket, so I'll be fine."

Beckham didn't look like he believed that for a second. He stepped forward, pulling his hands from his pockets as he somehow slid past without touching me, and took in the small space. I turned to watch as he surveyed the room like he was looking at a crime scene.

"Where's your stuff?"

I gestured to the luggage parked in the corner by the TV stand. "That's all of it."

He turned a disbelieving look on me, his gaze darting to my belly for the first time. Something in his eyes softened, sending warmth cascading all over my skin.

I mentally pinched myself to keep my defenses from melting.

As fast as he glanced at my stomach, his focus met mine again. "Parker."

"Beckham."

The stiff set of his shoulders relaxed a little, and I ignored the way it only happened after I said his name.

"You're not staying here."

I let out a disbelieving snort. "I don't really have a choice."

His jaw hardened as he chewed on the inside of his cheek, and I almost hated that I could see it so well with his five o'clock shadow. The mustache suited him. That I could admit.

"Yes, you do."

I crossed my arms, using my belly as a little shelf. "Whatever you're thinking, no."

His shoulders lifted in another half-assed shrug as he moved to the nightstand to grab my chapstick and wallet.

"What are you doing?" I demanded.

He crossed to my luggage, lifting it with one hand and tossing it onto the mattress. "Packing."

"Beckham."

He unzipped the luggage, not bothering to look my way. "Parker."

My arms fell at his response, hands slapping against my legging-clad thighs. We were falling back into old habits too easily, and that should've scared me. "At least tell me what your plan is."

He slid my wallet and chapstick beside my folded sweaters, and I tried to ignore the fact that he likely saw my underwear right next to them. "You're staying with me."

A loud, disbelieving laugh spilled from me without warning.

When he didn't so much as glance at me as he zipped the luggage and pulled it off the bed, I knew he'd lost his mind.

"You're serious."

He held the bag at his side, facing me. "Dead."

Nearly a minute of silence passed between us as I waited for him to tell me this was a joke. "Beckham, I'm not going to stay at your house."

"First off, it's a double-wide."

I cocked my head.

"Second, you're not staying here."

I set a hand on my hip, partly to show my utter annoyance at the fact that he was doing this, but also because I was tired of standing.

"Scared of something?" he asked, adjusting his grip on the handle. His tone told me he'd had the exact same thoughts as me—that it almost felt too easy between us, despite all the years we'd been apart.

"For starters, I have this." I waved a hand around my belly for emphasis.

He barely spared my stomach a second's glance before meeting my gaze again. "What about it?"

"I'm pregnant."

"Okay."

I heaved a breath. This was taking too long. I wanted to sit down and eat snacks and find some crappy, terribly cheesy movie on the tiny motel TV and fall asleep under the paper-thin sheets.

Okay, that wasn't *really* what I wanted to do, but it would probably beat doing whatever *this* was with Beckham.

"Maybe you've never gotten a girl pregnant before—"

"I haven't," he clarified quickly.

"—but there's a baby growing inside me," I went on. "A human." I leaned forward a bit, accentuating the word. "A *child*."

Beckham looked bored out of his mind, as if this wasn't news to him. "And...?"

"And? Eventually, he's going to come out."

His body froze as his eyes did that weird softening thing again. "It's a boy?"

I blinked. Blinked again. On its own accord, my hand found my belly. "Yeah. It's a boy."

His dark lashes fluttered and his Adam's apple bobbed like he was clearing away any emotion that had crept in. Then, like that little exchange never happened, he started walking toward me.

"Beck," I warned.

"Park."

I ignored the way the old nickname had my stomach flipping. "I'm *pregnant*." I very clearly overemphasized the word.

He stopped right beside me, and I turned to come face-to-face with him. "Where's the father?"

My jaw fell to the floor. "What is this, twenty questions?"

He shrugged. "You seem to think I don't know anything, so I'm asking. Where's the father?"

I shook my head. He was being unbelievable. I should've known the good ol' Beckham Bronson would come out to play at some point.

And why did I almost like it?

Beckham made a dramatic show of looking left and right before settling his captivating eyes back on me. Something looked lost in them, though. They felt a little hollow. A little sad.

"He's clearly not here with you for your father's funeral."

"My father was never a big part of my life, anyway."

He leveled me with a look, not giving in to my attempt at dodging his interrogation. If I didn't answer him, he'd never let it go.

"We're not together." I nearly smacked my forehead. I'd already told him I was single. *Of course*, we weren't together.

"He still got you pregnant."

"That doesn't mean he's this baby's father. Not in my eyes."

His gaze darted back and forth as he studied me, likely searching for any speck of anger or sadness at the admission. When he seemed to find none, he gestured with the luggage toward the door. "Let's go."

"Beckham—"

"This isn't up for debate. You're not staying in a motel in the middle of winter with no heater while you're pregnant. You need home-cooked meals, not some fast-food garbage. You need a comfortable, sanitary bed, and a heater that actually works—not some blanket you're likely not even supposed to be using." He'd somehow drifted closer, and I welcomed the body heat emanating off him.

I lifted my chin. "You don't even know how long I'm in Bell Buckle."

Nothing in his expression changed as he said, "Doesn't matter. You're staying at my place. For a week, a month, until after this baby pops out, I don't care. But you're not staying here."

I pursed my lips, hating him for so easily talking me into this. I did miss being warm, and if I was being honest, motel beds gave me the ick. I'd stayed in plenty of cabins and slept under the stars in nothing but a sleeping bag many times, but motels? That's where I felt like bugs were crawling all over me.

"This doesn't mean anything." I narrowed my eyes for emphasis.

"Not a thing," he agreed.

"Just a friend helping a friend," I added for further clarification.

Beck gave a curt nod. "Just a friend helping a friend."

As he walked me to my truck, neither of us mentioned that we'd crossed that line once before.

And I couldn't help but ask myself: What was stopping us from doing it again?

3
PARKER

I gnawed on my lip the entire drive to Beckham's double-wide. Questions about the last decade swirled around in my head as I followed his truck, begging to be voiced once I got out of my vehicle and came face-to-face with him again.

What had he been up to? Did he have a girlfriend? A job? Did he still ride broncs? How was his family?

Was it even my business?

Did he hate me for...everything?

I shouldn't have come back to the motel after my father's funeral. I should have gotten right back in my truck and driven far the fuck away. But where would that have landed me? I had nowhere to go. No one to help me care for this baby. And while the latter wasn't changing, having a roof over my head for the foreseeable future definitely added a semblance of safety to the situation at hand.

The way Beckham had been so adamant about me

staying with him didn't make me think I was a burden. Or at least, I hoped I wasn't. Beckham had always been sweet to me. And his home, coming into view as we turned down his driveway, was proof that he hadn't lost his humanity over the years.

The back door of my truck swung open as soon as I parked, and Beckham appeared, grabbing my luggage. My eyes darted to the bag before meeting his patient gaze.

"Ready?" His tone was calm, like he was approaching an injured animal and didn't want to spook it.

With a swallow, I nodded. He closed the back door and came around to my side before I could open it. As I swung my legs out, he took a step back, his shoulder leaning against the door so I could walk past him. Once I was a few feet away, he shoved it shut, then came to a stop beside me as I stared up at his home.

"Not what you expected?" he guessed.

I shook my head, my hands involuntarily coming up to rest on my stomach. "No. It's exactly what I pictured for you."

He let out a breathy chuckle. "A double-wide, huh? I didn't think I was *that* disappointing."

I elbowed his arm. "You're not disappointing, Beck. It's perfect."

The following silence had me glancing his way, spotting a frown tugging at the corners of his mouth before he continued onward to the front door. Once there, he set my bag on the porch and dug his keys out of his pocket.

After the door was unlocked, he shoved it open, gesturing for me to go first while he grabbed the handle of my luggage. I strode past him, taking in the space as I entered.

Despite appearing to be an older double-wide from the outside, the interior seemed newly remodeled. What looked to be faux white granite merged into the short backdrop of the kitchen while the cabinets sported a warm, honey oak color, giving a warmth to the space.

As we passed the kitchen directly beside the front door, I walked into the living room where a brown leather couch sat in front of another piece of oak furniture—the coffee table.

The bare space made it seem like he'd just moved in. That, or he was really bad at decorating, save for the giant longhorn skull hanging on the wall directly above the TV.

"Did you recently buy the place?" I asked, trailing a hand over the back of the couch. I looked over my shoulder to find him pausing at the entrance to a hallway. I did my best to ignore the way his muscles flexed under the strain of my luggage. His biceps always had a way of pulling me in, but now they were bigger. More toned. And that was only based on what I could see with his jacket on.

God help me when he takes it off.

He shifted the handle to his opposite hand before running fingers through his mussed-up hair. He'd abandoned his cowboy hat on the hook by the door. "Yeah, sort of."

I waited for him to go on, but when he simply stared at me, I offered a closed-lip smile. His eyes darted to my mouth before his tongue flicked out and over his lips, so fast I barely noticed it. Then he tilted his head in the direction of the hall, and I followed.

"I have a guest room," he explained as he stepped to the side by an open door, allowing me to walk in ahead of him. "It's not much, but it has an attached bathroom. No tub, though. If you want to take a bath, you can in mine." He set the luggage on the beige-and-ivory checkered comforter.

"That's fine. I don't know if I can take a bath anyway, with..." I trailed off, my focus moving down to my belly before back to him. "While I'm pregnant."

A line formed between his eyebrows, a look of worry washing over him before he quickly masked it. "I, uh, know someone else who's pregnant."

I gave him a curious look.

As soon as he noticed the look, he held his hands out, cheeks flaming. "Not because I just go around meeting pregnant women. Callan's girlfriend, Sage, is pregnant. She has another kid, a little girl named Avery"—his expression warmed at the mention of her—"so she might have some tips."

Nostalgia at the mention of his brother had me smiling. I never thought I'd hear about the Bronsons like this again, and now here I was, hearing their names like I'd never left. "Thanks. I'd really like that."

I hadn't realized how much I'd missed Bell Buckle. Now that I was here, the guilt of leaving all those years ago threatened to rip off the bandage I'd stretched over the wound this place had left. I hadn't had many friends when I lived here, save for the Bronsons, because my family were outcasts. Not for any reason other than my parents didn't like me hanging out with anyone. They had their secrets, and the last thing they wanted was their little girl sharing them with the town.

It was why Beckham and I mostly snuck around. Why I only saw Lettie, his little sister, and Brandy, her best friend, when I stopped by their ranch on my way home from school. Or the mornings after I'd stay the night in Beckham's bed.

All the risks I'd taken, all the sneaking around, was for Beckham.

Everything was for him. For us.

Until we both left.

The rustling of fabric had me flicking my gaze back to him, only to find he'd taken his jacket off and was slinging it over his shoulder. He rubbed at the back of his neck, the movement causing his shirt to rise slightly. I glimpsed the hard muscle of his stomach that dipped into a well-defined hip bone. The sight had me clearing my throat, turning away to hide the heat in my cheeks.

He must've noticed the sudden change in my demeanor, or maybe he felt the room shrinking like I did, because he stepped back toward the door, his face nearly looking pained.

"This isn't weird, is it?" I asked, stopping him before he could leave. At the motel, I was content to stew in the silence. But here? It was deafening, knowing he was barely four steps away, across the hall, with only walls separating us.

"I invited you here, Parker. It's not weird." His hand rested on the knob, and my focus shifted from his face to his arm. It was then that I noticed the tattoo on the inside of his left bicep.

"What's with the longhorn skull?" It was similar to the one I'd seen hanging in his living room.

The corner of his mouth twitched, as if my change of subject amused him. "Story for another time. Why don't you settle in? I've got some things I have to do."

Deflation hit me like a bullet. "Oh."

His features pinched. "It's not that I don't want to—"

"It's okay," I interrupted, not wanting him to feel guilty. "I'm the one intruding, anyway. You have your stuff to do." It was weird not knowing him like I did before. And yet, he was still the same Beckham. Just... grown up.

Guilt showed in his gaze, and I hated that I put it there.

He opened his mouth, but closed it again before landing on "Yep."

He hesitated, lips pursing like he wanted to say more. I wished he would.

He started to swing the door shut, and my hands twitched with the urge to stop him again.

Let him go, I told myself. *You're making a fool of yourself.*

I stepped forward, my control slipping. "Beck?"

He paused, the door nearly shut, and met my eyes in response.

"It's good seeing you again."

The barely visible tension in his shoulders seemed to dissipate instantly. "You too, Park."

Then he shut the door, leaving me alone.

I stared at it, listening as his boots faded back into the living room. A door shut, and I assumed he had left.

Slowly spinning around, I heaved a breath. The minimal decor of the room had a cute farmhouse feel, like he'd let Lettie and his mother, Charlotte, pick out the decorations and bedding.

The rug under the bed had hints of brown and green, pulling in warmth from the dark oak bed frame. There was a single plant on the dresser, but upon closer inspection, I found it was artificial. I rubbed a plastic leaf between my thumb and forefinger before trailing a finger along the wooden top of the dresser, making my way to the window.

I nudged the curtain aside, finding dust pluming into the air like a cloud behind Beckham's receding truck.

I really was alone in Beckham Bronson's house, then.

My gaze traced over the rolling fields that stretched for miles before admiring the looming mountains in the distance. Puffs of fluffy white clouds cast shadows over the land, their shapes indecipherable.

The sight stole my breath.

For all the memories Bell Buckle held for me, there were always enough good ones to outweigh the bad. For the longest time, I didn't know where my place was. I lived in my horse trailer with its attached living quarters for years, not knowing where I truly belonged, but feeling content all the same.

Leaving Bell Buckle had felt like the start of an exciting adventure. I'd never left home much before then, since my parents didn't like—and couldn't afford—to travel. Getting out of this town was the start of me truly finding myself. But now that I was back, staring at the landscape and reminiscing on all those times I saw that same mountain behind a smiling Beckham—standing tall while his brothers teased me and Lettie, watching over us as we cried and laughed and lived—I realized maybe I didn't have to go looking for my place after all.

I'd had a good life, despite the hardships.

My best moments were thanks to Beckham. When I'd come to his house crying over a fight my parents had gotten into, or when I'd sneak him into our house to watch a movie on his phone while my parents were passed out, he was the reason a smile always found its way onto my face after a storm—no matter how severe.

My palm rested on my stomach and I closed my eyes, inhaling deeply. I held it before blowing it out, then gazed out the window with a new outlook.

No matter what happened in the coming months, between my life and my baby, I knew without a doubt that everything would be okay.

It always was when Beckham was around.

4

PARKER

SIXTEEN YEARS OLD

"Where the fuck is your ring?"

The thunder did little to drown out my father's shouts. He'd come home an hour ago, and for the duration of that hour, he'd been yelling. At my mother. At the dog. At the beer for going warm on his way home from the liquor store—his routine pit stop after spending all morning at the bar. Outlaw's Watering Hole was more a home to him than this shack was. Although "shack" was giving the single-wide with holes in the roof and a decaying foundation a little too much credit. A shed would be warmer than this place. Probably quieter, too.

"I had to pawn it so I could pay the gas bill!" my mom shouted back.

They were always screaming.

As much as I hated my dad going out drinking and spending money we didn't have, at least when he was gone, the house was silent. My mom didn't talk to me much, unless it was to complain about the bills piling up or other adult responsibilities a parent should never put on their child.

The gas bill she'd pawned her only piece of jewelry for was from four months ago.

They turned the gas off yesterday.

"It ain't even fuckin' cold in here, Tris," my father shot back, the fridge opening and closing for the sixth time, like he couldn't quit checking to see if the beer had chilled yet.

It probably hadn't. I think the power was turned off, too.

We didn't have a TV, and I was told not to turn on the lights unless I absolutely had to. Instead, I had a flashlight. Too dark to brush your teeth? Shine the light in the mirror—lights up the whole bathroom. Making dinner past sunset? There's a lantern on the kitchen counter.

As a child, I thought it was normal. Until one time, when I was out walking at two a.m., I saw the Bronsons' house lit up like the Fourth of July. After that, I tried to avoid Beckham coming to see me after the sun went down.

I stared at my flip phone lying on the pillow next to me as lightning struck somewhere in the distance, causing another roll of thunder to shake the house. I'd mucked one hundred fourteen stalls to save up for that phone. It was cheap, it had a shattered screen, and the green was coming off the call button, but it worked.

A door slammed, but I didn't flinch. I was used to the

crashes that came out of this shell of a home, given that my parents threw a lot of things when they were angry with each other. Never at one another, but at a wall or the floor. For two people who could barely afford food on the table, they sure liked to break a lot of our belongings, as sparse as those were.

"That's because you're fucking drunk," my mom chastised from somewhere closer to my room. They must've made their way down the hall, my mom likely hot on his heels as he headed to their bedroom to change or piss or do whatever the fuck he usually did when he was wasted.

"I ain't fuckin' drunk!"

His denial was a slur.

I grabbed my phone off the pillow, rolling to my back and flipping the screen open and closed with my thumb. I didn't want to be here, but I also didn't want to call Beckham and have him hear the commotion in the background.

My only escape from all of this was either him or a walk on the back roads. When he discovered I went out on those empty roads alone, he told me to stop. I'd asked him why, and all he'd said was it wasn't safe for me to go by myself. I'd told him I couldn't simply call him every time I was sad, and he'd said I could.

He bought me a can of pepper spray the next day.

My screen lit up the room each time I flipped the phone open. A door opened, then slammed, then opened again. My dad was trying to get away from my mom, and she wasn't going to allow it. She liked to fight for some reason. I didn't see the appeal.

The bickering continued as they went back to the kitchen, and I took that as my hint that this would likely go all night. I had school in the morning, and it was already past eleven p.m. I'd never get any sleep at this rate.

Shoving off the bed, I grabbed my thin jacket to protect me from the rain. The temperature inside didn't vary much from outdoors, so I figured it'd be enough for a short walk while I called Beck. Chances were he was already asleep, though. He was a senior, myself a junior. We went to the same school, so some days he'd give me a ride. I always asked him how he'd slept, and he'd somehow always manage to include what time he fell asleep. I think he did that so I'd know I could call him late if needed. I still tried not to.

My parents were too busy arguing—my father buried in the fridge, my mother berating him where she stood at his back—to notice me leaving. Their shouts were too loud to hear the creak of the front door shutting behind me, or the broken screen slapping back against the frame.

The wind howled through the trees, the sky lighting up with another strike. I walked under a nearby oak, opting not to choose the carport as protection from the rain, as its pounding was only amplified by the metal roof. I flipped open the phone as my shoes squished wet leaves and pressed the number one. Beckham was the only contact I had on speed dial. He was the only person I called in general.

After hitting the fading green button, I held it to my ear, scanning the dark expanse around me. We were the only single-wide on this road for about a mile, and with us having no porch light or neighbors, the black night was suffocating.

Beckham answered after the fourth ring, his voice rough like he'd been sleeping. "Park?"

"Were you asleep?" I asked.

A distorted sound came from the background of the call, but it was hard to hear over the storm. If I had to guess, though, it was the sound of him sitting up in bed.

"No. Are you in the rain?"

My eyes froze on the telephone pole at the end of our driveway before I quickly cupped my hand over the microphone and my mouth. "No."

"I can still hear it, Park." Beckham sighed, likely checking the time. But he wasn't sighing at me. He was sighing because he knew exactly why I was standing in the middle of a storm. "I'll come pick you up."

"Beck, no, that's not—"

"You have your pepper spray?"

As if the weapon heard him, the weight of it in my pocket suddenly felt heavier. "Yes," I reluctantly admitted. Beckham would always worry about me, but I hated that carrying it made me feel like there was a reason he had to be concerned. Bell Buckle was a safe town. The only danger was being hit by a flying object inside my house. I was far safer out here than in there.

"You're outside your parents' place?" he asked, movement rustling behind his voice.

"Yes."

"Don't walk down that road, Park," he warned, knowing where my wandering typically took me. "I'm on my way."

I sighed, staring up at the branches hanging above me. Large droplets of rain splashed on my cheeks, the water icy. "Fine."

The line went dead, so I flipped the phone shut and shoved it in my jacket pocket. The fabric was damp, and it'd likely be soaked by the time Beckham got here, but that phone was an immortal brick. No matter what happened to it, it survived. I knew that because it'd once been the victim of my dad's alcohol-induced rage.

Not ten minutes later, Beckham's rusty truck appeared on the main road. He'd already cut the headlights, knowing the drill. It was almost embarrassing how often I called him for comfort, ending with him coming to save me.

I walked along the driveway that was more mud than gravel as he rounded the front of the truck to open the passenger door for me. I stopped, lifting my chin to find him studying me from head to toe.

"You good?" he asked. He was standing there in a black T-shirt that hugged his growing biceps just right. The rain rolled off his tan arms, but he didn't so much as shiver. A drop clung to the tip of his nose, more accumulating on the ends of his shaggy hair.

I nodded. "Yeah."

He tipped his head to the cab, and I got in. Once he shut the door, he came back around, climbing behind the wheel. The truck was still running, so all he had to do was shift into drive and we were off.

The heater was cranked, wrapping me in its warm embrace as the wipers worked overtime to clear the relentless rain from the windshield. Once we were a safe distance away, he flicked his headlights back on.

He glanced over at me, hand adjusting on the wheel. "Wanna talk about it?"

I stared forward, ignoring the water sliding off the ends of my hair and onto his seats. "Not really."

In my periphery, his chin dipped. It wasn't long before we were pulling up to his parents' house. As always, the porch was brightly lit—as if, even with the miserable storm looming over the fields, the Bronsons were untouchable.

Beck killed the engine, and we both opened our doors. He was at mine in an instant, holding it open as I slid off the now-wet seat. He paid the leather no mind as he shut the door and looped an arm around my shoulders, leading me up the steps. Crossing the large porch, he opened the front door for me, and we walked inside to a dimly lit kitchen. The light above the stove was always on at night. I knew because I was a frequent visitor in the late hours of the evening.

We didn't linger as he led me down the hall toward his bedroom. Charlotte and Travis, his parents, never minded if I stayed over. This being a small town, everyone knew the type of people my parents were. They didn't know exactly what went on behind closed doors, but it wasn't hard to guess that my home life wasn't the most fun. And the Bronsons being who they were, they'd never turn anyone away.

Even if it involved me sleeping in their son's room on occasion.

Of course, we'd fooled around. Beckham and I had been inseparable for as long as I could remember. I wasn't sure when we'd crossed that line. He kissed me once, in the small pond out on their property, and from that day forward, we just kind of...were. We kissed, we touched, we did a lot of things our parents likely didn't know about. We felt safe with each other, and while we weren't exactly *officially* dating, there was a level of comfort where we knew there was no one else. The whole town knew: Beckham and Parker were off-limits.

They could go after whoever they wanted, just not the two of us.

Beck closed the door to his room behind me, tossing his keys on the dresser while I peeled out of my wet jacket. I laid it over the back of his wooden chair that sat a whole foot away from his desk. I wondered if maybe I'd been wrong when I called him, and he hadn't been asleep but rather finishing his homework.

Without a word, he grabbed my hand and led me over to his bed. He laid down, pulling me with him. I rested my thigh over his, my cheek settling on his warm chest. I could still smell the rain on him, mixing with the hints of coconut and cinnamon that always wafted off him.

His fingers ran through my damp hair as he stared up at the ceiling. The small desk lamp cast the room in a gold glow, the distant strikes of lightning sending shapes flickering across the far wall every few seconds.

"My mom pawned her ring," I told him, the words quiet.

"Her wedding ring?"

"Mhm. My dad wasn't happy when he saw her bare finger."

Beck was silent, so I looked up to find his jaw working, like he was clenching his teeth. He didn't glance at me when he said, "Maybe if he'd get a job to pay the bills, she wouldn't have to."

He knew the position I was in at home. He just didn't know it involved flashlights and buttered bread for dinner.

"I know."

"Are you okay there?" He meant with food. With blankets and toothpaste and other necessities.

"We should be okay through winter," I told him. "She just paid the gas bill."

"If it gets shut off again, tell me."

When I didn't respond, his eyes finally met mine. Still, his jaw didn't loosen. "I mean it."

I'd tried telling him he wasn't going to pay my parents' bills before, but then he'd reminded me it wasn't only them who were enduring the life they'd created. It was me, too. And he wasn't going to let me live like that.

I only nodded, because he was right. I still didn't put it on his shoulders, though. He could take care of me when we left this town. Not while I was stuck in my parents' house. If they wanted to waste away, so be it. But I refused to let Beckham right their wrongs.

"I will," I lied.

Then I rested my cheek back on his chest, and he pulled me closer with his arm tucked tight around me. At some point, I fell asleep to the sound of his breathing. The familiar rhythm was the only way I could get any sleep as of late.

The next morning, he drove us to school.

And the next day, he brought me the wool blanket from the end of his bed.

5
BECKHAM

Did she even still like fettuccini Alfredo?

I mean, she had to, right? It was the only dish I knew how to cook as a teenager, so naturally, when she'd come over and I could practically hear her stomach growling, I'd make it for her. She always loved it, but now, as I stood at the stove stirring the homemade sauce, I realized maybe she only tolerated it because it was the only meal I was capable of not ruining.

I should've asked her before I'd run out of her room like I'd seen a ghost.

But I *had* seen a ghost.

I had convinced myself I'd never see her again. I was certain of it. Not a chance in hell had I ever thought her father would pass and his funeral would be held in Bell Buckle and she'd come back. Not only come back, but be willing to stay. Although the verdict on that was still up in the air. She'd admitted she wasn't sure how long she was staying here, but that meant she had nowhere else to go. Right? Or did she, and she had no deadline on returning?

These are the questions I should have asked, and yet when it came to Parker, my brain malfunctioned. Words went out the window and I couldn't do so much as form a coherent thought in her presence.

I thought about her constantly, but when I saw her standing there earlier today?

Fuck, I think *I* was the one that went to heaven.

As if my thoughts called to her, I heard her door open at the end of the hall, followed by slow footsteps coming this way. I focused on stirring the sauce, as if that would disguise the fact that I was thinking about her only seconds ago.

Her steps came to a stop, and I looked over my shoulder to find her rubbing her eyes.

"I didn't mean to fall asleep," she said, her voice slightly groggy. "Sorry."

She was so fucking beautiful, standing there in an oversized T-shirt, black leggings, and fuzzy socks. She must've changed into them before her nap, if the wrinkles in the fabric were any indication.

I forced my eyes back to the stove, because otherwise, I'd stare at her all night and ruin the meal. I still couldn't wrap my head around the fact that she was really here, standing in my house.

Pregnant.

"Don't apologize. It's been a long day. Why don't you sit down?"

Feet shuffled behind me before a stool scraped across the floor.

"Where'd you go earlier?" she asked.

I grabbed the drained noodles from the colander in the sink and brought them over to add to the pot with the sauce. "Had to stock the fridge."

"It wasn't stocked before?"

I shook my head, tossing the noodles and Alfredo together. "Just for me."

"You didn't have to buy me food, Beckham."

"You're pregnant." I opened the cabinet to grab two bowls, setting them on the counter before tugging on a heat-proof mitt and opening the oven. I slid out the tray of garlic bread, placed it on the stove, and turned off the heat. "I'm not going to make you shop for your own food here." I piled a hefty portion into a bowl, set a slice of bread on top, and slid it across the counter to her. "Parmesan?"

She blinked, like the question of whether she wanted cheese or not had taken her off guard. "Sure." She shook her head as if trying to clear her thoughts while I grabbed the block and began grating it above the bowl.

"Say when."

Her lips parted and snapped shut twice before she said, "When." Then her penetrating gaze landed on me, and I had to force myself to turn around to dish up my own bowl while somehow not dropping it all over the floor. "You don't have to feed me."

I shot a frown her way, setting my bread on top like I had hers. "Yes, I do."

She started to shake her head, but I set my bowl on the counter, braced my hands on the edge, and said, "I *want* to feed you. Let me take care of you."

She stared up at me, and I stared right back. If she wanted to battle, I'd battle, but I wasn't giving in. The least I could do for her, especially after her father passed, was make her food.

As if the invisible string holding us in place had snapped, we both blinked, looking away. I crossed to the fridge, grabbing two bottles of water and a Dr. Pepper. Closing the door, I walked back to my spot on the opposite side of the counter from Parker and set the water in front of her. Then, I cracked the top on the soda and placed it beside her bottle.

"I wasn't sure if you still liked them. It's not from the gas station"—my hand came up to rub at the back of my neck—"but I figured a can could make up for it until you can get one."

She zoned in on the soda, blinking like memories were flashing behind her eyes. They sure as hell were behind mine.

Growing up, after school, we'd stop at the corner gas station on the way home every day. She'd always grab a fresh Dr. Pepper from the machine, and I'd either go for an energy drink or a water.

"You remember the slushy machine they installed my sophomore year?" she asked, causing my bewildered gaze to snap to hers. I'd expected her to stay silent and dig into her meal, not bring up the past. I wasn't sure if there was any unsaid rule between us that said we shouldn't bring up old memories, so I didn't necessarily want to be the first to go down that lane.

"Yeah." I chuckled. "It broke two days later. You got to try one Dr. Pepper slushy. The first time, you were too scared to interrupt your routine to try it. I finally talked you into it the next day."

"More like you bullied me into it," she corrected, a smile lighting up her eyes. "You and Reed were so mean about it, I had no choice but to fill my cup with that watered-down soda concoction."

I arched a brow. "If I remember correctly, you ended up liking it."

"Until the machine broke!" She let out a small laugh, and it hit me how much I missed her smile. "Then I had to force this narrative into my head that it was disgusting so I wouldn't miss it."

I shook my head, incredulous. "That's a little insane, Park."

Her mouth popped open, the corners still tilted up. "It was good!" She glanced at my water, condensation already building on the plastic. "I'm surprised you didn't grab a beer. You were drinking them with dinner since before I can remember."

My shoulders stiffened at the reminder, my tongue darting over my lips before I dropped my smile and picked up my fork. "I'm a changed man."

Despite my focus dropping to the pasta, I could feel her studying me. I used to always be able to feel her eyes on me, and it seemed that never changed. Guess old habits did die hard.

"Who's this new Beck?" she questioned, almost more so to herself.

But I answered anyway. "I don't drink anymore."

The air in the room shifted, turning from playful to serious in mere seconds.

She picked up her own utensil, twirling it in the noodles. "There a reason for that?"

"Sort of," I offered, unsure how to put into words that I went on a bender I couldn't even remember the duration of because at the time, I'd have rather lost myself in a bottle than face the reality of my best friend being gone.

"Want to share?" Her fork was growing more full of pasta with each spin, a bite far too large for her to take, but she didn't seem to be paying attention to the food. Like I was the only thing she wanted to focus on.

I both loved and hated it, because if I got used to her being here, being real and right in front of me, I'd never want her to leave. Hell, I feared that was the case the moment I saw her at the funeral.

"Not really."

A simple nod, and she was scraping the pasta along the side of the bowl so it fell off her fork. Then she twirled a single noodle onto it and stared like it was the most interesting piece of food she'd ever seen.

I'd deflated her. Killed the mood. I seemed to be real fucking good at that lately.

"Park, it's not that I'm keeping anything from you—"

"You have no obligation to tell me anything. We're..."

Her words trailed off, but I knew what she was trying to say. The one thing that stood between us like a house fire, but neither of us had the heart to acknowledge. We'd both rather it burn us down in the process simply to avoid putting it into words.

"Not what we used to be," I filled in.

She nodded, and after a few strained seconds of silence, we began eating. I remained standing on the opposite side of the counter, not trusting myself to sit beside her and not want to inch closer to her. To purposefully knock my elbow against hers or brush my knee along her thigh. She didn't need complicated right now, and well...I was complicated.

"So, what are you doing for work?" she asked after finishing her bite of garlic bread.

"Right now I'm helping Wyatt at his mechanic shop. Other than that, I'm working here and there on my parents' ranch."

"No more rodeo?"

I forced a breath. Forced the next words, too. "No more rodeo."

She was quiet, like she expected me to go on. For her sake, for not feeling like I was hiding everything, I did. "It was time to call it quits. It's dangerous, you know? I was lucky I got out with minimal injuries. Not everyone can say the same."

Instantly, my throat tightened. I should've kept my fucking mouth shut, because she noticed the strain in my words and lifted her gaze to the side of my face.

I swallowed. Quietly tried to clear my throat. Sipped some water. "What about you? Any plans to go back to traveling and working on ranches after the baby comes?"

"Not really, no." She set her fork down, the metal clanking against the ceramic bowl. "I was making money off social media for a bit, but I need something more stable."

I finished the bite I'd taken while she spoke. "Like an influencer?"

She shrugged. Nodded. "Yeah. I post a lot about the western lifestyle and collab with brands. They pay me in return."

I smirked, finally mustering the courage to look at her again. The tiny freckles that dotted the bridge of her nose seemed heightened under the golden glow of my kitchen lights. Her blonde curls were frizzy, likely from her nap, but that only made her more beautiful. More real. Like I could finally let go of being scared to blink for fear she'd disappear.

"So you've got fans, huh?" I teased.

She laughed, and I think my heart skipped a beat. "Something like that."

Her eyes met mine, and we both froze. She searched my face, like she, too, was realizing I was actually here. In the flesh and in her presence.

It was fucking surreal, if I was being honest. Like being given a second chance after you'd accepted there was no hope.

"What?" Her voice was breathy.

I shook my head, my chest warming. But still, I

couldn't look away from her. "I just never thought I'd hear that sound again."

Those soft cheeks of hers tinged pink, and it was like the world stopped moving.

Parker Summerhill was back in Bell Buckle.

And I was going to find a way to keep her.

6

BECKHAM

The next day was yet another day where I had to remind myself to breathe. There wasn't a sense of panic in me that closed my lungs, but rather a brick sitting on my chest, weighing down the natural urge in my brain to suck in air and let it loose.

At first, I'd thought I might've developed some type of asthma. Maybe a breathing disorder where I needed medication to get rid of this pinched feeling in my sternum. But no. It was simply my mind being so bogged down by things I can't control that I forget to breathe deep enough.

Some days, it felt like I'd run a mile and couldn't fill my lungs to their full capacity, and I'd be scared I was suffocating. Others, I didn't breathe enough on instinct, so I'd have to remind myself over and over and over again.

I tried various exercises, but those didn't do much. I was drunk one time and tried meditating. All I did was fall over. None of that shit worked because it wasn't my lungs' fault. It was my brain. I was so lost in the depression some days that not even my mind wanted to put effort into keeping myself alive. Those days, I had to work overtime.

I'd come to learn the world didn't stop demanding things of you simply because your will to stay alive was dwindling.

Too wrapped up in tracking the rise and fall of my chest as I stowed the clean utensils in their rightful place, I didn't hear Parker leave her room. For some reason, I'd expected her to disappear overnight. I'd gotten so used to only imagining her voice that hearing it in person was like a shock to my nervous system.

Maybe the depression had rotted my brain into pulp, and I was hallucinating.

"You're so quiet," Parker remarked as she crossed to the fridge.

I bent to close the now-empty dishwasher, then faced her as she pulled a bottle of water from the shelf in the door.

"Just used to living alone, I guess." I leaned back against the counter, placing my palms against the edge. But that was false, because up until four months ago, I'd been mostly living with my best friend. "Did you sleep okay?"

"Yeah." She took a slow sip of water, a crease forming in the center of her forehead. "Did you?"

I ignored the question, focusing on her pinched expression. "Are you feeling okay?"

She nodded, averting her gaze and capping the bottle. "I get nauseous sometimes. In the mornings. It usually goes away after I've eaten something."

Guilt trickled in past the numbness. "I should've made you something."

Her eyes snapped to mine, lids narrowing. "No. That's not your responsibility."

I crossed my arms, slinging one ankle over the other as I waited for her to remember our conversation from yesterday.

"I appreciate what you're doing. I really do. But I promise I can feed myself. I'm not inept at taking care of my body."

This time, shame knocked on the unstable walls of my mind. "I didn't mean—"

"I know." She dipped her head to look at her bare feet. "This is weird, isn't it?"

My brows pulled together. "Why do you say that?"

She gave me an incredulous look. "Really?"

I didn't move, waiting for her to go on.

"I'm here. In Bell Buckle." She pointed to the floor. "In your house." She set a hand on her belly. "Pregnant. It's like a weird sense of déjà vu, and yet..."

Yet I wasn't the one who got her pregnant.

The unspoken words hung between us like radiation after a nuclear bomb. Our catastrophe was the last ten years and how they'd nonchalantly blown up in our faces, and we weren't willing to acknowledge them aloud. She'd changed. *I'd* changed.

There was no more eighteen-year-old Beckham and Parker.

I shoved off the counter, tearing a piece of paper towel from the roll. I opened the plastic case of blueberry muffins I'd bought at the store and placed one on the towel. After closing the case, I crossed the kitchen and held the muffin out to her like an offering.

"Nothing's weird about this, Parker."

She looked at the muffin, then at me. Warring thoughts brewed behind her captivating gaze, and I wished I could put them all to rest. She had nothing to worry about. Having her in my house was the one thing I knew for certain that I wanted right now.

"It's just like before," I continued. "You, me, against the world. Only difference is we've got a baby that has to finish growing before he can join our little duo. Though I guess then we'll be a trio."

Confusion crossed her features. "'We'?"

I dipped my chin in a nod. "We."

Hesitantly, she took the muffin from my outstretched hand. That look in her eyes, the one I'd seen so many times growing up, nearly pulled me under. It was like home and belonging looped into one dewy-eyed look. I'd fall right back into it if I could. Hell, I wanted to. But that was our past. Things were...different now. But for some reason, the more I looked at her, the more it felt like not much had changed in the last ten years.

If I didn't leave now, I'd start saying shit I probably shouldn't, and all that would likely do is scare her away.

"I was planning to go to Wyatt's shop this morning."

Like a rubber band snapping, her sense of hope vanished.

She cleared her throat. Nodded. "Yeah. I, uh—" She blinked, focusing on the muffin as she picked at the paper it was wrapped in. "I was going to look for a job anyway. I want to put some money aside for after the baby comes."

"If you need money—"

She nearly dropped the muffin as her whole body tensed. "I don't want your money, Beck. You've done enough for me already."

A thousand memories flitted between us. Her sleeping in my bed on the nights her parents wouldn't quit arguing. Me giving her my lunches at school when she had nothing more than a peanut butter sandwich. Us going to the pond to forget the world existed.

Life was simpler back then.

My lips rolled together. "Speaking of jobs." *Real smooth subject change—totally not obvious that discussing the past is difficult for me.* "How long are you planning to stay in Bell Buckle?"

"Already sick of me?" she questioned, but the teasing lilt in her tone fell flat.

"I could never be sick of you, Park."

As if she hadn't used my nickname seconds prior, as if we hadn't already been using them since the moment I walked into her hotel room, her expression saddened. Or maybe it was my brain screaming that she never should've left. That *I* never should've left.

"I'm not sure how long." She bit the inside of her lip, tugging it past her teeth before adding, "Is that okay?"

"You can stay as long as you need to." I grabbed my truck keys from the counter, palming them. "Do you have any appointments coming up?"

She shook her head. "I need to schedule them since I have to change doctors again."

"Again?"

Her fingers continued aimlessly busying themselves on the muffin as she clarified, "Yeah. I've kind of still been moving around a ton. It's not the most ideal situation for being pregnant, though. Plus, the bed in my trailer was hard as a rock."

"I hope the one here isn't too bad."

Her lips twitched before she avoided my gaze again. "No. It's perfect."

Then it hit me, what she'd said. "What'd you do with the trailer? And Tex?" Tex was the horse she'd bought as a teen, and given he was young himself when she got him, I had to figure he was still alive.

A look of guilt shone bright as she gnawed on her lip again. "I had to sell both."

"What?" The shock in my question was evident as my voice grew slightly louder.

Her eyes snapped to mine. "I needed the money, and I knew I couldn't stay in that trailer with a baby. Let alone give Tex a fair life."

"Where the hell is he?" That horse had been everything to her, and in turn, he was everything to me.

"A ranch in Montana. I know the people. He's okay."

I didn't so much as blink when I said, "Call them."

She narrowed her eyes on me, confused now. "I can't just call them, Beckham. They own him now."

"How much?"

"How much what?"

"How much did you sell him for?"

"Three grand."

The sigh that left me was heavy. I mentally started totalling how many shifts I'd have to work to cover the cost of getting Tex back. Then I remembered my winnings I'd set aside from rodeo.

Parker must've sensed what I was about to offer, because her eyes turned to slits. "No."

"Parker."

"I said no. Just leave it be, Beckham. *Please.*"

From the way her voice strained on her plea, her pain at selling him was obvious. I could get him back, I could drive there right now—

I forced myself to stop.

Parker told me to leave it, so for now, I'd leave it.

"Alright." My lips rolled together as I considered the possibility of overstepping. The last thing I wanted to do was scare her away. "I'll be back later today. You still have my number?"

She nodded. For some reason, that sent an electric shock to my heart.

I rubbed at my chest, backing toward the door. "Call me if you need anything."

"I will."

With one last look back, I left, making sure to lock

the door behind me in case she decided to go back to sleep. I couldn't imagine how exhausting it would be to travel so heavily while being pregnant. I was thankful she now had a home base to feel comfortable and safe in, rather than sleeping in that trailer—as much as the absence of it filled me with hurt on her behalf.

When I got to my truck, I hesitated with the driver's door open and pulled out my phone. I clicked Sage's text thread and began typing.

> Me: What was one thing you bought immediately and loved the most when you first got pregnant?

Sage began replying right away. With her staying home with Avery while running her own bakery from their house, she typically had her phone on her.

> Sage: Probably a pregnancy pillow. Why?

> Me: Just curious

> Sage: Do your brothers know you got someone pregnant?

I snorted. My brothers would be the last people to know if that were to ever happen. As close as I was with my family, they were all loudmouths. If the Bronson brothers knew anything, chances were the entire town of Bell Buckle knew, too.

Me: No, because it didn't happen

Sage: Did you get invited to a baby shower then?

Me: No, I'm not a woman

Sage: Men can go to those too, you know

Me: Can they?

Sage: You have a lot to learn if you have a baby on the way

Me: We'll discuss classes next time I come hang out with Avery

Sage: She keeps asking when you're coming next

Me: Tell her I'll take her for a ride this week. I gotta go. Thanks for the advice

Sage: I'm always a text away

Me: I know

She replied with an eye-roll emoji before I pocketed the phone and hopped in the truck.

As I started it, I realized that since my mind had been on Parker, I hadn't had to remind myself to breathe.

Maybe the air was a little clearer when she was

around. The skies a little less gloomy. And the constant worry in the back of my mind a little more eased.

7
PARKER

Was it embarrassing that I still had his number saved? Probably. Yet, when I'd nodded, he didn't seem surprised—and I had to believe it was because he still had mine, too.

Maybe I shouldn't have said yes to staying at his house. I should've grabbed my luggage and driven to some other town. Finding a place to rent would be difficult with my low budget, but it wasn't impossible. It was probably easier than facing these feelings slamming into us like a freight train with no control of its brakes. Nearly ten years clearly wasn't enough for us to move on—did either of us even want that? The only reason we'd parted ways was because our goals were leading us on different paths. Perhaps fate meant for us to find each other again, if only to see whether now that we'd gotten our fix out of the way—we might discover we never truly wanted this to end.

Whatever *this* was. I didn't even know if he had a

girlfriend, and I... I was a complicated case. Pregnant. Single. No place to call home. No job.

The list could go on and on.

Once I found out I was pregnant, I decided making money off social media wasn't enough. Sure, it paid whatever bills I had at the time, but it wasn't always stable. I could make thousands of dollars one month, and the next only a few hundred. It fluctuated too much, and I didn't want to put a child through that instability.

I'd stopped posting two months into my pregnancy. I could've kept it going as a side gig, but I had no new videos or photos of me riding my horse and exploring new ranches, and once the content I had prepped ran out, people were bound to get mad I wasn't making more. That was the hard part about putting your life online—once you started withholding things for privacy or other reasons, people felt entitled to know why. It almost made them hungry for more.

But I didn't want my baby online, and I didn't want all those strangers knowing I was pregnant, either. Being a social media influencer, people gave their opinions on everything, from the clothes I wore to the length I cut my hair. It got to the point where I couldn't even have a sunburn without everyone hounding me with information on what I should do and what I was doing wrong.

I could only imagine how they'd react if they found out I was pregnant, and that I wasn't with the father. They'd stalk me until they found him while simultaneously giving me advice on *everything*. I'd had my privacy stripped from me for far too long, and the last thing I wanted was to put a newborn through that.

All of those haunting thoughts flitted through my head as I stared up at the rusty metal sign for North State Auto. The thought of working here hadn't crossed my mind until Beckham mentioned the place, but Wyatt had always been nice to me growing up, so I figured it was worth a shot. He'd watched my back, same as the Bronson brothers, and for a while, he was part of the family, too.

I could only hope he still held that sentiment. I walked through the door, the bell dinging with my entrance, and hoped he wouldn't mind offering me a job. Even if it meant filing paperwork all day, I'd take it.

The door swung shut behind me as I took in the small space. I scanned the four gray chairs leading to the oak desk, and the man sitting behind it. Two computer monitors took up a majority of the tabletop, and a very thirsty plant was nearly falling off the chipped corner.

Wyatt spun around in his chair with a corded phone pressed to his ear. He held up a single finger to gesture for me to wait, then he froze, eyes bulging as he realized who was standing in the lobby of his shop.

"I gotta go," Wyatt said into the phone, not giving the person on the other end of the line the chance to object. He set the phone in the base and shook his head, disbelief coating his features.

"Parker Summerhill."

I smiled. "Wyatt Walters."

He stood, rounding the desk to pull me in for a tight

hug. I returned it, forcing myself to ignore the emotion building in my throat. He smelled like oil and grease with a hint of citrus hidden somewhere under all that.

"Where have you been?" he asked as he let me go. He took a small step backward, studying me like he couldn't believe I was standing here. I couldn't, either.

I shrugged. "Around."

"If that ain't the vaguest answer." He flashed his teeth with a grin before his gaze focused on my belly. "I didn't know you and Beck were—"

"No." I waved my hands awkwardly. "We aren't—"

He quirked a brow. "Really?"

I shook my head, at a loss for words. He really thought I was pregnant with Beckham's child? It was as if, to this day, the thought of me being with someone else wasn't an option for anyone. For the longest time, it wasn't. Until Daniel. But even then, we'd barely been sleeping together for a month before I cut things off. A couple weeks later, I found out I was pregnant.

"I'm looking for a job," I blurted, needing to change the subject. Explaining much of anything was futile right now. If I knew anything about the Wyatt I grew up with, it was that he'd want details on where I'd been and who I'd been with. If he assumed the baby was Beckham's, he'd ask when I was in Bell Buckle for that to have happened. And, well, right now, it almost felt easier for him to assume that than to ask where the baby daddy really was, and when he could slam his fist into his nose.

Beckham and Wyatt were similar in that they were both good at fighting out their problems.

I craned my neck, peering through the small window to the shop. "Is Beckham here?"

Wyatt shook his head, leaning his ass against the lip of the desk. "He told me he couldn't come by today. Said he had something to do. Which is fine, really. He's balancing a lot right now, so most days, he's just been stopping by to help when he can. That's what he's doin' at the ranch, too. He's just kind of..." Wyatt's gaze fell to his boots.

"Kind of what?" I pushed.

He grabbed a rag off the desk, fiddling with it. "Trying to figure shit out. He's been weird the past couple of months." He nodded at my belly. "Guess that might be why."

My brows furrowed. Beckham didn't know about my pregnancy until the other day, so that couldn't be possible. Whatever Beckham was going through likely had nothing to do with me, but I didn't offer that information to Wyatt. If Beckham wasn't opening up to him about whatever it was, I wasn't going to be the one to stir up drama.

"Right. So, about that job," I went on.

That nervous look in his eyes fell away. "You can't really lift heavy stuff, Parker."

"I don't know how to work on cars, so that's not a problem. I thought maybe I could do the desk stuff?"

The corner of his mouth crooked up, playfulness lighting his face. "Desk stuff, huh?"

I nodded. "Paperwork, phone calls. I don't know. I just need a job, Wy."

He sighed, tossing the rag on the desk before rounding it and plopping back down in his worn swivel chair. "Sage just quit the bakery. Maybe they have a job opening for you there."

I shook my head, approaching the desk. "I'd rather work for you."

If I had to work with pastries and coffee, I would, but a bakery seemed like the exact opposite of the type of space I'd enjoy. The delicateness that came with pastries was not my forte. Surprisingly, I felt more comfortable in a mechanic shop.

Wyatt's mouth pressed into a thin line before he sighed again. "I don't have much work for you—"

"Is that a yes?" I sounded too eager, but I didn't care. I was hopeful.

With a subtle shake of his head, he said, "Yes."

I smiled bigger than I had in months and rushed around the desk to wrap his shoulders in a hug. "Thank you, thank you, thank you."

He patted my back somewhat awkwardly, like he couldn't understand how I was ecstatic over a desk job. "Yeah, yeah. You're welcome. But no redecorating my office."

I pulled away, a grin still plastered to my face as I scanned the room. "This colorful place?" I ran a finger under a leaf on the drooping plant. "I could never. It's perfect."

He frowned. "You can start Monday."

"Monday's perfect. I'll bring my paints."

His frown deepened. "If you start drawing flowers on the walls—"

I waved him off, heading for the door. "No flowers. Got it."

"Or rainbows," he added. "Nothing girly."

I snorted. "Girly isn't in my vocabulary, Wyatt."

"You're wearing a dress."

I shrugged. "It's cute." I set a hand on the door, shoving it open with the ding of the bell before I glanced back at him over my shoulder. "See you Monday!"

He ran a hand down his face, mumbling something to himself.

The door swung shut behind me, and as I stopped at my truck to fish the keys out of my purse, I felt my phone buzzing. Pulling it out along with the keys, I scanned my notifications. Guilt hit me straight in the chest. I scrolled and scrolled for at least two minutes, scanning the countless comments on my last post—one that was posted months ago—of people asking numerous questions.

Where are you?

Are you okay?

Are you ever coming back?

Did you get in a horse accident?

What if someone kidnapped her?

What if she rode off a cliff?

Then came the hate.

She's dumb enough that she probably would ride off a fucking cliff.

Thank God, I was tired of seeing her on my feed.

She's not even pretty.

Her horse looks sick.

The influx of concern and disgust usually meant some other influencer or decent-sized account had posted about me, and naturally, people flocked to investigate. I'd turned my notifications off for a while after deciding to quit posting, but when the questions finally slowed, I'd turned them back on because I kept missing when old friends from my travels would message me. Every now and then, this would happen.

I'd debated deleting the app, but some small part of me still felt attached to the Parker I was when I found joy in social media. But with more popularity came more criticism, and I had to think about how all of that affected me and my baby. The stress of it all, keeping up with comments and messages, was too much.

Unable to help myself, I'd scrolled nearly to the bottom when my eyes snagged on a particularly weird comment.

You're so cute on such a big animal. Where do you ride those things?

I clicked the notification, curious if it belonged to some perverted man, or maybe a woman with a weird sense of complimenting people. But rather than my latest post popping up, it was one from two years ago—me sitting on Tex in a pond. I was wearing a light blue bikini top and denim shorts, my hair loose around my shoulders with my straw cowboy hat blocking out the sun.

I remembered that summer like it was yesterday, and

how I'd stood in the center of that pond, remembering all the times Beckham had been with me in the one on his parents' property. It'd been a sick, painful rush of déjà vu. But when my friend had turned the camera on me, I'd smiled. Even in the photo, it was obvious that it didn't really reach my eyes.

I didn't think it had in years.

The nostalgia of the photo had me locking my phone and shoving it back in my purse. Then I unlocked my truck and slid in behind the wheel. I straightened my dark blue dress that flowed down to my ankles, right above my low black cowgirl boots. I shimmied out of my sherpa-lined denim jacket and set it on the passenger seat. Despite the chill in the air, I felt clammy.

Being back in Bell Buckle was a lot. Maybe too much.

But I knew one thing for certain.

Seeing people from my past lifted a weight off my shoulders. The community of Bell Buckle was always close-knit and willing to help one another, and the job opportunity at Wyatt's was proof that the town still held that charm.

And for the first time since I found out the news, I felt like I had a strong chance of being the best mom I could be.

8

BECKHAM

The moment I shifted my truck into park in my driveway, my phone buzzed. Then buzzed again. And again. I grabbed it off the passenger seat, watching as multiple texts filtered in, one after another. I scrolled to the bottom, holding my thumb on the screen so it'd stop moving as I tried to read the first text from Wyatt.

Wyatt: Incoming

Immediately after his text, our family group chat began to blow up.

Lettie: When were you going to tell us Parker was in town?

Lennon: You guys can't say I'm the closed-off one now

Lettie: That's Reed

Reed: Don't bring me into this

Callan: Wait, Parker is in town?

Brandy: You already brought yourself
into this, Reed *fist emoji*

Oakley: Who's Parker?

Sage: I'm wondering the same thing

I ran a hand down my face, seriously debating turning off my cell. Instead, I decided to tackle that issue later. The dark gray clouds looming in the evening sky told me I had minutes to get these things inside before rain would begin coming down in buckets.

I got out of the truck and shoved my still-buzzing phone in my pocket before closing my door and opening the back one. While balancing five boxes of various granola bar flavors in the crook of my arm, I folded a massive pillow in half and tucked it under the other elbow in order to loop my hand through the grocery bags. My hip bumped the door to close it before I made my way up the steps of my porch.

The boxes threatened to topple to the ground as I shifted to grab my house key. Somehow, none of them managed to fall as I unlocked the door and twisted the handle, pushing my way inside. Once I was in, I kicked it shut and crossed to the counter to set everything down. With my hands on my hips, I heaved a breath, surveying the damage done today.

Not a single thing on my list had been for myself, and for a split second, I thought I'd gone overboard. That once Parker saw what I did today, she'd think I was overstepping and run off.

With a shake of my head, I forced those thoughts aside.

Bell Buckle didn't have major shopping centers, so I'd called off work today to go on a small road trip to the only place I could find that carried pregnancy pillows. While I was there, I'd grabbed whatever else I didn't think Bell Buckle had—and then things they most definitely had, but I wanted to get today, anyway. Fancy granola bars for the mornings when she felt nauseous before eating, prenatal vitamins in case she didn't have any or needed to stock up, lotions, bubble bath, eye patches.

Really, I didn't know what she wanted or needed, and now that I was thinking about it again, I'd definitely gone overboard. I was practically setting her up for a spa day.

A flash of light had my gaze moving from the counter to the living room where the TV was on, but the volume was so low, I could barely hear it. Leaving the items in disarray, I crossed to the couch to find a sleeping Parker with her legs curled up and her head on the armrest.

I frowned at her bare arms and feet. Despite the heat being on, it was still less than comfortable to sleep without a blanket. Reaching for the throw draped over the back of the couch, I gently laid it over her, making sure it covered her toes.

I should've left it at that, but before I could help myself, I crouched to get a better look at her. Her calm presence warmed something in my chest, and while I'd known what missing her felt like, having her here in front of me was almost more painful. Because if she was back, there was a high probability of her disappearing again.

Carefully, I moved a stray curl off her cheek, tucking it behind her ear. Her breathing shallowed out for a moment before her eyes flicked open.

"Beckham?" Her face scrunched before she glanced at the window behind me. "What time is it?"

"Five. You fell asleep watching TV."

Her focus moved to the TV before she rubbed her eyes and propped herself up on an elbow. The movement made the blanket fall down her arm, and she grabbed the edge, rubbing the fabric between her fingers. "You put a blanket on me?"

"You looked cold."

Something in her expression melted away, replacing itself with a look I couldn't quite place. "Thank you."

I dipped my chin and forced myself to stand. I was too close to her. So close that I could reach out and cup her cheek. Or take her hand in mine. Both seemed wildly inappropriate and right all at the same time.

"I got you some things," I said as I walked back to the

kitchen. Behind me, the colorful hue from the TV disappeared, indicating she'd turned it off.

I turned around at the counter to find her making her way over.

"What's all this?" she asked as she surveyed the mountain of items.

I opened my mouth to list everything off, but snapped it shut when I remembered she could see what it all was easily. She meant why. *Why* did I get my childhood love all these items to make her more comfortable in her pregnancy?

That was a question even I couldn't answer.

"I figured you might want a pregnancy pillow—" I began.

"You know what a pregnancy pillow is?"

I lifted my focus from the items to find her shocked expression on me.

"Well, I didn't until Sage informed me on some pregnancy...stuff."

She crooked a brow, stifling her smile.

"What?" I asked.

She shook her head. "Nothing. That's just... That's cute you asked her."

My cheeks heated, and I didn't miss how her eyes fell to the blush. I quickly cleared my throat and moved to the fridge, rifling around to grab makings for dinner.

Instead of acknowledging her calling what I did *cute*, I said, "I also made you a key."

"For your house?" A hint of surprise laced her tone.

I set the various ingredients beside the stove before

pulling out seasonings for the chicken. "Yes, for the house."

She moved behind me toward the fridge. "You didn't have to do that."

"How do you expect to get in if I'm not home?"

The door to the fridge closed, and the telltale crack of a soda can tab sounded. "I mean, I could have gone and had it made myself."

I waved her off before spinning around to grab the buffalo sauce from the fridge. Instead of seeing the plain white exterior of my refrigerator, I came face-to-face with Parker. Our eyes held for a moment before I broke the stare.

"I'll have to buy more of those to feed your habit."

She cradled the can, smiling. "I'm trying not to have as many with the pregnancy, but I just can't help myself sometimes. I like a little treat."

I crossed my arms and leaned a hip against the counter, forgetting the dinner while distracted by her. "And today is celebration enough for a treat, huh?"

Her grin widened as she tucked stray curls behind her ears. "Wyatt is letting me work at the shop."

"On *cars*?" Parker could do an oil change, sure, but she wasn't very savvy with the rest. At least, she didn't use to be. I supposed a lot could change in the span of ten years.

A breathless laugh escaped her. "Gosh, no. I'd somehow break them worse than when they came in. He's letting me do the office stuff."

Okay, so she wouldn't have too much extreme labor

to deal with while carrying her baby. That made me feel better. "That was nice of him."

She took a sip of her soda. "I'd ask where you were when you said you were going to the shop today, but all of this is explanation enough." Her eyes darted to the items still in disarray.

I shoved off the counter, crossing to the fridge in a second attempt to grab the buffalo sauce. I'd be happy to get nothing done if it meant I could stare at her all night, but that would mean she wouldn't have dinner, and a starving Parker was not my goal here.

In three strides, I was directly in front of her. She blinked up at me, frozen in place. Only the can of Dr. Pepper separated us, and I nearly wanted to tear it from her grasp and toss it in the sink to get even an inch closer.

It'd take nothing to lower my lips to hers and refresh my tongue with the taste of her. Nothing to set my hands on her waist and feel her. To breathe the same oxygen as her. To back her into the wall and go back to old ways.

But nothing was too much. Nothing held so much weight; it was nearly crushing. It'd take nothing, and yet, it'd change everything.

Her lips parted as she tilted her head back. Was she thinking the same thoughts I was? Imagining being back in my arms? But that was silly to think—no matter how much we dreamed, it never led us to the same place. Our splitting ways for ten years was proof of that.

My body leaned forward the slightest, like she was my center of gravity and I couldn't resist the pull. I might've imagined it, but her breath seemed to hitch. My eyes caught on her mouth, on her pretty pink lips and that faint freckle right above the corner that I loved so much. One inhale and I could smell her. Vanilla with a hint of almond. I knew that because I'd studied her for so many years that even her scent had been ingrained in my being. I never knew if it came down to her shampoo or the deodorant she used or maybe the perfume she spritzed, but whatever it was, I'd missed it.

And awakening that part of my senses nearly choked me.

"I have to grab the buffalo sauce," I forced out, my voice pitched so low I barely recognized it.

She blinked out of her haze, seemingly as stuck in the bubble that was us as I was. "Right."

She took a small step to the side, and I reached around her to open the fridge. Her shoulder brushed my chest, the small kitchen not leaving much room for movement. Every nerve in my body went on red alert, a live wire igniting the skin beneath my shirt.

My hand wrapped around the neck of the glass before pulling the bottle out and shutting the door. When I stepped back, I looked down at her to find her features pinched, like she'd become aware of our point of contact as much as I had.

"What's for dinner?" Her question was nearly a squeak.

"Buffalo chicken with rice and coleslaw."

"Oh."

Why did naming a fucking meal feel like such an intimate thing right now?

Forcing myself to snap out of this, I turned and headed back to my spot at the counter. I pulled out a cutting board, then got to work prepping the chicken breasts.

"I'll put the groceries away after I get this started," I told her, trying to make conversation so the tension in the air would clear the fuck out.

"I can do it," she offered. Before I could protest, I heard the clink of her can being set down, and she began shuffling things around.

The silence while the two of us got to work was deafening.

"My siblings are probably going to want to see you," I said to fill the quiet.

"They know I'm here?"

"You saw Wyatt. The whole damn town probably knows you're here now." Wyatt wasn't a blabbermouth, but news spread fast in Bell Buckle. He'd likely told one person, and it spread like wildfire. I knew for certain it hadn't been anyone from the funeral, because the topic of Parker had only been brought up after her trip to the shop today.

Once the chicken was coated in seasoning, I moved over to the stove. Parker had moved to the opposite side of the kitchen, placing boxes and other dried goods in the small pantry.

I set a pan on the stove and turned the heat to medium-high, drizzling some oil in before bringing the breasts over.

"I don't mind seeing them," Parker stated.

"I know. They're just...a lot. They've all got their partners, so it's, like, a family of forty now."

Parker's silence spoke volumes as I set the chicken in the heated pan. I didn't want her to think I was trying to hide her for any reason.

"I don't want to overwhelm you, is all," I went on.

"Because I'm pregnant?"

I grabbed the tongs, needing to give my hands something to do. "No. Because they're going to ask you a million questions, and I don't want you to feel obligated to give them answers."

The pantry door swung shut, and I glanced over my shoulder to find her elbows on the counter and her teeth digging into her bottom lip.

"Speaking of..." she began.

"Oh, no. Tell me, what did you manage to do in the couple of hours you were out of the house?" Parker was good at getting herself in a pickle, but she was good—usually at getting out of it, too.

"Wyatt *might* think the baby is yours."

My entire body froze. If that's what Wyatt thought, then that's what the entire town was led to believe. Unless he hadn't been the one to spread the news of Parker's arrival, then someone might have simply seen her pregnant and not thought twice. But Bell Buckle being the town that it was, that was highly unlikely.

Everyone who was around when Parker and I were kids knew that we were destined for marriage. Though that didn't end up happening, I wouldn't put it past them to try and piece her reappearance together with that baby being mine.

Was that really such a bad thing, though? The father wasn't around, and by the sound of it, he wouldn't be coming by at all. I didn't want Parker to be subject to the scrutiny single moms seemed to get. People were so quick to judge when they didn't know the situation, to encourage someone to stay even if the environment wasn't healthy, all because of fucked-up values.

"Okay." I pulled a meat thermometer from the drawer.

"Okay?" Parker repeated. "That's it?"

I shrugged. "Is that a problem?"

"He's not your baby."

"He doesn't belong to the man who stuck his dick in you and decided he wasn't ready for a child. So, as far as anyone needs to know, he's mine."

Her mouth opened and closed like a fish out of water. I think I was speechless, too. Who the fuck was I, coming in and claiming that baby as my own? In a perfect world, of course he was. But in *this* world? Well, I had no fucking idea what to call this.

"All I'm saying is that I don't mind running with that narrative if you don't."

"We can tell them the truth, Beckham. You don't have to sacrifice yourself for me and my baby."

I set the tongs on the counter a little too hard. "Sacrifice? Parker, you already know I'd fucking die for you. You don't think I'd do that for your baby, too?"

She straightened. "I know you would. But this is my problem, not yours."

"You've always been my problem, Park. And if you think I've got nothing to lose, well, I'd have said you were right a few days ago. But now? I have you to lose."

Sadness swirled in her eyes. "What does that even mean?"

I knew she meant the first part of my statement, but I ignored it. That was a story to unpack another time. But even bringing it up had a weight landing on my chest like a ton of bricks. A thick, pungent scent filled the air, and I remembered the chicken.

"Shit." I grabbed the tongs and flipped the chicken over. The top was slightly charred, but not unsalvageable.

Parker moved from her spot. "Do you need help?"

I shook my head, turning the heat down a bit. "I've got it."

She stopped in her tracks, and I met her gaze. She probably had so many emotions warring around in that little head of hers, and here I was, making things worse. We needed a subject change before I said shit I'd regret, like how I wished she would sleep in my bed so I could feel a little less alone on the nights I couldn't sleep.

"I saw your profile," I said, turning the stove fan on low.

"You did?"

I nodded. "Didn't know you were *that* popular, Park. I'm a little jealous."

Her nonresponse had me looking over to find a smile

on her lips, cheeks rosy. "I'm surprised you haven't seen it before. I figured you would've looked me up at some point."

I shrugged before grabbing a pot for the rice. I was doing this all out of order, but Parker was distracting me, and honestly, I didn't care how long it took to cook this meal. I could stand here talking to her all night. "I tried not to."

Seeing her happy and living her life, even through a screen, would've hurt too much.

"I looked you up."

I busied myself with the rice and water, measuring each. "Yeah?"

"Yeah. I was just...scared to reach out. I guess? I didn't know if you would've wanted that."

I lit the burner before turning my full attention on her. I didn't tell her I would've loved to have heard from her. I didn't admit I thought about where she was constantly, and whether our trips would ever line up. I didn't mention how I looked for her everywhere I went, even knowing she could easily be hundreds of miles away. Parker was always on my mind, and the only thing preventing me from confessing that was the fear that I wasn't always on hers.

"I always want to hear from you, Park."

My admission had her cheeks burning hotter. As if a light had been switched, she cleared her throat and stepped back. "I should go shower before we eat."

"There are extra towels in the hall closet if you need them." Lettie had forced me to have extras of everything

—bedding, toilet paper, washcloths, you name it—saying I needed more on hand than just one of each thing.

She offered a small thanks before disappearing down the hall.

I stood there cooking, wondering why the fuck I still couldn't keep my thoughts straight around her.

9
PARKER

My growing stomach stared at me in the mirror, and I stared back at it. Every day, the size turned more from looking like bloat to looking like...I was carrying a baby.

My baby.

Not anyone else's but mine. The thought scared me sometimes, knowing that the other half of this baby didn't care enough to be here for him.

That was the thing about life. It built you up just to tear you right back down. I was in shock when I found out I was pregnant. Awestruck when I found out I was carrying a boy. But when Daniel told me he wanted nothing to do with raising a child? I was numb.

A few short months later, I got the call that my father had passed.

It was bittersweet that he'd left this world before my son could come into it. On one hand, I should've been looking forward to bringing his only grandchild to meet him. On the other? I was thankful I wouldn't have to one day explain to my son why he didn't visit his grandfather often. Why we celebrated holidays alone. Why, when other kids were getting cookies from their grandparents, we were bracing for confusion and violent outbursts from ours.

Alzheimer's could be a shitty thing. Every day was different from the next. As time went on, I got more reports of my father's episodes until I'd asked to stop knowing altogether. I'd witnessed his wrath enough times growing up that I knew visiting wouldn't have helped. He may have remembered me, but it was a version of me from the past. And the way he'd treated me, nothing good would have come from it. I didn't think I could handle seeing him like that, anyway. Which was selfish of me, really. But I'd come to learn over the last few years that in order to protect my peace, I had to think of myself.

But when those two little lines popped up, that shifted, too.

Now, only he mattered. And I'd do anything to keep him safe.

Knuckles rapped lightly on the door to my room. "Parker?"

I adjusted my sweater over my bump, tugging the hem a little harder than necessary to make sure it didn't crawl back up. I'd need new clothes soon, but I didn't have the budget right now. Hopefully, that'd change in the coming weeks.

"Yep?" I grabbed my purse off the end of the bed.

Beckham stepped in, leaning a shoulder against the doorframe. "Do you want a ride to work?"

The scent of hay and rain wafted through the room. "Did you go to your parents' ranch this morning?" It was barely seven thirty.

He nodded. "My brother's had shit to do, and I didn't want to leave my dad to feed on his own."

My hand tightened around the strap of my purse at the mention of his family. "What time did you wake up?"

He tucked his hands in the front of his jeans, his back to the frame now. "Four thirty."

"Oh." I chewed the inside of my lip, forgetting the reason he'd come in here.

"Why? Wish I would've woken you up?"

I looked up from my duck boots to find him smiling, though a crease had formed between his brows. "No. Waking up that early sounds like hell right now. But…" I bit the inside of my cheek. "I would like to see them."

He straightened a little. "Yeah?"

"I miss them. Miss your mom." Charlotte Bronson had never once blinked when it came to taking in a rescue case—whether of the horse or people variety.

The deep line disappeared, and now his face only held a bright smile. "Yeah. She misses you too."

"She does?"

"They all do, Park. Only reason they quit asking about you is because I couldn't take it anymore."

The admission may as well have been him ripping my heart from my chest and stomping it into the floorboards.

"I'm sorry for leaving."

He shrugged. "I left too."

"But you had every intention of coming back. I..." I'd been content with the idea of leaving Bell Buckle behind. The good and the bad. And all for what? Some years of traveling from ranch to ranch around the states, just to end up knocked up and a single mom?

Would my fate have been different if I'd stayed?

Would this be Beckham's baby?

Why did part of me wish it was?

"Didn't think you'd end up back in my house?"

Pregnant with another man's baby held unspoken onto the end of his sentence, but for some reason, he had taken to hiding his feelings about my pregnancy.

"Exactly." I ran my hands down my jeans that barely buttoned.

"That's okay. Sometimes things don't go as planned, but we shift."

I didn't miss the way he averted his eyes when he said it, how all traces of his smile fell and I was left looking at a shell of the Beckham I'd seen moments ago.

My pregnancy brain wracked my memory until I remembered why he was in here. "That ride you mentioned?"

His gaze met mine again, a spark of hope in those hazel depths.

"I'd love that."

———

Beckham's phone chimed with at least five texts on the drive over, and after the fifth, he silenced it. I'd chosen to ignore them, my mind instantly going to the worst-case scenario. That it was his girlfriend.

But why was that the worst case? We weren't a thing. We wouldn't be a thing. And yet, the air still felt charged around him. Like one spark and we'd go up in flames.

He parked in the lot and I got out, waiting for him by the hood.

"Do you have a girlfriend?" I blurted when he came to a stop beside me, hands in his Carhartt jacket's pockets.

He looked like I'd hit him with a bat. "What?"

I gestured to the phone tucked into the inner pocket of his jacket. "Was that your girlfriend texting you?"

His mouth twitched. "Jealous, Park?"

I could see the hint of amusement on his face.

This was just what I needed—a reason for him to tease me.

"No. I'm only curious so I know not to—" I snapped my mouth shut.

His growing smile was downright devious. "Know not to what?"

My hands did some weird, extremely awkward movement through the air before I stuffed them in my coat. "Nothing."

He pressed his lips together like he was holding in a laugh, and I scowled.

"Stop that."

"You want to know if I have a girlfriend."

I let out a growl of frustration—yes, a growl, because Beckham made me lose all sense of humanity. "Yes! I want to know. Happy?"

"Very."

I waited for his answer, rolling a piece of lint between my fingers as I did. But then he turned and continued toward the door.

"Aren't you going to answer me?"

He grabbed the handle, pulling it open, and faced me. "No. I don't have a girlfriend. Haven't in ten years."

Well, if the cold hadn't sucked the air from my lungs, that sure would have.

"Oh."

God, why was I always speechless around him? One answer and the past was slamming into me over and over again, a blaring red sign screaming, *Warning! Your pregnancy hormones already have you acting crazy, and now you're hanging out with the one guy that makes you* literally *crazy. Beware!*

He gestured to the shop, and I forced my feet to move, slipping past him into the heated lobby.

Had he slept with anyone since me? And if he had, why did I feel a pang of jealousy at that thought, when we both knew damn well I'd slept with someone? I wasn't purposefully trying to be celibate over the years, but when all I did was travel from ranch to ranch, helping out old cowboys and tough women, I didn't have much time for flings.

"Have you slept with anyone? Since we parted?" I

mentally cursed myself after the question slipped out. Where the fuck had my boldness come from today?

None of this was my damn business.

"In terms of sex, no." He stepped in behind me, letting the door fall shut, and started taking off his jacket. "But I've fooled around."

I shoved the pinch of jealousy away. I had no right.

"Okay. Who was texting you?" I asked, and winced. Curiosity was my arch nemesis today.

He hung his jacket up on the rack, pulling his phone out from the inside pocket. He clicked on the screen, squinting down at it. "Lettie. And Brandy. Sage." He scrolled a little more. "Bailey. Oakley."

"So, everyone," I surmised.

He nodded, locking the phone and shoving it back in the pocket. His smirk had me knowing what was coming next. "Why so many questions this morning?"

"Just trying to catch up," I chirped.

He blinked a few times, likely waiting for me to add anything of value to that poor explanation. When the silence stretched, he said, "They want to see you."

"When?"

"If they had it their way, it'd be now. But I want you to do this on your timeline, not theirs."

I took a steady inhale. I was eager to see everyone again, and their new partners, but I knew what came with seeing people from the past. It wouldn't only bring up the good, but it'd dig up the bad, too. All those times I joined them for dinner and fought back tears because we never had nice meals at my house. When I'd broken my arm, and Charlotte hadn't hesitated to pay the medical bill.

"Tonight?" I offered. No matter what, I'd have to relive what I'd left in Bell Buckle. I might as well nip it in the bud before I could think about it too hard.

Beckham studied me like he might be able to read whether I was looking for an out. I wasn't. "You still want to go to the ranch for this?"

I nodded. I missed that place.

"Just don't go to the bar," Wyatt said, his sudden appearance causing me to jump. Beckham seemed to track my reaction before we both faced Wyatt where he was coming in from the back door.

"Why not?" I asked. "Something happen to Outlaw's Watering Hole?"

Beside me, Beck's teeth ground together. "Wyatt."

"He's got a drinkin' problem, ya know." Wyatt sat in his chair, swiveling it around and shaking the mouse to wake the computer.

"What?" My eyes flew to Beckham to find him stiff as a board.

In my periphery, Wyatt seemed to freeze. "Shit, Beck. I thought she knew. She's got your baby and all, so I thought—"

Beckham raised a hand, stopping him.

The room was suddenly tense, the air too thick.

"I'll just leave you two to it." I didn't look to see Wyatt leaving the way he'd come. The sound of the door shutting was the only indication he'd left.

Beckham turned my way, but I couldn't read his expression. Guilt? Concern?

"Parker—"

"Were you going to tell me?"

"Tell you what? There's nothing *to* tell."

"A drinking problem, Beckham! That's a pretty big fucking deal."

"I *had* a drinking problem."

"That doesn't just go away overnight."

"I quit drinking, so yeah, it does."

"Why?" I had no idea why I was mad; I only knew that I was. It felt like he'd been hiding it, even though I hadn't been around to know about it in the first place. All those years, so many things happened, and I knew none of it. The reminder of all that lost time stung, making me more upset than I should've been. "It got that bad you had to full-on quit?"

He ran a hand over his jaw. "I had a wake-up call, so yes, I chose to quit."

My eyes widened. "A *wake-up call*? What does that even mean?"

"I punched my brother." His tone was flat, like there was no emotion inside of him aside from a hint of regret.

"You *what*? Which one?"

"Reed."

That was the last name I'd expected. Reed and Beckham always got along growing up, despite making everything a competition. What the fuck had changed in the last ten years?

Not only had he turned to alcohol, but it had gotten so bad that he'd punched his own brother?

What the hell was happening?

I tore my hands through my hair, spinning around to face the wall. I silently counted to ten.

Beckham knew my dad was an alcoholic. Knew how bad he'd gotten. He knew all of that, and yet that was how he'd chosen to end up.

"Parker. Take a breath."

I spun on him. He'd come closer, only a foot separating us now. "Tell me why you did it."

He looked ashamed of himself, and that had me nearly breaking. "I was mad."

"Because of the alcohol," I filled in.

"No."

"There's no other reason, Beckham!"

"Yes, there is."

"Then tell me."

Pain washed over his features like a waterfall, and he was trying not to drown in the current. "Park."

"Tell me, Beckham." I swallowed back the knot in my throat. "No secrets, remember?"

"Fuck, Parker. Because of you!" He ran a hand over his hair, fingers digging into his scalp. "Because Reed brought you up to get a rise out of me, and it worked."

My lashes fluttered, processing what he'd said. "Why would you punch your own brother over me when I hadn't been here in years? You didn't even know if I'd be coming back."

He laughed, though it held no humor. "Don't you get

it, Parker?" He stepped closer. "I never stopped thinking about you. Every fucking day, I wake up, and I think of you and—" He cut himself off, but I tried not to look too far into why. Who else did he think of when he woke?

"It's always because of you."

I shook my head. "My dad—" I choked out.

"I know." He grabbed both my hands, cradling them in his own like I was the most fragile person on this planet. "I know, Parker. I was in a really dark place. Reed helped me. My family helped me. I'm getting better every day. I'm never drinking again. *You* will never go through anything like that again."

Despite it all, I believed him. Beckham had never lied to me, and I had to trust that was the one thing that hadn't changed over all these years.

"Promise me," I whispered, unable to muster more than that.

He moved even closer, our clasped hands grazing both our stomachs now. "I promise."

"Are you okay?" I asked, because I couldn't not worry about Beckham. Even hundreds of miles apart, I worried about him.

He lowered his head, placing his forehead to mine, and nodded. "I'm okay."

And that was enough.

It always was.

10

BECKHAM

I tossed the wrench in the toolbox, a loud *clang* ringing out through the shop. Parker deserved to know. About the drinking. About Garrett. About me. For that reason alone, I couldn't be mad at Wyatt. But his way of outing me, paired with replacing the fuel pump on this '72 Camaro, had me damn well frustrated. More so at the car, but the semantics didn't matter.

"What'd that wrench do to you?" Wyatt asked, running a stained rag between his grease-covered fingers.

"Nothing."

"I said I was sorry, Beckham. I don't know what else to say."

"I wanted her to know. I just..." I braced my hands on the front fender of the car, staring in at the engine.

"Wanted to tell her another way," he filled in.

"What other way is there to tell the girl you'd do anything for that you ended up just like her father?"

Regret hit me in the gut, stealing the air from my lungs. I never should've drank that much. Never should've turned to alcohol to fill the hole Garrett's death had shot through my chest.

Four months later, simply thinking about him still made me want to scream. To tear my hair out and beat myself up and sob for hours. *Garrett should be here.* He should be fucking breathing, giving me shit for falling off a fucking horse. Not under so much dirt that I couldn't hear his laugh.

Grief chose the wrong fucking times to rear its ugly head. I didn't *want* to grieve. I wanted my best friend.

"Beckham?"

I shoved off the car, swiping away the tear that'd fallen. "Yeah?"

"I asked if you were good."

I pinched the bridge of my nose before sliding a hand down my face. Counted my breaths because Garrett couldn't. "Yep."

Wyatt studied me as I closed the hood and started to clean up the mess from the day.

"I apologized to Parker, too," he stated when I tossed a handful of trash in the can.

"She accept it?" Parker was sweet, but she had heavily fortified walls. Her parents put them there, and she didn't let them down for just anyone.

"Yeah. Told me to keep any details about you out of my mouth around her."

That piqued my interest. "Why?"

He shrugged before setting a box of oil filters on the shelf. "My guess is she wants to hear it all from you."

My focus moved to the door that led into the office that doubled as the shop's lobby. Had she been sitting in there thinking about me all day, like I had her?

"Maybe take her on a date," Wyatt suggested.

My gaze shot to him. "What?"

He crossed his arms, splotches of grease dotting his tan skin. "Take some time to catch up with her."

"She's living in my house. There's plenty of time to do that there."

He shook his head. "In a neutral place, Beckham. She's not going to open up if she's surrounded by your things, feeling like she doesn't belong there."

"For someone who doesn't think before he speaks, you've sure got a lot of wisdom."

He sent a frown my way. "Thanks. But complimenting me won't get you a raise."

"I'll have to try harder next time." Despite the teasing, Wyatt had a point. Parker likely felt out of place. Even though I'd told her she was more than welcome to stay, I'd seen her hesitancy in opening cabinets or closing doors. Like she didn't feel comfortable enough to treat the place like her own. "I'll figure something out with Parker."

"You better, man. She's carrying your baby. And by the way"—he arched a brow—"when did that happen?"

I rubbed the back of my neck, not knowing if Parker had told him anything I needed to keep in line with. This whole ruse was going to be harder than I thought. "Few months ago."

It wasn't entirely a lie. She did get pregnant a few months ago. Just not by me.

Every time I remembered that little fact, my heart stung a little worse, my jaw clenched a little tighter. Someone else had the audacity to get her pregnant and then up and ditch her. I needed to know who the fuck he was so I could find the fucker and shoot him in the goddamn dick.

"Woah, there." Wyatt held up his hands, taking a step back. I blinked back into reality, out of the red haze that always came over me when it came to protecting Parker, and noted him taking caution of me like one would with a bear. "Sensitive subject, I take it."

I grunted. Paused. Maybe comparing me to a bear was the right thing to do. I was damn sure starting to sound like one. "Something like that."

"Alright. Well." He grabbed his hat from the work-bench and popped it on. "Thanks for the help today. I probably don't need you around till next week."

Next week? I didn't want that. I wanted every excuse I could take to be around Parker. Wanted a reason to talk to her, even if it was only for her to order a truck part.

"But," Wyatt went on, casually walking across the shop toward the door, "because I know you probably want to be around your girlfriend, I tacked on an extra client this week so you have a reason to be here."

"She's not my girlfriend."

He wrapped a hand around the knob, patting me on

the shoulder with the other. "You keep telling yourself that, buddy."

Before I could send some smart-ass retort his way, he opened the door that led to the lobby. I followed after him, stopping short when I saw Parker and her big eyes staring up at me from the swivel chair.

"Good day?" she asked. For a moment, it felt like we were the only two in the room.

I'd done my best to avoid coming in here for the sole reason that she'd hate if I kept checking in on her. Parker was strong, and I had to keep reminding myself of that. But seeing her pregnant, growing an entire baby inside of her, awoke some feral need to take care of her at all times.

"Other than Beckham giving me shit for calling him out?" Wyatt asked, his back to the exit. "It went smoothly."

He already knew how her day was, so he didn't ask. He didn't have a reason to avoid that desk. He'd come and gone like he always did, while I'd holed up in the shop like some broody wet puppy.

"I'm going to head out. Lock up on your way out?"

I nodded in Wyatt's direction. "Will do. Drive safe."

"You, too. See you two tomorrow."

Then he was gone, and we were alone.

The small space felt like a live wire. Every flutter of her lashes, her small intakes of breath, the way her eyes held mine so intently—like she had a million things to say and didn't know how to say them—all of it had my skin buzzing and my head a mess.

"How are you feeling?" I asked, figuring that was a good place to start.

She offered a closed-lip smile before reaching forward to turn off the monitor and stand. "Good. And you?"

"Good." For the first time in a long time, it wasn't a lie. "You still want to see my family tonight? I can always postpone—"

She stepped out from behind the desk, setting a hand on my chest. "I want to go."

Every cell in my body froze, raising its head to the feel of her. When we'd touched earlier, it had felt the same. I wanted nothing more than to pull her into me and skip all the rest. But I didn't know if that's what she really wanted, and I wouldn't be selfish enough to add that to her plate. She had enough to deal with already.

She removed her hand from my chest, staring at the place it'd once been like she'd felt it too. "Sorry."

"Don't be."

Being this close to her gave me too much opportunity to do exactly what I wanted to, so I moved to the coat rack by the door. I grabbed hers, handing it to her when she followed, before sliding my arms into my own.

"Sage knows someone is pregnant, but no one knows that it's you. I don't know if Wyatt told them anything, so..." I didn't know how the fuck to ask if she wanted me to pretend around them, too.

A look of shame crossed her features, and she ducked her head as she tugged her jacket on. Her left arm got stuck halfway through and she wiggled it to try to rectify it, but her attempt was futile.

"Here." I walked around her, straightening the sleeve and tugging it a bit so she could maneuver herself into it more easily.

"Thanks." She messed with the cuff like it needed fixing. "I should probably get new clothes soon. These are getting a little tight."

"The girls would probably love to go shopping with you," I offered. I'd have volunteered to go with, but she likely wanted space from me. We were living in the same house and working at the same place. The last thing I wanted to do was suffocate her.

She slowly turned in place, our chests brushing when she came face-to-face with me. "I'd love that."

I nodded, but I didn't really know what I was nodding to. Not as her eyes sucked me in and a thousand flashes of memories blared in my head. Her riding me in my truck. Her laughing on her horse. Her crying on the side of the road instead of being at school. So many versions of Parker, and I'd loved all of them. This version, though... She was almost a stranger, and I hated it. Same Parker, but...different.

Her voice was quieter, the red of her cheeks brighter, the hope in her eyes deeper, as she said, "I'm ready to go."

But even with her words, I couldn't force myself out of this stupor. My hand moved of its own accord, brushing a stray strand of hair behind her ear. She wore gold studs today, the color bringing out the flecks of yellow in her hazel eyes.

I hadn't realized I'd drifted closer as she whispered my name. "Beckham."

It was a warning and a plea. Confusing and alluring. Would it be so bad if we went back to how things were before she left? Would she hate me if I tried?

My phone ringing in my jacket didn't give me the chance to try.

With a sigh, I stepped back and pulled my phone out. "Yes?"

"Lettie's asking how far away you are. Charlotte needs to know when to put the casserole in the oven," Bailey said. A horse whinnied in the background, and I suspected he was out feeding the animals their dinner.

"We're leaving the shop now." My tone was a bit harsh when I should've been thanking him. He'd unknowingly stopped me from making a grave mistake. How did I know that testing the waters wouldn't result in Parker leaving? Right now, she and the baby came first. I could settle for my fist in the shower and just the thought of her. Hell, I'd do that forever if I had to.

"Alright. I'll tell her. Don't drive like an idiot."

"To a family dinner? Never. I drive like a grandpa."

"You don't have to tell me twice. I already knew that."

I frowned before we said our goodbyes and hung up.

I pocketed the phone, finding Parker staring out the glass door to the parking lot. The setting sun cast rays of rich pink across the black asphalt, reflecting hints of strawberry hues into the lobby.

"That was Bailey," I explained. "Lettie's impatient."

"Just like always," Parker noted, a hint of sadness in her tone. She looked at me over her shoulder, and I closed the distance. Reaching a hand around her, I shoved the door open. The burst of cold air had her wrapping her arms around herself. The sight made me remember all those times I'd picked her up at the end of her driveway: cold, hot, crying, antsy.

"Just like always," I repeated.

I followed her to my truck after locking up the shop and held the passenger door for her while she got in.

Finding out who got her pregnant and abandoned her could wait. Kissing her could wait. All of it could wait if it meant she was here.

I was tired of missing memories.

11

PARKER

Beckham had tried to prepare me for this dinner as best he could. Growing up, the Bronsons were like a warm blanket after a long, cold day, wrapping you in their embrace and giving you sanctuary. There was never a day where I didn't feel at home in their house. But tonight, I worried I wouldn't have the same feelings, and I'd have no choice but to mourn the loss of it.

Back then, I fit in. Now I was walking into a house half full of people I knew, and half full of people who were complete strangers. Beckham's siblings had formed their own relationships over the years, and my only hope going into this was that they all accepted me, and that none of the Bronsons resented me for leaving Bell Buckle.

"It's going to be okay," Beckham affirmed, setting a hand on my thigh to stop the bouncing. We were heading up the driveway to the main house, and the sight of it, even from this distance, had a bowling-ball-sized emotional pit dropping to the base of my stomach.

"You don't think they'll hate me?"

He aimed a frown at me, the look laced with concern. "They've been asking about you like crazy, Park. I wouldn't take them being eager to see you as them being pissed off."

I picked at the side of my fingernail. "I've missed them. And I know we have to have the hard conversations, but I just..." I dropped my head. "I could really use the good right now."

His hold on my thigh tightened slightly. "Is there something you need to tell me?"

I looked up to find his body stiff, his grip on the wheel white-knuckled. "What do you mean?"

He shifted, but the movement seemed forced, like he was trying to loosen his muscles. "About the asshole who got you pregnant and left."

My heart started racing at the mention of him. "You're bringing this up now?"

He heaved a breath before shaking his head. An internal battle raged behind his eyes. "I need to know, Parker."

"Know what?"

"Did he hurt you?"

My eyes widened. Daniel had never been abusive, but when he found out I was pregnant and I planned to keep it? Well, he hadn't been happy, and that may have slipped into his physical reaction to the news.

"No."

"Are you lying?"

"Beckham, now's not the time."

He let out an incredulous, humorless laugh. "You're lying to me."

The hurt behind that statement sent knives digging into my conscience as regret quickly hit me. "He didn't hurt me before. But when he found out I was pregnant, he recommended I get an abortion, and I told him I wouldn't get one." I'd thought about that option for all of two minutes before I shoved the idea into a locked box. The moment I saw those two lines appear, I'd cracked. The hard facade I tried to uphold in certain situations was nowhere to be found at that moment. I *wanted* this baby, regardless of who the father was.

His hand spun on the wheel, leather creaking below his grip. "What'd he do?"

"He pushed me."

Thankfully, we'd made it to the end of the driveway. Otherwise, I was sure Beckham would've hit the brakes right in the middle of the road.

"He did *what*?"

His eyes held the promise of death. There was no question about it.

"I think I was in his way—"

"Don't make excuses for that asshole."

Shame had me casting my gaze to my lap again.

"Did you fall?" he asked, softening his tone.

I nodded. "I went to the hospital that night, just to make sure everything was okay." I met his stare again. "The baby is okay. And I never saw Daniel again."

Beck's teeth ground together before he tore a hand through his hair and moved his focus out the windshield. He was staring at the ranch, but it was like he wasn't really seeing it.

"Beckham, I'm okay." I set my hand on the one he still had on my leg. "None of that was your fault." Because I knew Beckham. Knew he'd blame himself if he could, because holding that responsibility was easier to him than accepting he had no hand in stopping the bad things that happened.

"I should've never let you leave," he whispered.

"And what were you going to do? Stuff me in your truck while you went off to ride broncs?"

"If it would have kept you safe."

But both of us knew that wasn't even close to a possibility. We were both too eager to be free to be contained. It was what had torn us apart.

Through the windshield, I saw the front door swing open, and a little girl with long brown hair came barreling out in short sleeves and fuzzy slippers. She shouted something as she bounded to the truck.

"What do you want to tell them about the baby?" Beckham asked, his tone low despite his eyes lighting up at the sight of the girl.

"They think he's yours?"

"If Wyatt talked to them, then yes."

"And if he didn't?"

There was a long, heavy pause, and our gazes met.

Beckham would sacrifice everything for me, but I didn't want him to pretend for my sake.

"If you want me to say he's mine, I will."

He showed no hesitation, and it made my chest sting.

But I didn't get the chance to answer as a woman who looked nearly identical to the girl appeared on the porch, tears in her eyes and a pained expression on her face.

Beckham was out of the truck in an instant, leaving his door wide open as he met the little girl halfway. He scooped her up, hurrying toward the porch and up the steps. Seconds later, Callan emerged, coming to the woman's side and setting a hand on her elbow. The two men studied something on her hand while the little girl buried her face in Beckham's neck.

The sight had my heart skipping a beat.

I climbed out of the truck, quietly closing my door and then Beckham's before crossing to the porch. My approach felt like I was imposing on a private family matter, and the knowledge that I wasn't part of it had me blinking back tears. I blamed the pregnancy hormones.

"You need stitches," Callan stated as he inspected her hand.

"Cal, it's fine," the woman insisted.

As I hit the top step, I saw the blood dripping down her arm.

"He's right," Beckham agreed. "That cut won't heal right on its own."

"But Avery—" she started.

"I've got her." Beck ran a hand up and down the little girl's back.

The woman looked from Beck to Callan before

settling her gaze on me. Her eyes widened before her mouth popped open. "Oh my gosh! I'm so sorry. You must be Parker. I'm Sage, Callan's girlfriend."

She went to hold out her hand, but stopped as she remembered she was pressing a rag to her bleeding finger.

I waved her off. "It's okay. Keep pressure on that. It's nice to meet you, Sage. Sorry about the..." I glanced at the blood dripping down her arm.

"I was cutting fruit when Avery ran out here like a bat out of hell because she saw Beck pull up. I thought her scream was because she got hurt, and the knife must've slipped when I looked up." Her focus moved behind me before turning to me and Beck again. "Did you two come together?"

I looked at Beckham to answer that, but he stood there stiff as a board with Avery sniffling in his arms. I wasn't sure when she'd started crying, but I was sure she felt guilty.

"We did," I answered, and braced for the barrage of questions. *Are you dating? Is this his baby? When did you find time to get together, let alone have a baby?*

"We should go," Callan urged, placing a palm on Sage's lower back.

His suggestion had a trapped breath loosening from my chest.

Sage sent a sympathetic look at Beckham. "Are you sure it's okay? I know this dinner was for Parker, and the last thing I want to do is take any attention away from that."

He frowned at her. "Sage. You accidentally cut your-self. This wasn't some malicious plan. Please, go. I'm more than happy to watch Avery."

Something about her hoping she hadn't ruined the night had me wondering about her past—if there was a pattern there, and if this worry came from somewhere deep.

"We'll send you updates," Callan said, leading Sage toward the porch steps.

"Mama," Avery called out, reaching for her over Beck's shoulder.

Callan squeezed Avery's hand while Sage reached up on tiptoes to place a kiss to her cheek. "I'm okay, honey. It's not your fault. Mommy's just clumsy sometimes."

"Like me?" Avery sniffed.

Sage nodded, a reassuring smile on her lips. "It must run in the family."

After they departed, Beckham turned to me and opened his mouth.

"Don't apologize," I said quickly.

He snapped his mouth shut and lowered Avery to the ground.

I smiled down at her. "You must be Avery."

She nodded, rubbing puffy eyes.

"You know"—I lowered myself to a crouch in front of her, ignoring how it was becoming more difficult with my growing belly—"I've accidentally cut myself plenty of times."

"You have?" she asked.

I held out my arm, pointing to the scar on the inside of my elbow. "This was from barbed wire."

She studied it, angling her head to get a better look. "Mama said never to play with that."

I dipped my chin in agreement. "Your mom's right. It's super sharp. But the important part is that it healed." I dropped my arm, meeting her gaze. "Your mom's going to be okay."

Her bottom lip puffed out. "I just don't want her to be in pain."

Beckham ran a hand down the back of her head. "Your mom's strong, Aves. Just like you. She'll be good as new once they stitch it up."

She craned her neck to look up at him. "Will the stitches hurt?"

"Maybe. But after, she'll feel a lot better."

He didn't sugarcoat it, and Avery seemed to appreciate that as she gave a firm nod.

"Now, run on inside. We're right behind you," Beck said.

She gave him a quick hug around the waist before darting inside the farmhouse. When the door clicked shut, I turned to find Beckham studying me.

"You ready?"

I inhaled a steadying breath, nerves seeping right back into my bones. But even as my palms grew clammy, I knew this was what I wanted.

"I'm ready."

12

BECKHAM

Parker's movements seemed hesitant as we stepped into my parents' house, and rightfully so. Not only had it been a long time since she'd seen my family, but she was also pregnant. All of that resulted in dozens of questions I was sure she didn't know how to answer.

As soon as we passed the threshold of the front entry, Parker stopped. The entire room did, too. One glance turned into four, which turned into all eyes on her.

"Parker!" Lettie exclaimed breathlessly, like she'd been just as nervous before our arrival. Had they thought she'd bail? That her presence was only a rumor?

Lettie crossed to her, not sparing Parker's stomach a single glance as she wrapped her arms around her. Parker returned the gesture, and the sight warmed something inside me.

Lennon, my oldest brother, stood in the living room with his arm around his girlfriend Oakley's shoulders.

Reed was in the kitchen with his girlfriend, Brandy, a platter of buttered corn placed in front of them like they'd been working on it when we walked in.

"Well, look who it is," my mom said, setting a pair of tongs down on the counter by Reed and Brandy.

I quickly shot her a look warning her to take it easy, but she waved me off and swooped in right as Lettie stepped away. Parker was stiff as a board as my mom's arms wrapped around her. But as my mom ran a hand in circles over her back, Parker loosened, melting into my mom like she was the roots of the family tree Parker had missed so dearly, grounding her in the storm that was her life.

I'd run headfirst through pounding rain and dangerous blizzards time and time again to save Parker from the flood. This house had always been her safe haven, and Charlotte was her umbrella from the pain.

Parker wouldn't be alone in any of this, and my mom hugging her like she hadn't been gone a day was proof of that.

The two parted and my mom squeezed Parker's hand, a tear-filled smile on her face.

"Are you doing okay, sweetie?" my mom asked.

Parker nodded, looking like she was holding back her own tears. "I'm okay."

My mom sent me a speculating look to confirm, and I dipped my chin. I didn't allow myself to live in a world where Parker *wasn't* okay.

"Parker, this is Oakley," Lettie started, toning down the excitement a bit as she gestured to the auburn-haired woman who was now beside her. She could likely tell this was a big step for Parker, and I appreciated my sister for not hesitating to loop her in.

"Hi." Parker sent Oakley a soft smile. "I'm not sure what they've told you about me, but in case it was bad" —she narrowed a teasing glare on me before continuing —"I was best friends with Beckham growing up."

I crooked a brow. "Is that what we were?"

Parker gave me an all-knowing look, a blush painting her cheeks, before she fell into easy conversation with the girls.

After introductions and warm welcome-backs, my mom packed us all around the dining room table. With the sun setting earlier in the day, it was too cold to enjoy dinner on the porch tonight—her favorite place to see her large family laughing and smiling as they dug into a home-cooked meal. We could bear it with the heaters on, but she'd likely kept us inside for Parker's and Sage's sake.

All through dinner, the obvious was avoided. Parker was pregnant, and no one brought it up. I wasn't sure what to expect out of my family with that, but it was coming. I only wished I knew when so we could both prepare. Hell, we should've discussed logistics well before arriving here.

Once dinner was done, Parker insisted on helping the girls clean up. Meanwhile, my brothers forced me to join them on the front porch. I'd been reluctant to leave Parker's side for the fear she'd be ambushed alone, but Lettie had sent me a reassuring look before I slipped out the door with my jacket on and baseball cap pulled low.

Lennon leaned his elbows on the wood railing, beer beside him, as he stared out at the barn faintly illuminated by the lights on either side of the barn door. Reed had his arms crossed and a frown aimed my way. He had every right to be a little hard on me right now. I'd been spiraling for months, and now I showed up to dinner with a pregnant Parker. He likely thought she'd been the source of all of my troubles the past few months. It didn't help that I hadn't been entirely honest with them about Parker over the years. Telling your family the truth about the girl you fell in love with could be tricky, so I'd lied about some things to save myself their concern.

Bailey was taking small sips of his beer, giving his hands something to do. We all felt a little awkward. A little off. But Bailey especially, because as far as he knew, I'd been in contact with Parker while she was gone. And that...was a lie.

"Alright, out with it," I said, stuffing my hands in the pockets of my jacket. "You all have something to say, so say it."

The three of them exchanged glances. Bailey shifted on his feet, Lennon avoided looking at me, and Reed was straight scowling.

"She's pregnant," Reed stated. There was never any fucking around with him. When we were younger, he and I loved to get into loads of trouble around the ranch. Then something changed in him, and women became a sore subject. Being with Brandy was slowly changing him, but it'd take a lot for Reed to stop being so damn broody.

I gave him a blank stare as if that fact wasn't obvious. "She is."

A cricket chirped somewhere below the deck. A cow lowed out in the field.

Bailey clanked his beer down on the table and slapped his hands together. "Okay. I don't like this." He pinned me with his gaze. "We're all wondering"—he did some weird hand motion—"how."

I tilted my head. Waited for him to go on.

When I was met with nothing but silence and expectant stares, I said, "Well, when a man and a woman—"

Lennon took a long sip of his beer while Bailey held a hand up and interrupted. "We all know where babies come from."

"Okay, then you know how she's pregnant," I concluded.

Reed's frown couldn't have gotten deeper if it tried.

"Is the baby yours?" Lennon asked, finally speaking up and shoving off the railing.

I rolled my lips together. Parker and I had discussed it in the truck, but we hadn't come to a final agreement because of Sage's injury. Either way I put it, I could end up upsetting her. And that was the last fucking thing I wanted to do. I didn't want her to have to deal with the onslaught of questions about the father if I said the baby wasn't mine, but I also didn't want to stake that sort of claim if she didn't want me being that figure in the baby's life. At least, for now.

"He's as mine as he'll get." There. That was good enough.

Reed let out a disbelieving half-ass chuckle. "We all know that baby isn't yours, Beckham. My question is, why does the whole goddamn town think it is?"

"It's a boy?" Bailey asked right after.

"It's a boy," I confirmed before directing my attention at Reed. "How do you know he's not mine?"

"You wouldn't have been in such a shitty downward spiral if Parker had been in town," Reed grumbled.

Lennon nodded his agreement.

"What's this, gang-up-on-Beckham night?" I knocked back my water, emptying the bottle. "Where's Callan when I need him?"

"Did you know she was pregnant?" Lennon asked. His look of concern softened me up a bit, but not enough.

"No." And if I had thought she was off happy with some other man, it likely would've tipped me over the edge. I lost Garrett, but losing Parker for good, too? There were only so many things a man could handle.

"So that's not why you punched me?" Reed arched a brow like he didn't believe it.

"I punched you because you hit a sensitive topic just to get under my skin," I gritted out.

Bailey sipped his beer, watching our interaction like we were some form of entertainment. "If you ladies want to hash it out—"

"How's that sensitive topic treating you, Beck?" Reed's question was quizzical, but it didn't take a genius to figure out why he was pushing this. "She comes back into town, pregnant—"

"Leave her out of your goddamn mouth," I bit out.

"Feeling protective because she's pregnant with some other man's baby?" He kept at it, teetering on the fine line that was nearly nonexistent when it came to Parker. Someone so much as thinks of her wrong, I punch them. End of fucking story.

"What'd she do to end up on the run from the baby daddy, Beck? Think to ask her that? Find out what you're getting yourself into?"

My fist clenched, muscles pulsing with the urge to reenact what I'd regretted doing for months.

"I don't plan to hurt him."

All heads swiveled to find Parker's silhouette filling the doorframe.

Lennon cursed while Bailey let out a low whistle. Reed, on the other hand, had the brains to look regretful.

"If that's what you think I'm here to do, to make him clean up some mess I was involved in, it's not. I came to Bell Buckle for my dad's funeral."

Shock lit all their faces. Not many people in this town cared for Parker's father, so aside from the outsiders who attended his funeral, Bell Buckle had stayed in the dark about his passing.

"That's whose funeral you went to?" Bailey asked me.

I nodded.

"I was going to leave after," Parker went on.

"She has nowhere else to go," I clarified. "She's staying with me. In my house." I sent Reed a hard look, solidifying the fact that yes, I was going to fucking protect her. That's how it'd always been with Parker, and that's how it was going to fucking stay. I was well aware the man who'd gotten her pregnant had pushed her, but she'd told me he hadn't hurt her before. Some part of my brain told me not to believe it. Parker was a pro at hiding her pain all so she could see those around her smile. She never wanted to bring the mood down. But fuck, couldn't she just tell me the truth so I could kill him and get on with it?

"Don't take this out on Beckham." A small hand rested on the swell of her belly, and in the faint light from the house, I could see the goosebumps on her arms from the cold. She shouldn't be out here without a coat, but I wasn't about to interrupt her to tell her that. "I told him I could leave, but he insisted I stay. I've been traveling to different ranches since I left this town. I always stuck to that plan. But that changed when I got pregnant, and then I found out my father passed. I didn't come here with some malicious intent to take advantage of Beckham, if that's what you're thinking."

Reed lowered his gaze to his boots. "That's not what I thought, Parker. Beckham's been going through something, and the last thing he needs right now is another responsibility." He threw a hand my way, concern flitting across his features. "Fuck, a few months ago, he could barely feed himself. Now you're here, you're pregnant, and he's Beck. He'll always take care of you. There's no question about that. We just don't want him losing himself again."

Unspoken words hung in the thick air. Like whether I was even capable of helping her when I could barely help myself. Whether this was the right thing for me to be doing when I'd just shown my family how unstable I was. Whether I was able to be around Parker, pregnant with someone else's baby, and not lose my damn mind.

Spoiler: I lost my mind the first time we kissed as teenagers. Never got it back. Didn't think I wanted it back if I could.

"So... Which is it? Is the baby his?" Bailey asked, clearly losing us with the emotional bits.

"No." Parker's answer hurt for some reason, even though it was the truth. I wanted that baby to be mine. Wanted to be the guy who was with her when she saw those two lines pop up. Wanted to go to every appointment, every ultrasound, and talk about how cute our baby was. How proud I was to be a dad.

But none of that was real.

This was our reality.

Lennon's eyes narrowed slightly, skeptical. "Wyatt start that rumor himself, then?"

A flush lit Parker's cheeks and she stepped out of the doorway, coming closer to me. "No. Uh, I did."

Bailey's brows shot up. "Holy shit, P."

"I didn't mean to," she added quickly, wrapping her arms around herself. "He assumed, and it went from there."

"Yeah. Spread like wildfire," Lennon mumbled.

"So, what? You're gonna clear it up?" Bailey asked.

Reed was quiet now, likely brooding in the fact that he hadn't gotten out everything he wanted to say. That, and he likely felt bad for Parker overhearing our conversation. Brothers could give each other shit, but we didn't loop girls into the mix.

"I'm fine with it," I said before Parker could confirm.

She shook her head. "You don't need to—"

I pinned my gaze down on her. "We can discuss it away from my brothers and their never-ending peanut gallery." Eyes back on my brothers, I said, "Anyone asks, that's what you go with. I don't want any other rumors spreading about Parker."

"You mean, besides this one," Reed muttered.

I shot him a glare, but before I could rip him a new one, my phone buzzed in my pocket. Slipping it out, a text from Callan lit up the screen.

Callan: We're still waiting for the doctor in the back. Sorry it's taking so long. Avery okay?

A glance inside the front window showed Avery sitting on Oakley's lap, head resting against her shoulder.

Me: She's good. Looks tired, though. I can bring her to my place, let her sleep over

Callan: That'd be a lifesaver. Mom has a spare booster in the truck. I'll come get her in the morning

Me: Sounds good. I'll let you know once she's all tucked in

Callan: I owe you

Sliding the phone into my jeans pocket, I looked down to find a worried Parker staring up at me. "How is she?"

"She's okay. Just waiting for the doctor." I couldn't fight it any longer as I wrapped an arm around her shoulders and tugged her close. Her skin was ice as I said to the guys, "We're gonna head out. Avery's staying at my place since Cal and Sage are going to be there for a while."

"How many stitches?" Bailey asked, a white puff of air forming with his words from the cold.

"Not sure yet." I turned Parker in the direction of the door, but she stopped me. She set a hand on my arm, and I dropped it.

She stepped in front of Reed, and he met her gaze. "I know you worry about him. But I'd never intentionally hurt your brother."

"He hasn't been the same since you left, Parker."

His response pissed me off, and I nearly stepped between the two before he added, "But I have hope this time. Just...be gentle with him."

Reed took the number-one seat for the hardest to

break of the Bronson brothers, but over time, Brandy had softened him. I really should thank her, because if he had said anything to upset Parker, we would've had a redo of this past summer.

Parker tilted her chin up, so much promise in those eyes of hers. "I will."

13
PARKER

Soft snores filtered in from the back of the truck as Beckham slowed at the turn for his house. I'd figured Avery would fall asleep on the way, if the number of yawns before we left were any indication. I could play off my silence as being considerate while she slept, but really, I was nervous.

I hadn't been sure what to expect from the conversation with his brothers, but Reed being pissed wasn't on my bingo card. Sure, the man had always been a grump, but never toward me. That, paired with how I hadn't felt like I was imposing until I walked in on them talking about me, had my emotions on edge.

I'd put on a brave face, but with my hormones, I was doing all I could to hold the impending tears at bay.

After parking in his usual spot, Beckham came around to open my door before doing the same to Avery's. He didn't hesitate as he reached across the sleeping girl to unbuckle her and gently scoop her into his arms. I quietly closed both doors and tried not to focus on the way Beckham's biceps flexed with Avery in his hold.

Like he'd done it a dozen times, he unlocked and opened the front door using the hand under her legs, then swung it open to let me in first. I slipped past him, and he nudged the door shut before heading down the hall in the direction of his bedroom.

Not a single word passed between the two of us.

While I waited on the couch, I checked my phone. A text from two hours ago popped up.

> Axel: How are you holding up? You and the baby doing okay?

A strange sense of calm washed over me with my cousin's check-in. He'd been doing that every so often since I told him I was pregnant and navigating things on my own.

We'd known each other existed while growing up, but with the feud between our fathers, we never met. With free will and the desire to reclaim the things my parents had robbed me of, I'd found Axel's sad excuse for a Facebook profile and reached out. It'd taken him weeks to respond—something about how technology wasn't his thing and his teenage daughter was the reason his profile existed to begin with. After that, I'd driven to Midnight Valley to meet them. He was a single dad, so he understood the struggles I would be facing doing this on my own. The difference was Annabelle was sixteen now, and lived for giving him headaches and heart attacks.

I hoped my experience would be a little bit different.

> Me: We're okay. I'm back in Bell Buckle.

> Axel: Visiting or staying?

> Me: Both?

I could imagine him shaking his head at his phone, a frown on his face. His little town was eccentric. Neon lights lit their streets, the nightlife in Midnight Valley invigorating as ever. During the day, Axel fit in. But at night? He came alive. The whole town did.

> Axel: Wouldn't have expected anything less. If you need anything, call me. I mean it.

I could tell Axel had been worried when he found out I was traveling solo. It was probably a normal feeling, having a teenage daughter and all, but I assured him I was okay. Just because the remainder of my close family was dead didn't mean I had nobody left.

I shot a text back, then let curiosity get the best of me as I opened the account I was trying to ignore. My notifications had run wild with my silence, and the red bar at the top confirmed as much. Rather than scrolling through those, I clicked a few of my posts, glancing at some of the top comments. One in particular caught my attention. Stopped my heart for a beat, too.

The same man who'd left the comment about me on

my horse had typed: *Anyone know where her family lives? Just wanna check in.*

I reread the comment at least ten times before closing the app and tossing the phone on the other end of the couch.

No one online knew I was from Bell Buckle. I'd kept that part of my life a secret for a reason. Yet his interest had me gnawing on the inside of my cheek, worried someone with the wrong intentions would find me here.

Down the hall, Beckham quietly shut the door to his room and padded toward me in the living room, socked feet silent on the floor. His appearance had me wiping any trace of worry off my face and shoving the comment out of my mind.

"Does she sleep here often?" I asked from my spot on the couch, readjusting my legs so they were bent as far as they could go. The bulge of my belly pressed against my thighs.

Beckham grabbed two waters from the fridge before joining me. He plucked my phone from the cushion and set it on the coffee table before taking his seat. "I watch her for Sage and Callan when they have appointments or need a minute to themselves. Depends how tired she is from the day or if they're late getting home."

I glanced down the hall, noting he'd laid her in his bed and not the guest room. I assumed she stayed in the guest bedroom when I wasn't here, which meant...

"I can take the couch tonight," I offered, feeling bad that he had no other options.

He shook his head, his mouth a firm line. "No."

My forehead scrunched. "I'm not going to let you sleep on the couch because I'm in your guest room. I'm appreciative of you letting me stay here, but I can't upend you completely, Beck."

His stare was hard, setting in stone that there was no room for negotiation. "You're not sleeping on the couch, Parker."

He held the water out to me, and I took it.

"Well, neither are you," I declared defiantly.

He uncapped his bottle and brought it to his lips, eyes on me as he drank. I watched his Adam's apple bob. His lips wrapping around the opening. His hand gripping the plastic before he brought it down to his lap.

The smirk on his mouth told me he noticed me staring.

"What do you suggest, then?" he asked, a cocky lilt to the question.

My eyes narrowed in challenge. "Sleep with me."

He choked out a breathy laugh. "You askin' or demanding?"

I crossed my arms. Cocked a brow. "What'd it sound like?"

His little half-smile nearly melted me to a puddle. "You got bossy, Park."

"I got tough."

His gaze roamed down my chest to my legs, taking his time with his slow perusal before meeting my stare again.

I swallowed.

"So what you're saying is you won't hesitate to throw a punch if I end up on this couch tonight?"

"If fighting's where we have to take this, I'm not above it." My shoulders lifted in a casual shrug.

"Fightin' with our clothes on or off?"

His words had my cheeks flaming. Had me shifting on the cushion as my core heated and my pussy pulsed.

What the fuck was he doing?

"Beckham—"

He brought the bottle to his lips but didn't throw it back. "I'm only joking, Park. Don't get your panties in a bunch." He drank.

"I'm not wearing any."

Water flew, a cough sputtering from his lips as he choked. "Jesus, Parker."

I cocked my head, fighting my smile. "What?"

"Warn a guy next time. Could've fucking killed me."

I shoved off the couch, holding my shoulders back a little more to pop my breasts out. I wasn't sure why I did it—my growing chest didn't need more attention than it was already calling. Then I walked past him, heading down the hall.

"I still get cold at night," I called over my shoulder, quiet enough not to wake Avery.

A sigh sounded from the living room before a muttered, "Of course, you do."

Teasing Beckham was fun.

Felt a little like old times.

A little dangerous, too.

———

I opted for a silky tank top and my underwear. The bottoms were no different than how I typically slept, and Beckham was well aware of that with our history of sleepovers. The top, however, was a luxury I rarely indulged in. Matching pajama sets were expensive, so I chose old T-shirts and no pants most nights. But tonight was about riding the edge.

My nipples were perky and hard, my breasts larger than ever before with the pregnancy. And as the door opened and Beckham appeared, he noticed.

"Fucking hell, Parker." He scrubbed a hand down his mouth and shifted his gaze to the floor.

I pulled the covers back and crawled in on the far side of the bed. "What?"

"You want to attend another funeral this week? Because that's the path we're heading down."

With my back to the pillows, I pulled the comforter right below my ribs. "It's just like old times."

His eyes darkened. "*Old times* was me ripping those panties off you and fucking you all damn night."

I nearly let out a squeal at the sudden boldness of his statement.

His focus darted to my cheeks that were surely the shade of a cherry before moving to my mouth.

"Stop biting your lip," he demanded.

My teeth quickly popped off it. I hadn't even realized I was doing it.

He was quiet as he scanned the bed. The floor. The entire room, like there was somewhere for him to hide.

"If this is going to work without us touching, there need to be rules," he said.

"Who said anything about us not touching?" I asked innocently.

He narrowed his eyes on me, then crossed to the bed.

He grabbed the edge of the blanket, and I eyed his clothes. "Sleeping in jeans and a T-shirt?"

He frowned. "I don't want to wake Avery by getting a pair of sweats."

I wiggled until I was lying flat on my back, staring up at him. "Sleep in your underwear."

I swore I heard him whimper.

A second later, he unzipped his jeans and shucked them to the floor, along with his shirt. The veins in his arms bulged, like he was restraining himself. One look at his body had me doing the same.

Holy. Fucking. Shit.

Beckham Bronson was a goddamn sex god.

Hard muscles rippled down his abdomen. A well-defined V disappeared into his boxers, along with a faint freckling of hair, where my eyes then met with a much-bigger-than-I-remembered imprint of his cock.

This time, I did squeal. Shutting my eyes, I quickly flipped onto my side so my back was to him. Not a moment passed before a hand was on my arm, tugging me back flat. My eyes opened to find Beckham hovering over me.

"You think it's fair you get to stand before me in your underwear and I can't do the same?" he questioned.

"Completely fair," I choked out. I was suffocating in memories of him naked with me.

He cocked his head. "What's wrong, Parker?"

"Hot." I swallowed, attempting to compose myself. "I'm hot."

His gaze caught on my lips. I stopped breathing. "I thought you were a cold sleeper."

"Not anymore," I squeaked.

He was slowly getting closer, and I didn't think he realized it. "We're only going to sleep next to each other."

I nodded quickly, briefly regretting not letting him sleep on the couch. I'd been a fool to think we could restrain ourselves in this bed. Especially in an environment we were all too comfortable in.

Together. Thinly clothed. Under the sheets.

"You're going to stick to your side of the bed, and I'm going to stick to mine," he went on.

Another nod.

"We can do that, right?"

"Right," I agreed.

I did not, in fact, stick to my side of the bed.

Waking up wrapped around his body the next morning was proof of that.

14

BECKHAM

SEVENTEEN YEARS OLD

Early September in Idaho felt like an entirely different planet.

Trees would turn rich shades of red and orange, mixing with the wildflowers and tall grass. Everywhere I looked, a new color palette emerged, sucking the breath from my lungs and leaving me in a state of awe.

That was how it felt every time I looked at Parker Summerhill.

Beautiful. Happy. Mine.

We never established titles, but as she lay beside me in the meadow by the pond, daisies and bumblebees scattered around, those were the three words that came to mind.

Beautiful with her sun-kissed cheeks that deepened the shade of her freckles.

Happy after I made love to her in the grass.

And mine. Because no way in hell would she ever be anyone else's.

Her hands were crossed over her stomach, her delicate floral skirt ruffled around her thighs from my time between her legs. Her blonde hair was in perfect disarray, fanned out around her with specks of grass and flower petals caught in the strands. And her pink lips were curved at the corners, satisfied and content.

"You ever wonder what the birds are doing?" she asked, gaze stuck on the cotton candy clouds hanging high above us.

This time of year, the air stayed warm until the sun went down. The chirps and buzzing around us were slowly getting fainter and fainter as the wildlife prepped itself for sleep. But I planned to stay here all night. Between Parker's legs. My mouth on hers. Her body beneath mine. We didn't need blankets or a roof. Not when we had each other.

That was enough for me.

"Preparing for winter," I answered.

She shook her head. "I mean where they want to go next."

"South," I deadpanned.

She smacked my arm playfully. "Be serious, Beckham."

I grabbed that arm, tugging her on top of me. She giggled, hair falling into her face.

"I *am* serious." I brushed the strands behind her ears so I could get a better look at her face. I could never tire of it. "Serious as I've ever been."

"You think they wanna reach for the stars like us?" she pondered.

"Baby, I don't need the stars. Not when I have you."

Her lashes fluttered with the roll of her eyes.

"Fine," I relented. "Ask me again."

Her golden-brown gaze pinned me in place. Parker had a thing for dreaming big, and now was one of those times when she got lost in that head of hers. What I'd give to have even a second inside her pretty little mind.

"They say *reach for the stars* like it's some unachievable thing," she went on.

This was what we did. She got quizzical about the world. I got hung up on her.

I entertained her every time.

The cycle repeated itself.

"Yeah?"

"Yeah." Her chin tilted back as her eyes met the fading sky. The sunset lit her something pretty, pinks and oranges painting her tanned skin in a mirage of perfection. "I think I'm just gonna keep on reaching till I get there."

I smiled. "What's that look like?"

A little shrug. "Traveling outside of Bell Buckle. Finding myself. Living the life I didn't get to live being here."

My eyes fell while hers stayed pinned to the clouds. Her words were a blow she wasn't intending to land, but they did nonetheless. Parker was meant to fly, and she believed her parents clipped her wings the day she was born. Maybe they did. But I didn't want to be like them.

Didn't want to hold her back from experiencing the world. If Bell Buckle wasn't enough, I'd only encourage her to seek more.

Unfortunately for me, though, *Parker* was enough. I didn't need ocean views or thousands of acres. I only needed her.

"What does it look like for you?" she asked, finally dropping her attention back to me.

"Horses," I answered, not wanting to tell her the truth and make her feel bad. If Parker wanted to dream, I'd count the fucking sheep just so she could.

A crease formed between her brows. "Like rodeo?"

I shrugged. "Sure. Got some friends that wanna ride broncs. Why not?"

Behind those eyes, she seemed to hold something back. But then she leaned down and pecked a kiss to my mouth. "You'll be the best damn bronc rider this side of the Mississippi ever saw."

I tugged her to me, drawing the kiss deeper. "You gonna watch me fall on my ass?" My hand fell to hers for emphasis, squeezing the perfect flesh through her skirt.

"For as long as I'm here," she murmured before tangling her hands in my hair and slipping her tongue in my mouth.

And for the first time in my life, while I kissed the girl who hung the moon and the stars, I wondered if I was enough.

15
BECKHAM

My phone's spot on the coffee table was a heavy presence on my conscience as I fought the urge to pick up the device. My hands itched. My mind was warring. But most of all, my heart hurt.

The worst part was that I should be on fucking cloud nine right now. I lay in bed with Parker and ended up with her in my arms by morning. What more could I want right now?

It was a stupid question, because I was greedy, and all I wanted was to text my best friend and tell him I got her back. I held Parker in my arms, and I didn't fuck it up.

Garrett's phone was still connected. His mom never stopped paying his bill, and if one day she decided to, I'd take it over. She kept it plugged in on the nightstand in his childhood bedroom so if either of us wanted to hear his voice, we could call and listen to his voicemail. What we were doing to ourselves was cruel, but no one really taught you how to grieve. Did you move on completely, erasing everything but the memories that inevitably would fade? Or did you leave reminders of him around so that when you missed him, you could ease the ache in some way?

I think that was why I hadn't mustered the courage to tell my family about his passing. Their lives were completely separate from my life in rodeo, which made it easy to hide it. But I didn't want my processing of all of this to be rushed by society's pressure to go back to normal.

There was no *normal* after you lost someone, anyway.

There was just existing, and finding ways to cope.

Parker in my arms last night, her breasts pressed up against my chest with only the thin material of her tank top separating us—that wasn't coping. That was living a fucking dream.

If someone had told me months ago, "Hey, don't waste away, asshole. The love of your life is going to come back," I likely would've punched them in the face —much like I had with my brother—and told them I'd do whatever the fuck I wanted. Because that's what happens sometimes when people grieve—they get angry.

"Is your favorite color still green?" Avery asked, arranging her colorful plastic horses around the mini bale of hay I'd made her with leftover baling twine and broken pieces of straw. She had a whole farm set at my house, complete with a barn, tractors, and an arena.

We'd finished the breakfast Parker had prepared for

us this morning: a heaping pile of waffles covered with strawberries and whipped cream, alongside some slices of bacon. Now, Parker was cradling her Dr. Pepper on the couch while she watched Avery and me play imaginary farm animals.

"Hmm," I hummed, setting the toy dog by the water trough. "I think today it's yellow."

Avery scrunched her nose. "Why do you change it so much?"

"It's only fair to all the other colors," I told her. It *definitely* wasn't because Parker wore a pale yellow crewneck today.

"What's your favorite color?" Avery asked, looking over her shoulder at Parker.

She smiled. "Mine's yellow, too."

"No one in my class likes yellow," Avery said, a little disappointed.

"Well, now you've got two people who do." I scruffed her hair, and she swatted my hand away with a toothy smile and a giggle before we went back to playing.

"Where'd you get that longhorn skull from?" Parker asked, gesturing with her drink to the one sitting on the wall above my TV.

"Uncle Beckham said it used to be his friend's," Avery answered.

Intrigue lit Parker's expression. "Really? Which friend?"

"An old one," I answered gruffly. "Avery, why don't you go get your coat? I think your mom and dad will be here soon."

"Okay!" She shot up and was out of the room in a flash.

I began tossing her toys back in the bin I kept stashed in my wooden TV stand.

"It's nice looking," Parker acknowledged, standing from her seat to get a better look.

To this day, we still didn't know how it survived the accident fully intact.

"Are you okay?"

I looked up to find Parker tracking my movements as I put away the toys.

"Yeah. Are you?" I responded.

"You seem different, Beck."

With the rug now clear, I set the bin back in its spot and stood.

"Ten or so years will do that to a guy."

A line formed in the center of her forehead, doubt shining between the cracks. "Yeah, but you were never like…"

I stepped into her space, instinct causing me to grab both of her hands and grip them between us. "Like what?"

She shook her head, not in denial, but like she was clearing the fog swirling around in her thoughts.

"You never answered me," I murmured.

The crease deepened. "What?"

"Are you okay?" I asked again.

She looked down at her belly brushing my shirt and our hands grasped on either side of it. Then her eyes lifted back to me. "You're holding my hands."

My thumb moved like the past was fueling it forward, brushing across her knuckles. Memories of me holding her hands just like this, under a wide-open sky filled with stars. Of when I'd help her down from my truck bed after ravishing her. "I am."

"Beck." My name was barely a whisper.

"Park."

Her head moved subtly from side to side.

And just like that, we fell into the past. Into over a decade ago when she was mine and I was hers and we were unstoppable.

Maybe history would repeat itself.

I'd never wished harder for a statement to be true.

A knock on the front door had her sliding her hands from mine and taking a step away. A bouncing Avery emerged from the hallway, coat falling off her slender shoulders.

"Is that them?" Avery squealed.

"It should be." I glanced once more at Parker to be sure she was alright before heading for the door. Avery skipped alongside me, beating me to it.

"Can I open it?" Big, round eyes bored up at me. "Pleeeassee."

I couldn't help my smile. I didn't know how Callan restrained himself from buying her the world. "Go for it."

In a flash, the door was torn open and Avery was running at her mom and dad. She was gentle as she hugged Sage, then Callan lifted her by the armpits and tossed her in the air before setting her on his hip.

"Did you have fun?" Callan asked, tucking her unruly hair behind her ears.

Avery nodded like she'd somehow found my stash of sugar, and proceeded to ramble on and on about everything we'd done.

Callan listened intently while I waved Sage inside. Cal already knew Parker from our childhood, but Sage and she were complete strangers.

Parker had moved to the kitchen to busy herself, but promptly stopped her wiping of the counter when she saw Sage.

"Parker," Sage said, flashing a sweet smile.

Parker quickly wiped her hands on her leggings. "Sage." Unexpected relief coated her tone. "How's your finger?" She moved to quickly hug Sage, and something about her going right in, past a handshake, had me fighting a smile.

"Doing fine. Just a few stitches, nothing major." She lifted her finger to show it off after Parker stepped back.

"Thank goodness. I was worried." Parker's gaze flicked from her finger to me before settling back on Sage. "We'll have to get together sometime. Have Beckham give you my number, and we'll talk."

"I'd love that," Sage replied. "Just keep him out of that shell he crawled into for a few months, will you? It's nice having this Beckham back." She shot me a wink.

Relief washed over Parker's face. Whether it was from Sage's ability to not acknowledge her pregnancy or the prospect of having a friend in this, I wasn't sure. But I was damn happy to see it, either way.

Sage quickly said her goodbyes and joined Callan and Avery on their walk to the truck. As soon as the door was closed, Parker went back to wiping the counters.

Her silence was deafening.

"What?"

She lifted a shoulder. "Nothing."

I frowned. "Parker."

She stopped, leaving her hand on the towel as she faced me. "'Out of that shell'?"

I sighed. Of course she caught that.

"It's been hard since I quit rodeo," I explained.

She stared at me like she was waiting for me to go on, and when I didn't, she resumed her cleaning. "Okay."

I wanted to tell her more. Tell her *all* of it. But it hurt too damn much to even try to speak the words.

I grabbed my keys and left before I could crack, feeling like the biggest piece of shit for not confiding in her.

We used to be that for each other. But that was the kicker, wasn't it?

Parker and I were in the past.

And this was my reality.

———

Later that day, the cool breeze drifted through the browning fields ahead of me. I'd forgotten a coat, but I needed the bite of cold to ground me. If it didn't, I feared I'd end up in my nightmares instead of here, sitting in the grass on my parents' ranch.

I'd taken one of their horses and led Bucky beside me until we crested the far hill. I needed the distance today —the physical isolation—because mentally, I was suffocating.

Both horses grazed beside me while I watched the sun inch closer to the horizon with every inhale.

Bucky was a retired bronc. I'd been scrolling Facebook one day when I saw he was going up for auction. Having experience with my mother's nonprofit, Bottom of the Buckle Horse Rescue, it was a no-brainer that he'd end up in a kill pen and shipped off to slaughter.

Bailey and Lettie had been up at the auction house in Montana, so I'd called my dad first thing to be sure they grabbed that horse.

Now, I couldn't be more damn thankful I had.

Bucky was a walking reminder of Garrett. One of the few things I had left of him.

Garrett and I had learned all we knew on that horse. Sure, in rodeo, you rode every damn level of crazy, but Bucky was the go-to at some of the local clinics.

Sometimes I wondered if that horse felt the loss of Garrett. If he could feel it in the breeze or the hollowness of the trees. If he, too, noticed how everything around us felt like the life had been sucked out of it. Or maybe it'd only been sucked out of me. Maybe I was projecting my grief, the emptiness so strong, it felt like the air was nonexistent.

A speck of something cold and wet slid down my cheek, and I swiped it away. The hole in my chest seemed to grow every time I let myself think, but all those articles I'd scrolled through online said to embrace the emotions. Not to bottle them away and stew in them.

It was a hard pill to swallow, given I grew up thinking men shouldn't cry. That it made us weak. Pathetic.

So who the fuck was I to sit here sniffling over him?

I tore my gaze from the drifting clouds to Bucky, where he was pulling the grass up around my boot. Hatchet, one of my dad's horses, grazed farther away, both of their manes fluttering in the wind.

Everything around me was moving, living, thriving. I simply felt frozen. Like time had ceased all movement four months ago, and this pit in my stomach was incurable. I often wished the clock could reverse just a little bit more before it stopped, to a time when Garrett was smiling.

God, what I'd give to hear his laugh again.

A rustle behind me had me sniffling and clearing my throat, wiping my cheeks once more for good measure before I twisted.

"Heard your brothers were hard on Parker," my dad said as he gently tugged the reins. He wasn't one for a ton of words, usually reducing himself to grunts and frowns, so the unexpectedness of his visit, especially way out here, made me weary. Did he think something was wrong? Or was this one of those times where he'd be bluntly honest and tell me I was being a fool?

His horse stopped, and he dismounted. Letting the animal do his thing, he lowered himself beside me.

"She forgave them," I told him. Parker was too good to hold a grudge against many people.

My dad was silent as the sky reflected in his blue eyes. His mustache was unmoving, but I could see the frown he always wore beneath it.

After what felt like minutes, he spoke. "Is the baby yours, son?"

My gaze fell to my scuffed boots. "No."

Neither of us moved a muscle. I'd never been more grateful for my dad's silence than right now.

"You wanna tell me what's been goin' on?" he asked.

I'd spoke too soon.

My eye caught on a particular cloud in the sky, all puffy and fake-like. Out of all the people I thought I might dump my feelings on, I wouldn't have guessed it'd be my dad.

"You don't wanna tell me, that's fine," he grumbled. His voice was hoarse with old age and time spent yelling at cows—and his sons—on the ranch. "But don't peg me as a fool to not know where you got that from."

Forehead creased, I turned to meet his gaze.

"Don't keep things from the people you love just because you think that's how your ol' pops battles with his own struggles," he went on.

"What struggles, Dad?"

His cheeks moved like he was rolling his lips together beneath his thick 'stache, and he swallowed. Another few minutes of silence, and he was shoving to a stand and setting a hand on my shoulder.

"Even cowboys cry, son." He squeezed. "Only the brave ones can accept that."

Without another word, he walked over to his horse, grabbed the reins, and hefted himself into the saddle.

And as he disappeared in the distance, heading back toward the barn, I disappeared somewhere else.

Into the horizon.

With tears in my eyes and Garrett on my mind.

16

PARKER

Driving an hour to an appointment to check on the baby wasn't ideal, but I hadn't wanted to run into anyone at the clinic in Bell Buckle and have to explain everything. People in small towns were nosy, even if they didn't try to be. And with my social media presence, plus having grown up in this town, it was inevitable they'd have all sorts of questions.

Beckham may not have kept up with my profiles, but with eight hundred thousand followers—a majority likely being from the west—someone in Bell Buckle was bound to know what I did for a living.

It was nearly dark now, a light drizzle having started on my way home. Even after all these years, I still knew these roads like the back of my hand. I navigated them with ease until I pulled onto Beckham's property and killed the engine. I hurried inside, raising my arms over my head to protect myself from the rain as best I could.

Twisting the handle, I was thankful the front door

was unlocked as I slipped in and shut it behind me. With my back to the door, I found Beckham sitting on the couch, stiff as a board.

"Hey," I breathed, shoving my slightly damp hair off my forehead. The strands would definitely frizz.

"Hey." Beckham stood, hands on his hips and lips rolling together like he was working up the courage to ask something. He sent a brief look to the ceiling like it'd give him strength, then met my gaze. "Where'd you go?"

A breath rushed from my lungs, thankful that was all. I shoved off the door, moving to the sink in the kitchen to wash my hands. "I had a doctor's appointment."

After scrubbing and drying them, I turned to find him staring.

"Why didn't you tell me?" he asked, sounding hurt.

"I didn't know if you'd care," I responded hesitantly.

His eyes nearly bulged from their sockets before he ran a hand over his mustache and down his jaw. He spun, then paced a little before freezing again. "What would ever make you think I didn't care about your appointments?"

Truthfully, I felt like a burden walking back into his life, pregnant with another man's baby. "Looping you into the appointments felt like too much."

He chuckled. A dry, humorless sound. "'Too much'?"

I opened my mouth. Snapped it shut.

"You drove yourself?" he questioned.

I nodded. "Who else would have driven me?"

He blinked rapidly, dragging another rough hand

down his chin. Before I could see if those were tears building, he took off down the hall.

His bedroom door shut quietly, and a muffled *thud* followed. I couldn't tell if he wanted space, but I also didn't want to leave him alone with whatever feelings my appointment had stirred up. Was he that upset I hadn't invited him?

I kicked my shoes off and padded down the hall, stopping at his bedroom. My fingers wrapped around the knob, stilling for a moment before I slowly turned it and cracked open the door.

Beckham's back was to me, his hands gripping his hair punishingly. On his bed sat his baseball hat, squished and forgotten.

"Beckham?" I whispered.

His head shook back and forth. "I'm sorry, Park." His swallow was audible, his back muscles flexing through his shirt as he dropped his hands to his sides. "It's not you, it's just—"

I opened the door the rest of the way and walked until my belly pressed against his back. My arms wrapped around his torso, pulling him to me. He froze as I rested my cheek against him.

"Don't be sorry." Apologetic was the last thing I wanted him to feel when it came to me. *I* should be the one apologizing.

"You shouldn't be in here right now," he whispered.

"There's nowhere else I'd rather be," I replied.

After one long minute of worrying he'd force me out,

Beckham twisted in my hold until his chest was to me and wrapped his arms tightly around my shoulders.

I melted into him as he hunched his back and buried his face in my hair. A sob wracked his body, taking me by surprise and ripping my world in two.

My hand moved on instinct, smoothing over his hair as his tears soaked the shoulder of my shirt. His sobs could create an ocean in this room and I'd still hold onto him. If Beckham was hurting, there wasn't a chance in hell I'd ever let go.

Both our knees buckled and we lowered to the floor. My legs fit perfectly over his to where I was straddling him, and he nuzzled his face deeper into the crook of my neck. Hot tears ran down my chest, staining my skin with his pain.

I wanted so badly for him to talk to me. To tell me what was hurting him so I could fix it. But that wasn't fair of me to ask when I wasn't being completely transparent with him.

So for now, I'd hold him. Wipe the tears from his cheeks and fix his hair.

Once his body stopped jerking from the sobs and his sniffles became further apart, I leaned back slightly, setting my hands on his cheeks and lifting his head.

His bloodshot eyes and glistening cheeks had me fighting back my own tears.

"Never go alone again," he pleaded in a broken whisper.

"I won't," I promised.

I brushed his cheek with my thumb, wishing like hell I could read his mind.

"I'll drive you."

I nodded. "To every single one."

His eyes fell to my lips, and they parted on their own accord. His focus shifted between my mouth and my eyes like he couldn't decide if he wanted to stare at me forever or close the distance.

Both options scared me, but not because I didn't want Beckham. I couldn't put this baby on him and force him to be a dad to some other man's child.

I wanted him to talk about his feelings and tell me what was going on, but I also didn't want to dig him a deeper hole than he already seemed to be disappearing into, so I asked the first thing that popped into my mind to attempt to brighten his mood.

"Do you want to see the sonogram?"

His brows pinched together before he realized what I was asking, then he nodded. "Of course."

I lifted slightly, tugging the photo from the back pocket of my maternity jeans. I flipped it around so he could see, and when his attention shifted to it, I nearly passed out.

Weight had never been so visibly lifted from a man's shoulders. Eyes had never lit up as brightly as the sun rising in the morning. Hearts had never beat as vividly as mine did now.

Showing him this photo of my son might have been a massive mistake. It didn't distract us from our proximity, not in the least. All it did was make me want to tuck this little paper into his wallet and ride him until the sun came up and the cows started mooing.

New tears welled in his eyes and he quickly wiped them away with the back of his hand before they could drop. His throat bobbed over and over before he met my melting gaze. I feared I might turn into a puddle, right here and now, and all I had to blame was the past and these damn pregnancy hormones.

"This is your son," he stated, pure awe in his voice.

I nodded.

Then he simply took my breath away when he lifted his free hand and glanced at my belly. "Is it okay if I...?"

I nodded again, never feeling the phrase *loss of words* more than I did right now.

His large, callused palm met the fabric of my shirt and the warmth of him seeped right through it, penetrating my stretched skin and working its way to my heart. My pulse wasn't racing. It wasn't slow, either. On Beckham's lap, with the feel of him touching me, I was calm. Content.

Falling.

His hand moved slowly, tracing my small bump like it was the most precious work of art he'd ever seen. With his soft touch combined with that pure look of adoration, I feared I'd need to put a lock and key over the organ in my chest.

He sniffled, then shook his head. "Sorry."

I wiped another falling tear away with my thumb. "Don't be sorry."

His eyes fell to my hand before he met my stare again. "Did your appointment go okay?"

"He's healthy as can be. I'm twenty weeks now."

His eyes widened. "Don't you get your anatomy scan at twenty weeks?" He'd clearly been doing his research.

I dipped my chin, guilt hitting me like a bullet. "I did today."

He let out a quiet curse, and without thinking, I set both hands on his cheeks. "Don't be so hard on yourself."

"It's hard not to when you're doing these things alone, Park."

"I'm not alone." My hand covered his over my belly. "I have him. And now I'll have you there with me, too."

My two boys.

I was tearing myself to pieces with that thought, sending a wrecking ball through the rational part of my brain, as if I wanted instinct to take over and let me land in his arms.

Would it be so bad?

"Do you want to talk about it?" I asked, quieting my voice and letting my hand on his cheek slide back between us. I didn't want the topic of my baby to dominate our space when he was clearly struggling and needed someone to talk to.

He seemed to contemplate it as he chewed the inside of his cheek before landing on, "Not today."

I nodded past the closing of my throat. Maybe he didn't feel the same as I did. Maybe he didn't want us to go back to how we used to be.

And that was my answer as to why it'd be so bad.
To hear Beckham reject me...
I didn't think I'd survive.

Shopping options in Bell Buckle were...limited. When I told Beckham about my plans with the girls to go shopping for new clothes, he insisted on playing chauffeur. Somehow, on the ride to the nearest bigger town, I'd convinced him to drive home and that I'd get a ride back with Lettie. After promising we'd leave before dark, he gave in.

Now, we sifted through racks of clothes at a little boutique Sage had found online. I'd already found two pairs of jeans I loved, but unfortunately, they wouldn't fit over my belly, and I wasn't sure if my size would change after I had the baby—so I decided to pass and hope they were still here by the time I lost my baby weight.

Brandy was over by the single dressing room with Oakley while Lettie and Sage stuck close to me.

"Do you know the sex?" Sage asked me, pulling out a violet sundress and holding it up to get a better look at it.

"Boy." It was the first they'd asked about my baby,

and I didn't think their avoidance of bringing it up came from a place of uncaring. I got the impression they didn't want to pester me for information, but honestly, I wanted to talk about it. For an entire four months, I was alone in this pregnancy. Sure, it was nice to talk to Beckham about the baby when he asked, but he couldn't relate to the way a woman's body changed. Or some of the other pregnancy-related...things.

"Do you know yours?" I asked Sage.

"Not yet. We're doing a gender reveal on the ranch in a couple weeks. If you'd like to come, I'd love to have you there." Sage set the dress back on the rack, checking for other sizes.

Her mention of a gender reveal had my heart squeezing. I'd learned my baby was a boy off the doctor's app on my phone. There was no pink or blue frosting hidden inside a cupcake, no confetti falling from a popped balloon.

I was over halfway through this pregnancy, and I feared I'd mourn every second of it. The big milestones, the bump photos. I hadn't done any of it because I was more focused on finding places to survive rather than enjoying the time spent growing my baby.

Would he one day resent me for not celebrating him before he was born?

Sage paused her rifling through the hangers. "Are you having a baby shower?"

I snapped my attention to her, not having realized I'd zoned out. Curiosity was etched on her features, like she didn't understand why I seemed sad.

I quickly went back to looking at a few shirts folded on the table in front of me. I had no idea what to say. *No, I don't have anyone to invite because my family is all dead and the closest relative I know of lives hours away and has a daughter of his own.* "I wasn't planning on it."

"Oh my gosh." The clap of Lettie's hands had me jumping. "You two can have a baby shower together! Brandy, Oakley, and I can plan it."

"It could be farm-themed," Oakley offered.

The clothes seemed to be forgotten as Oakley and Brandy came to join us.

"I don't want to take away from Sage—" I started.

"Do not even think about finishing that sentence," Oakley interrupted, bright green eyes pinning me in place.

"I'm due in April," Sage informed me. "When are you due?"

"February." Being two months apart from her somehow eased some of my worries, like I wouldn't be in the newborn trenches alone. I had no idea what I was doing despite the countless books I'd been reading, and knowing Sage already had experience being a mom comforted me.

"Let's plan it for January then," Lettie decided.

While the girls got to talking about their ideas for the farm-themed shower, I headed over to a corner with various styles of bralettes. Wires were becoming more and more uncomfortable every day, so I figured switching and getting a bigger size might help ease some of the pain in my breasts.

I set my sights on a more deep-cut one, looking through the drawers to see what colors they had in stock.

"It's a lot, huh?" Sage's voice had me looking up from where I was crouched.

"There are so many colors to choose from," I said with a light chuckle.

"There are." Sage's lips flattened into a small smile. "But I meant the baby."

I paused, taken off guard by her seeming to want to talk on a deeper level. While traveling, so many conversations I had were superficial. I was never in one place long enough to form lasting relationships.

"It is," I admitted, using the edge of the table to help me straighten.

"I was a single mom before I met Callan," she told me.

My heart squeezed at the thought of how hard that must've been.

"Avery and I had to make it on our own after moving somewhere new." Her gaze fell like she was remembering all of it before locking eyes with me. "But no one is more strong than a mom trying to make a better life for her child."

I nodded, any words I might've been about to say escaping me. It was hard to think I'd be doing so much of this alone, let alone speak about it.

"Do you know who the dad is?" she asked, her tone soft, like she didn't want to scare me away, but also wanted to make it known she was here if I wanted to talk.

My fingers messed with the strap of the bra in my hand. "I do."

She dipped her chin in acknowledgement before shifting topics. "Do you have any names picked out?"

All I felt was relief that she didn't press further. So many people only started a conversation to gain information from it. So little actually wanted to only talk.

"I haven't really thought that far ahead yet." Hell, I'd barely thought about the baby's wardrobe. I was so focused on finding doctors for appointments, and then my dad's funeral came up, that everything was slipping through my fingers at a pace I couldn't keep up with.

"Do you?" I asked.

"We've floated some around, but Callan wants to look our baby in the eyes before he settles. He says that'll help him decide," she explained, a look of nostalgia crossing her features, like maybe she once fought as hard for happiness as I was right now.

"Does that work?"

She shrugged, setting a hand on the table beside us. "It helped with Avery. I was the only one involved in picking out her name, and I was scared I'd pick wrong."

My mouth puckered in thought, but I didn't want to press for more.

She must've noticed my curiosity, because she clarified, "The man who got me pregnant wasn't all too eager to help plan for the baby. That included bouncing around names."

Empathy hit me straight in the gut. Sage seemed so

sweet, and hearing she'd had that experience was painful. "I'm sorry."

She waved me off. "It's in the past. Callan has made up for it." A smile split her lips before it faded again. "If you're in a similar situation, Parker…"

I gnawed on my bottom lip, trying to figure out how to explain this. "I didn't have a great childhood, so I always told myself that if I had kids, it'd be when I was ready and able to make their lives amazing." My hand instinctively went to my stomach. "He's not coming at the most ideal time, but when I was faced with the choice of raising him or having an abortion, I couldn't choose the latter. Those two little lines woke something up inside of me, and from that moment, I knew I'd do anything to protect my baby."

With a deep breath, I looked longingly at my belly before continuing. "He didn't want me to have this baby. He didn't want any financial ties, no 'burden,' as he called it. But he had never hurt me, despite often being a selfish prick."

"Until he did," Sage stated quietly. Of course, she could see the signs. She'd probably been through worse.

"Until he did," I confirmed.

She set a gentle hand on my arm and leaned closer. "You're not alone in this. Names come and go, but your love for your baby won't. It'll be there every hard day to nip you in the ass and remind you that you can do hard things." She squeezed. "Don't force the process. I'm sure once you hold him, you'll know. You're not failing, Parker. I promise."

Because even though we'd been simply talking about names, she could tell it was more than that. It was the crib, the type of bottles we'd use, how I wanted my labor, whether I could even keep a baby alive, how I'd deal with diaper rash or his first tooth coming in. And Sage was right. I wasn't alone for any of that.

If I chose to stay in Bell Buckle and raise my baby here, I didn't think there'd ever be a single day I'd be alone.

"Can we talk about pacifiers?"

Sage's smile gleamed. "Of course."

With the sun setting on the horizon, I waved goodbye to Lettie as she backed out of Beckham's driveway. Once she turned onto the road, I closed the front door to Beckham's double-wide and pressed my back against it, shutting my eyes and dropping the shopping bags. My head rested back as I couldn't help the smile that bloomed.

I had a *good* day. With girls who I'd known since childhood, and new ones I felt just as comfortable with. They'd never once treated me like I was impeding on their shopping trip. Instead, we laughed and smiled and gave each other opinions on outfit choices. They'd listened intently when I told them stories of my travels, rather than zoning out or acting disinterested. Sage and I had talked babies for so long, I was surprised the others didn't get sick of us.

It felt nice to learn things that hadn't stemmed from Google or a pregnancy book. As informational as both were, there was nothing like getting tips from another mom.

The whole day, I'd forgotten my phone even existed, and it felt like taking a deep breath after being underwater for too long. With social media having been the way I made a living for so long, I was constantly on my device doing everything under the sun. Responding to DMs, editing a video, emailing about a brand deal—it was all exhausting and time-consuming, but for a while, I loved it.

The silent house slowly seeped in, and I popped an eye open, scanning my surroundings. The kitchen light was on, but I wasn't sure if Beckham was here. Granted, he would've left it on for me even if he'd left. I tugged my phone out of my purse to check for any texts, but only saw a few from the girls in our group chat saying they had a fun day, and that we should do it again sometime soon.

Despite it having felt good to be off my phone all day, curiosity won out, and I found myself with the Instagram app opened. The icon in the corner was maxed out with likes, comments, follows—all of it. It was no secret that other influencers had taken to coming up with theories about my silence online, pushing new people to my account to see if they could crack some mystery. As if it was illegal for me to live my life and not broadcast it online.

When I'd first decided leaving social media was the

best course of action, I'd posted a quick story about taking a break. Of course, people were nosy, and everyone wanted to know why. Now, every accusation was being thrown around—the biggest being that I was either knocked up or in prison.

Their imaginations ran wild, that was for sure.

Deciding to ignore all of those, I tapped into my messages and found countless requests from new people. I scrolled and scrolled, my mind numb to all the questions and speculations. My thumb ceased its movement as I stopped on one from an account with no profile picture. They didn't ask where I was, or whether I was alive, or throw assumptions at me. The message began politely. That fact had me clicking into it.

And instantly regretting it.

Hi, Parker. I hope you're doing well. You've been quiet online for so long, and as a concerned Good Samaritan, I'd like to know your address so I can order a welfare check. No drop in from a stranger. Strictly professionals. This would ease my worries a lot. Thanks.

I stared, unblinking, at my phone for what felt like minutes before blocking the account and deleting the message. Somehow, finding a complete stranger asking where exactly I lived seemed far-fetched. People were nosy and frequently overstepped, but going as far as to ask for something so private? With the profile looking brand new, I could only guess whoever messaged me was someone who'd known me before.

My heart stopped at the thought of Daniel trying to

find out where I was. But he'd wanted nothing to do with this baby, so the possibility was unlikely. Right?

I shoved off the door and grabbed my bags after pocketing the phone, beelining for my temporary room. Whoever it was, Daniel or not, they weren't getting that piece of me. Besides, even if it was someone I knew, I wouldn't give up Beckham's address with the possibility of it being exposed online.

Halfway down the hall, Beckham's bedroom door opened and dim light spilled into the hall. I nearly tripped as I stopped, my palm slamming against my chest in a poor attempt to calm myself.

"You scared the shit out of me," I panted.

But then I was breathless for a whole other reason as Beckham stepped out of his room wearing only a towel. His chest was glistening, water droplets coasting over suntanned skin. Dew stuck to his mustache, thick strands of wet hair hung in his forehead, and his eyes devoured me.

"Sorry. I was just coming out here to grab a clean shirt," Beckham explained, gaze roaming over my body like he was checking to make sure I was still whole. "Did you have a good time with the girls?"

I nodded, gulping. "Yep."

A crease formed between his perfect brows before he cataloged my hand still flat against my chest. "You okay?"

I nodded again, more frantically this time, and attempted to move past him. But his double-wide was outdated, so the hall was narrow, and all I succeeded in doing was wafting his scent full of mischief and temptation toward me. I paused, shoulder to his chest, to look up at him.

How in the fuck had he gotten so much hotter over the years?

"I'm just going to bed, so…"

"It's five p.m.," he stated.

My mouth popped open before I set a hand on my stomach and clarified, "The baby and shopping has me exhausted."

"You want to take a bath?"

My mouth went dry as the first thought that hit me was getting in it with him.

"No," I blurted.

He looked taken aback by my abrupt response.

"I don't want to fall asleep in the bath," I added quickly.

Beck's tongue ran over his bottom lip before his eyelids grew heavy and he leaned in. His breath warmed my shoulder, sending goosebumps down my spine. "I could keep you awake."

My knees nearly buckled.

Pregnancy hormones had me nearly jumping at the proposition, and I swore they were making me crazy.

"Beck…" His name was a whispered plea on my lips.

His nose grazed my cheekbone, his eyes hooded. "Yes, Park?"

I couldn't make my mouth form the words to tell him this was dangerous. We were playing a risky game of revisiting the past when our futures weren't built to clash.

Almost like he could sense it on me, he stepped back, leaning a shoulder against the doorframe. He crossed his massive arms. His towel was slung so low, I nearly sent up a prayer hoping it'd fall just an inch to give me a little something more to think about later.

His penetrating stare bore into me like I was something to be studied and he'd forgotten how to read. I *wanted* him. He could *tell* I wanted him. But this was more than him and me.

At the end of the day, I wasn't sure I could put the burden of my baby on him. To ask him to raise some other man's child? It'd be selfish.

I had my time to do what I wanted. Now, I had to be an adult.

I only hated that it meant I wouldn't get to follow my heart. But I loved my baby enough that I'd sacrifice everything if it meant giving him a stable, happy life.

I broke our eye contact and made it to my room by sheer will alone.

18

BECKHAM

I could still smell Parker in the hallway when I left my room shortly after our run-in. I'd pinched myself just to be sure I wasn't dreaming, because no amount of time in her presence would convince me this was real. That I was this lucky to have her back in Bell Buckle.

She was making me crazy, yet I didn't want her anywhere else but here. Sure, maybe I had to lock my door at night to stop me from crossing the hall and reminding her how good we were together. And maybe I regularly jacked off in the shower solely to alleviate the pain she was putting me through. But that didn't mean I wanted her gone.

I only wanted the invisible line between us to disappear.

For her to give in like I wanted to.

What were we waiting for? Parker and I were written

in the goddamn stars, and here she was sleeping in an entirely separate room.

That reason alone was why I was currently up for the second time tonight, refilling my reusable bottle with ice-cold water. I'd had to have chugged more than a gallon over the last couple of hours in an attempt to distract myself from the idea of barging into her room and telling her she was never leaving again.

Being in such close proximity to her earlier had not been a smart move—I could admit that. All it'd done was dig up the memory of her little gasps when I touched her body. The sight of her mouth had me remembering her lips parting when she came. The scent of her dredged up how she'd coat my sheets and old shirts for weeks.

Parker was everywhere then, and she was every-where now.

After taking the biggest swig known to mankind and capping my water bottle, I headed back down the hall, clicking off the kitchen light on my way. My hand had just closed around the knob on my bedroom door when I paused at the sound coming from behind Parker's door.

A gasp echoed in the still night, causing me to set my bottle on the floor and cross the hall. I leaned an ear against her door—to make sure she was okay, of course —and waited. Seconds later, another gasp, this one louder and a bit quicker.

Without thinking, I tried the handle, and when it turned, I shoved open the door. My feet moved three steps before I stopped. And nearly fell.

Parker shot up in bed, the blanket grasped to her chest. "Beckham!"

"Are you okay? Were you having a nightmare?" My eyes scanned her for any signs of distress, and when they found her other arm was hidden beneath the blanket, I choked. "Were you...?"

"Yes!" she exclaimed.

My cheeks lit up like fire. "Oh."

I couldn't tear my eyes away from what I knew was under the blankets. Her hand, right between those legs I knew so well. Did she have a toy? Why did I want to find out?

"Do you need help?" I croaked.

Her jaw nearly unhinged itself as her eyes widened. She snapped her mouth closed before wiping the look of shock off her face.

"I think I can do this by myself."

"Oh, I know. I'm just better at it."

Her brows shot up.

"Don't you remember, Park?" I asked, my voice taking on a husky, raspy edge.

Her throat bobbed on a swallow, her lashes fluttering.

The corner of my mouth hitched up. "You do."

My feet began moving, and I nearly forgot I wasn't wearing a shirt. My gray sweats hung low, and without the presence of underwear, I was certain my erection was no secret.

I reached the side of the bed, sliding a finger along the comforter. Parker looked at me through hooded eyes as I wrapped my fingers around the edge.

"Do you still like being played with?"

"Beckham." Her voice was a warning and a plea.

I began slipping the blanket over her legs, exposing her bare thighs to me. She wore an oversized T-shirt, but with what she'd been doing moments ago, the hem was up past her hips.

As soon as the blanket exposed her, her breath hitched. I think mine stopped altogether.

But I didn't look. Not yet. Instead, I used my other hand to tip her chin up. Her lips parted as I leaned closer, all while my fingers released the comforter and slid up her smooth inner thigh.

"Tell me to stop," I murmured.

Not a single sound passed those plump lips.

"Tell me you don't want my help getting you off."

This time, she let out a soft, barely audible moan. Her head tilted back more, our noses nearly touching now.

"Tell me, Parker."

Her eyes moved between mine. "Don't kiss me."

My forehead creased in question.

"Kissing is too much, Beckham," she admitted, quieter this time.

"Is this too much?" My hand bumped hers out of the way, and I fucking *whimpered* when I felt how wet she was. She'd dragged her hand up to her clit while playing with herself, so I did the same. My pointer finger circled the rim of her entrance before sliding up the center of her pussy. As soon as I reached her clit, she was gasping.

"No," she panted, utterly breathless. Breathtaking. All of it.

Fuck.

"You're telling me I can touch you?" I clarified. If she didn't want this—want *me*—I'd stop. I'd lose my mind doing it, but I would.

She nodded.

"I need your words, Parker."

"Yes," she breathed.

With her permission, I began circling her bundle of nerves slowly, carefully at first before adding more pressure. I wanted so badly to refresh my mind of the sight of her writhing beneath me, but I didn't want this to end. Maybe it was the heat of the moment driving her to wanting my hands on her, and if that was the case, I wanted to savor this moment and not miss a damn second of it.

So many things had been swiped out from underneath me in an instant—the body of a horse, the love of my life, my best friend. I couldn't let this be one of them.

I'd worship her for hours if she'd let me. Teeter her on the edge only to bring her back down, over and over again.

Her eyelids fluttered closed for the briefest moment, lips parted, and a moan stuck in her throat before she pinned her eyes back on me. She looked wild and ravenous, and I wondered if she thought of our past as often as I did.

I braced my other hand beside her head, gaze

roaming down every inch of her body until it stopped where my fingers disappeared between her legs.

She bent her knees slightly when she realized where I was looking, her thighs trying to press together.

"I-I have stretch marks now—"

My eyes flew to hers as my fingers stilled. "Don't hide from me."

Her lashes fluttered while those cheeks turned more rosy than before. "I just... I don't look the same."

"You think I do?"

She stared at me, seemingly speechless, so I reluctantly removed my hand to grab the waistband of my sweats. I tugged them down, exposing my hip bone farther, all the way, until the side of my thigh was showing. The gnarly scar was on full display.

She inhaled sharply before shoving up on her elbows. "What happened?"

"Was helping some buddies corral a loose bull. He charged me, sliced his horn right into my leg."

So much concern shined in her eyes. Did things like this happen to her when she was gone? Had she been injured, and I'd been clueless?

"I'm sorry," she whispered.

I shook my head, readjusting my sweats before leaning back into her space. "I didn't show you to get your sorrow. I showed you because I want you to know that time changes us. You're not judging me for that scar, are you?"

She shook her head. "I would never."

"I lo—" I cleared my throat and set a palm over her

bare thigh, erasing the word I was about to say from my vocabulary. "I like your body because I like you, Parker. It's not one or the other. And these marks?" I squeezed her leg before climbing onto the bed and situating myself between her legs. "I'm obsessed with them because they're you."

I couldn't help myself—not even her *no kissing* rule could stop me—as I dragged my tongue along her inner thigh. Her little gasp, combined with the squirm of her body, had me pressing a hand to her belly on instinct to hold her in place. For the briefest moment, I froze. And then the feral need to make Parker feel like she was caught in the goddamn clouds took over, and my other hand moved. Two fingers slid inside her, and she arched her back. I looked up to find her mouth parted while she watched me.

"Can I kiss you here?" I murmured, flattening my tongue against her pussy.

She hurriedly nodded, a breathy "yes" slipping out.

"What about here?" I circled her entrance.

Another desperate nod. "Yes. God, *please.*"

"And here?" I finally brought the pad of my tongue to her clit, and she arched farther toward me.

"Beckham."

"Yes, Parker?"

"Just fucking touch me already."

The corner of my mouth twitched with a smile knowing Parker Summerhill was begging for me. Almost ten years later, this hadn't changed.

"If you insist." My lips pressed to her clit and I sucked

the bundle into my mouth, flicking it with my tongue. She moaned louder this time, hands gripping the sheets before she brought them to my head and weaved her fingers into my hair.

"Your mustache—" she choked out.

I popped my mouth off her clit. "What about it, Park?"

Her head was resting back, her eyes closed like she was in heaven. "It feels so fucking good on my skin."

"You should have told me sooner." I lowered my mouth to her again, tongue dragging along her pussy before I found her entrance. I spit on her, and the gasp it elicited blended with her next moan.

I sat up on my knees, her hands skating down my chest, nails leaving marks behind. My fingers never left her, and I watched as she writhed because of my touch. I rooted myself in this moment and swore to never forget it as I watched her fingers tangle in the sheets, tugging and threatening to tear the fabric.

I slid two fingers in and out of her at a steady pace, knowing it was making her ache for more. Even when she came, I didn't think I'd be able to stop. Touching Parker was addicting, and forcing myself to part from her would be punishing.

"*Beckham,*" she pleaded.

I'd missed my name coming out of those pretty lips like she couldn't get enough of me.

I quickened my pace and added a third finger, dropping my gaze to watch as I fucked her with my hand. She was so fucking wet, her pussy glistening in the gold light of the bedside lamp. I crooked the ends of my fingers in a beckoning motion, and she arched her back farther.

"You still like that," I murmured, a bead of sweat sliding down my forehead. I wasn't overextending myself in any way, but *fuck*, she made me hot.

"Yes," she panted.

I shoved in as far as I could, bending my fingers farther, and stroked that sweet spot deep inside her. The moan that erupted out of her was enough to have *me* going over the edge.

I shifted, my dick rubbing against the stretched fabric of my sweats. My hand shot out to the mattress to hold myself up. Parker hadn't noticed, not with her eyes shut.

"Look at me."

Her lids flew open and she met my heavy gaze. I shifted my hand, pressing the pad of my thumb to her clit.

That crease in her forehead deepened, her mouth parting farther. My other hand moved to grip her thigh, needing her to ground me before I lost it.

In seconds, she was clenching around me and throwing her head back. The sight of her was intoxicating, and when I shifted forward again, I knew there was no stopping it. Not with Parker unraveling because of me.

With her moans still echoing in the air, I loosened what little control I still had and came. I bent forward slightly, hanging my head as I tried to stifle my quickening breaths. My eyes pinched shut, my teeth digging into my bottom lip.

I was coming in my goddamn pants, and she hadn't even touched me.

As her breathing settled, I forced myself to slide my fingers from her. I trailed the tip of my pointer down her inner thigh, painting a B into her delicate skin.

One glance down revealed evidence of what I'd done. How utterly feral she made me.

Internally, I cursed.

"What's wrong?"

Her small voice had me moving my attention back to her, where she was now perched on her elbows and looking utterly spent.

I opened my mouth to tell her nothing was wrong, because really, nothing could be in this moment, but then her eyes fell to my lap.

Her brows rose. "Did you...?"

"Yeah." I ran a hand through my hair before dragging it over my mustache. I could still taste her sweetness there. "I did."

The room was silent before she moved into a sitting position, pulling the blanket over her lap. The knowledge of that secret B still staining her skin had me hard all over again.

"Beck—"

"Don't say that was a mistake," I begged. I couldn't handle it if she did.

Her lips smacked shut before she went on. "I wasn't going to."

I gave her an incredulous look.

"If this is going to become some sort of habit between us..." she went on. The flush of her cheeks was still bright and distracting, but I forced my brain to focus. "We have to set boundaries."

I choked. "Boundaries?"

Her eyes narrowed. "Yes."

"You want to tell me not to touch you? Pass."

She frowned. "Not like that, Beckham."

"You can't establish rules between us while you're not wearing any pants."

She crossed her arms, trying to look tough, but all it did was make me smile. "Maybe we can discuss this tomorrow, then. Besides, I can't focus either when all I can think about is licking your cum off your thighs."

Air caught in my throat and my eyes turned watery as I sputtered a cough.

She smirked, like her plan had worked.

"Fine. Tomorrow, we'll discuss this." I held up my fingers and slid them in my mouth. My tongue lapped up the remnants of her before I pulled them out with a *pop* and aimed them her way. "But mark my words, Parker. You're not depriving me of this again."

She rolled her eyes, her teasing clear on her face. "We'll see."

I shoved to a stand, planting my hands on my hips. Her eyes dipped to the impression of my hard dick through my sweatpants—and the wet spot that had formed there—before meeting my stare.

"It's bedtime, Parker."

"Is it?"

My brows lowered. "Test me tonight, and see just how much of a rule follower I am."

"We haven't established any yet," she said.

"You said no kissing. Or have you forgotten?"

She plopped back on her pillows with a huff. Maybe she was as opposed to boundaries between us as I was. But if she thought it was best, I'd play along. I'd test her every second of our time together, but I could feign obedience.

For now.

"Goodnight, Park."

"Goodnight, Beck."

But I didn't sleep after I left her room. Not until I came all over again in my shower, only the thought of her beneath me spurring me forward. I dreamed of her, too.

Dreamed of breaking every little rule she thought she could put between us.

19
PARKER

My finger tapped an unsteady beat on the kitchen counter the next morning. I had no idea what to say to Beckham. These rules I was so adamant about were few and far between, not a single one making sense in my mind.

Why couldn't we kiss? Because I thought that was going too far? His fingers inside of me, his tongue on my clit, was *too far*. And I really thought keeping our mouths apart was what would keep our minds on track?

Sure. Great plan.

Familiar footsteps sounded from down the hall, and I turned on the stool to find Beckham strolling toward me. He looked like an entirely different man this morning— no heavy eyes or strained inhales. He was...lighter. Brighter. Happier.

This was not going to be easy.

"Good morning," I said.

"Morning," he replied, leaning an elbow on the

corner of the counter merely a foot from me. He was wearing a new pair of sweats, the shade a bit lighter, and a tight-fitting white tee. "So, these rules."

My eyes flicked to his intoxicating biceps before I cleared my throat and straightened my back. "Right." My fingers dug into my knees, my nerves on fucking fire. "Should we be doing this?"

"Define 'this.'"

I narrowed my eyes on him. Of course, he was going to make me spell it out. "The messing around." My hands made nonsensical gestures. "The touching."

He arched a brow. "Touching, huh?"

"Beckham," I chastised.

His shoulder lifted an inch. "It could be more than that."

"No," I blurted.

His eyes widened for a split second before he masked his surprise. And was that...disappointment?

"This is already a lot to try to navigate." My palm rested on my stomach, a tiny kick bumping against me.

His gaze moved to my hand and he visibly softened. "I know. But this is between us, Parker. We can get through anything."

"Can we?"

So many unspoken words and emotions flitted between us, it was nearly suffocating.

"So, the rules," he repeated.

"We already established no kissing," I started, and he nodded. "And I don't think we should touch each other in public."

The muscle in his neck jumped before he dipped his head in a nod. "Okay."

"This is just messing around, right?"

He nodded again.

"I don't think it should go further than that, then," I said.

His forehead creased. "Further?"

"Sex. I don't think we should have sex."

His expression cooled, but he flexed his fingers. "Okay."

I stared, waiting, like he might add some of his own input to this. But he remained silent.

"Do you have any rules...?"

"I'll take what I can get of you, Park. I'm not going to add any more restrictions to that."

Shock mixed with a world's supply of guilt rendered me speechless. "Beckham," I whispered, the word pained.

The spark that was there moments before faded, and he lowered his head. "It's all good." He met my gaze again, a small smile pasted on his lips. "Like I said, I'll take what I can get."

I hated this. Hated the weird in-between we seemed to be stuck in. But I couldn't offer him more, not when us getting together meant him taking on the responsibility of my son.

"Speaking of..." I focused on my fidgeting fingers. "I think I should find somewhere else to live when the baby comes."

His silence had me looking up. His eyes hadn't left

me, and he ran a rough hand down his mouth. "You really think that's best?"

"Isn't it?"

"No." There was no hesitation in his answer. No reservations.

"Beckham, I'll have a *baby*."

"Okay."

"Why are you being so nonchalant about this?"

"Because you're acting like this is all some complex scenario that I might not be able to handle. When have I ever backed away from anything when it comes to you? When have I ever made you think I wouldn't be there for you through everything?"

"This isn't just me anymore," I said quietly.

"Who else is this about then? The asshole who got you pregnant and walked away because he was scared of what his own actions caused?"

I shoved off the stool, our chests nearly touching. "All I am right now is baggage, Beckham."

His hands cupped my neck before snaking up to my hair. He angled my head up so I had no choice but to look at him. "Don't you ever say that about yourself."

A tear slipped down my cheek, and I batted it away. I hated how easily I cried these days. "It's true."

One of his hands slid out of my hair to rest on my belly. His touch warmed me from the inside out, and I wasn't sure if it was my baby or the butterflies causing my stomach to flutter.

"This is all too much," I quietly admitted, the words

barely coming out through the tightening of my throat. "I'm not ready."

"Yes, you are." His thumb stroked back and forth. "When have you ever not conquered what life's thrown at you?"

A small laugh sputtered from my lips. "This isn't a choice between vanilla or chocolate ice cream, or whether I should ride with my spurs or without them. He's an entire human." My gaze fell to my stomach and Beckham's hand resting on it. His fingers tightened in my hair. "What if I mess him up?"

A shake of his head had me lifting mine. "You won't."

"And if I do?"

"Then we'll fix it."

His answer was so sure, as if he wasn't at all freaking out about the fact that I was supposed to push this baby out of me in a few months, come home, and raise him. I focused on that fact, and not how he'd used the word *we*.

"I don't even have a permanent place to raise him," I admitted, shame coating the statement.

"Yes, you do."

The finality in his tone had me meeting his gaze again. "You have answers for everything, don't you?"

A heavy breath left his lips. "I try, Parker."

My hand cupped his cheek. "I know." I edged closer to be sure he was really hearing me when I said, "I appreciate you."

Seconds passed before, finally, he dipped his chin. His eyes darted to my mouth and then he stepped away from me. "Don't be so hard on yourself. He can feel it."

My lashes fluttered as his words processed. It felt like I'd been hit with a hundred-mile-per-hour wind and spun upside down. "You've been reading baby books, haven't you?"

His cheeks flushed. "If the internet counts as books, sure."

My lips twitched with all the words I wanted to say but shouldn't. "You don't have to do research for me..."

A crease formed in the center of his forehead. "I'll always take care of you, Parker. You know that."

"I know." And that was why this was so hard. Because the longer I stayed here, pregnant and alone, the more he'd help. The further involved he'd get. The harder it'd be to walk away when this game of pretend was all said and done. I'd been here for weeks, and we still hadn't talked about before—when the two of us parted and we thought we were done for good.

Was it too much to bring up?

Would we implode and truly be ruined forever if we did?

Our past held so much of us together, and it was too much to think of right now. Too heavy a topic when I already couldn't handle the reality at hand. I was barely holding myself together with a frayed string and dwindling strength. All I heard growing up was how strong other mothers were. How they sacrificed for their family. Letting my emotions get in the way would only show how weak I really was, and if there was anything I wanted this baby to know, it was that his mother would always be there to face any storm.

So I took a deep breath. Ran my hands over my clothes. And set my shoulders back. "We have to get to work."

———

For the past four hours, Beckham has made excuse after excuse on things he needed from the office. A pen. A notepad. Water. Erasers—at least three of those now. He came in four times asking me to reconfirm what they needed to work on with the old Dodge Charger sitting in the garage. As if brake pads and an oil change were that hard to remember.

At this point, I nearly expected it was him every time that door opened, so when the hinges squeaked for what had to be the twentieth time today, I grumbled, "What is it this time?"

"Bad day?"

Wyatt's voice had me snapping my head up from the paperwork laid out in front of me.

"Shit. Sorry. I thought you were—" I shook my head. He didn't need to know I was being snarky with Beckham. Sure, he probably noticed his multiple disappearances, but the last thing I needed was for our drama to be the talk of the town.

"Trouble in paradise?" Wyatt wiped his grease-stained hands on a dirty rag before plopping into the chair across from me.

I set the pen down. "Everything's dandy."

He sucked in air through his teeth. "See, I know

women. Got a lot of 'em that come in here with car problems and pretend it ain't pissin' 'em off. That right there"—he aimed a finger my way—"ain't dandy."

I reclined in the chair with a sigh. "And what? You want me to confess all my *car problems*"—I used air quotes around the phrase—"to you?"

He held his hands out in a *duh* gesture. "Hit me with it."

I shook my head at how ridiculous he was being. I was sure the last thing he wanted to hear about was girl problems. "How about, instead of that, we discuss maternity leave."

"What's there to discuss?"

"Well, I'm going to save up as much PTO as I can for after the baby comes, since I'm sure I won't qualify for the full maternity leave with my short employment here and all. I'll have childcare by the time it runs out so you won't have to worry about a baby crying in your lobby."

He frowned, narrowed his eyes. In a blink, his entire demeanor had changed. "You really think I'd make you give up time with your newborn to come file paperwork?"

I blinked, his question taking me off guard. "Well, I need money—"

He held up a hand. "You're going to be a mom, Parker. Fuck the job. It'll be here if you want it back, but not until you're ready." He leaned forward in his chair, rag gripped in a fist. "No fucking way am I going to make you miss out on those moments."

My heart pinched. "But Wyatt, the money—"

"Whatdya need money for? Ain't no one in Bell Buckle gonna let you be homeless, especially not that lovesick puppy currently listening through the damn door."

Something metal clanged to the ground just outside the door, confirming Wyatt's suspicions.

"I can't just mooch off everyone," I stated. "I need a stable income to care for my baby."

"So I'll pay you while you're on leave."

I opened my mouth to retort, but he beat me to it. "It's standard. You get a portion of your pay while on maternity leave. No fucking law, rule, or policy is going to tell me how much that portion is, so consider all of it yours."

Clearly my pregnancy was taking a toll on my brain, because what he was saying couldn't seriously be true.

"For how long?" I managed to get out.

"How long you need it?"

Slowly, I sat forward, hands braced on the armrests. "Wyatt."

He simply stared, like this wasn't the most ridiculous idea ever.

"People go through hard things. Wreck your car, forget to pay a bill, have to move houses. But no one should have to hold the load of raising a baby all on their own. My dad did it for me and my brother. Did a shitty job at it, but he did it. I only ever wished someone would've given him a damn break in life, so maybe he would've given us a break, too." He stood, pocketing the rag. "You stay home with your baby. Raise him to be the best little man he can be. I'll do you this favor, if you do that for me."

Wetness pooled in my eyes as words escaped me. He waited, giving me a moment to compose my thoughts.

"I will."

Satisfied, he dipped his chin in farewell.

When his hand grasped the door handle, I added, "But only for six months. I won't take any more than that."

He looked back at me, and the hardened, dirt-smudged man smiled. "Deal."

20

BECKHAM

My parents' house looked like a pink-and-blue bomb had gone off. Streamers, confetti, plates, and napkins. Somehow it all blended flawlessly with the rustic charm of the Bronson ranch.

Sage's gender reveal theme was boots and bows, and I had to give it to them—it was a damn cute idea. Parker stood on the opposite side of the house from me, talking with the girls about something I couldn't decipher. Not that I was trying to read her lips. My entire focus was homed in on her belly under the swell of her light pink dress. How her hand came up to rest on the bump while she spoke. How she looked like a fucking angel standing there with the light shining in from the window behind her.

The woman made me so damn parched, I was already on my fourth bottle of water since arriving here with her two hours ago. We'd come together, and it'd nearly killed me when I helped her down from my truck and had to let go of her hand. No public intimacy had been her rule though, and if following it meant I could have her in the privacy of my home, I wouldn't break it.

"Travis just looked at me like I was some sort of fucking animal," Bailey went on, telling a story about some shit that happened on the ranch yesterday.

Lennon chuckled, already on his second beer. "One day, my dad's going to decide to never let you come back."

Bailey smiled. "My life's goal is to catch that man off guard."

Lettie sidled up next to him, leaning into his side as he wrapped an arm around her. I hadn't even noticed her cross the room. "Oh, that's your life's goal, is it?"

Bailey leaned over to press a kiss to her cheek. "That, and ruining every surface on this ranch."

Lennon made a gagging noise, a dribble of beer sliding down his chin. He wiped at it with the back of his hand. "I do not need to know that shit."

Bailey's smile only grew as he took a sip of beer.

"Beck," Lettie said, grabbing my attention. "You okay?"

I looked down to find a furrow in her brows. "Yeah. All good."

She always worried about her brothers, the same way we were all protective of her. But the past few months, her check-ins had become more frequent.

I guess that's what happened when I lost myself to alcohol.

"He's just a little distracted," Bailey chimed in.

Confusion marred Lettie's forehead before her eyes followed the direction I was facing. Realization replaced the creases. "Oh."

I shook my head. "No. Don't 'oh' me like that. There's nothing going on."

"She's living in your house," Lennon pointed out.

"Thanks for the reminder." I shot him a glare.

"Are you guys—" Lettie started, but I cut her off before she could finish that question.

"No." I tugged my cowboy hat lower. "She needed a place to stay, and I have an extra room. It's as simple as that."

"Is it ever as simple as that between you and Parker?" Bailey mumbled into his drink before tossing it back.

"Yes," I said at the exact same moment Lettie answered, "No."

We sent twin glares at each other.

"You guys are insufferable," I muttered.

The front door opened, and Brandy popped her head in. "The reveal is ready!"

Sage's face lit up as Callan intertwined their fingers, immediately leading them outside. Parker's gaze met mine briefly before she followed Oakley out. My feet were moving before I could think to stop them, and I heard Bailey utter behind me, "It's definitely not that simple."

While we all gathered outside, I didn't even try to hide the fact that I was searching for Parker. As soon as I found her, I made my way over and didn't stop until I was by her side.

"You doing okay?" I asked, my hand brushing hers. "Do you need anything?"

"I'm okay," she whispered, eyes trained on the barn ahead of us.

"If you need a minute..."

She shook her head, pinky nudging my hand.

Seconds later, the doors to the barn were shoved open by Reed and Brandy, and little shrieks of excitement came from the girls. Brandy held a thumbs up past the doors, and hooves sounded. Slow at first, and then they picked up to a trot before Avery appeared on Boots, the horse Callan got her. She had the biggest smile on her face as she emerged from the barn, pink balloons billowing behind her where they were attached to the back of the saddle.

Cheers and clapping sounded from the group, my mom and dad turning to hug each other. Tears filled the former's eyes while my dad smiled wide as ever. Sage and Callan instantly ran for Avery, where she pulled Boots to a stop. Callan reached up and swooped her down, spinning her in his arms before the three of them hugged.

My brother was having a girl.

I couldn't help it as moisture gathered in my eyes. I looked down to find Parker with the biggest grin on her face. She turned her attention on me, eyes gleaming, and I might've imagined it, but I think her fingers wrapped around mine for the briefest moment. I wasn't sure, though, as every time I got caught up in the reality of her standing before me, everything else faded away.

At the same time, she was bringing me back. Rooting me to the present and showing me light could be found, even when my head was stuck in a pit of darkness.

———

I lost track of how much time had passed since we arrived at my parents' house. All I knew was that the sun was setting, and I was happy.

Parker had excused herself from the front porch a while ago, and I was trying not to let my concern show. She couldn't possibly be in labor...right? She was over five months pregnant now, and while I knew scares could happen, I got the feeling she hadn't disappeared due to those types of complications.

Even so, if she was fighting a mental battle right now, getting lost in herself, I didn't want her to be alone in that. She might think she had to hide those types of things to keep up the image of being strong—but like myself, she had to learn that being low was okay, too. Not every day, every moment, were we capable of pasting on smiles.

I excused myself from my family, who were all gathered around the long table. Reed's eyes tracked me as I moved, and I only hoped he didn't follow me. The family had, for some reason, tasked him with keeping an eye on me over the last six or so months. While we had our share of disagreements, I'd gotten the sense he was tired of playing the overbearing big brother role. I wouldn't be surprised if they'd all made a pact to watch me today, though, between the drinking and the baby stuff.

After a quick search through the house, I found it was empty. A glance at the back sliding door showed it was cracked, a chilled breeze making its way inside. I crossed the room, planning to close it, when Parker's form took shape at the railing on the porch. Little pieces of hair were floating around her face, her cheeks slightly red from the cold. From where I stood, I could only see a portion of the side of her face. Her arms were crossed where she leaned on the wood in front of her, her ivory sweater pulled tight around her to ward off the chill.

Slowly, I slid open the door until I had enough space to slip out. I wasn't quiet as I closed it and moved to her side. Still, knowing I was there, she continued to stare out at the land. Faint oranges and purples mingled with the horizon, only minutes of the colorful canvas left in the day. With the darkening landscape, the outdoor lights strung up across the porch began burning brighter, casting a golden glow over the worn wood.

She didn't speak, so I didn't either. Instead, I fought the urge to pull her into my side as I followed her line of sight.

Minutes passed before she said, "Do you ever feel like time is moving too fast?"

I looked down at her, finding her gaze still hooked on the darkening landscape. "All the time."

She seemed to think on that a moment before saying,

"What if this is my only pregnancy, and I'm sitting here blinking and missing it as it flies by?"

I swallowed, because if I had it my way, and this pregnancy went well, she'd be pregnant a hundred more times. Babies with her had always been my dream. "Do you not want more kids?"

Glassy eyes met mine. "Do you really think anyone will want me after I've had another man's baby?"

I do, I almost said, but stopped myself right before the admission passed my lips.

"You're having *your* baby, Parker. And that doesn't mean you're tainted. It means you grew an entire human, and you're beyond fucking strong for doing it. Any man that doesn't see that, send them to me." *Send me any man that talks to you. I'll show them what happens when they go near my Parker.*

Her lips rolled together before she broke our stare. "I just don't want to regret missing these moments. Women have photoshoots, gender reveals, baby showers. They decorate a room and pack a hospital bag. All I've had time to focus on is myself. I'm already selfish, and he's not even here yet."

I cupped her chin, forcing her to look at me. "Don't ever say you're selfish. You're doing the things you need to do to ensure your child has a good life when he comes into this world. None of that is selfish. But you also can't forget about you. We'll make all that happen, if that's what you want."

Her eyes welled with tears, but they didn't fall. "It's too late," she whispered.

"It's never too late." My focus darted to her glistening lips.

Her breathing seemed to deepen, her cheeks reddening further as she noticed where I was staring. "We can't kiss." The statement was barely audible, like she didn't want to be reminded of it either.

"I know," I murmured.

But that didn't stop my thumb from running along her cheek. It trailed down to the line of her jaw and tipped her head back. Her bottom lip puffed out as her mouth parted and her eyes became heavy.

"I don't want you to be upset because of the gender reveal. Because it *will* happen. Everything you want, I'll make it come true. I promise."

Her lashes fluttered closed before they opened and landed on my mouth. "Beckham..."

"Yes, Park?"

"Please distract me."

Those three words revived me. Lit a flame only Parker could ignite.

My hand carefully grazed down her neck, her pulse jumping at the pads of my fingers. I trailed them over her collarbone, down the dip of her dress, until my rough palm caught on the fabric of her pink dress. I cupped her breast, squeezing.

Her sharp intake of breath nearly brought me to my knees.

My other hand gripped her upper arm, turning us so her back was to the railing, and mine was to the house. I kneaded her breast before sliding inside her dress to cup the flesh.

"Not wearing a bra to my parents' house is danger-ous, Park," I whispered, my lips brushing the shell of her ear.

"For who?" Her words sounded drunk with arousal already.

"Me. You. Both of us. Fuck." I rolled her nipple between two fingers.

Her head tilted back farther, the column of her neck exposed. I leaned in to inhale her scent.

Fuck, fuck, fuck.

This wasn't good. We were in public, and this was out in the open, and her neck looked so damn kissable—

"Please let me kiss you," I begged.

Her head shook side to side, hair falling over her shoulders. Her knitted sweater slid down her biceps, exposing more skin.

"Parker, *please.*"

With one hand braced on the railing, she moved the other to her dress and tugged. Both breasts were exposed now, nipples pebbled from the cold.

"Only there," she instructed breathlessly.

Not wasting a single second, I dipped my head. I couldn't help myself as my lips brushed her neck on my way down. Couldn't stop my tongue from tasting her sweet skin. One hit, and the thin ice I was standing on threatened to shatter.

Her hands tangled in my hair, nails digging into my

scalp as I wrapped my mouth around her nipple and sucked. My other hand cupped her opposite breast, massaging and pinching and squeezing.

I felt her body tighten, felt how her legs clamped together and her skin turned feverish.

While I sucked, my free hand moved between her legs, against the fabric of her dress.

Her belly jumped when I made contact with her pussy, then she spread her legs the slightest bit, allowing me room to get to her clit.

I slid my fingers up her pussy before circling the bud. I wondered if she was wearing panties, and one swipe at where a seam should be had my dick twitching.

"No panties, either, Park?" I mumbled against her breast. Her tug on my hair had me going back to sucking quickly. More desperately. Because that's what I was for her. *Desperate*.

"They show lines," she managed to get out between breaths.

"They would've made this harder, too," I added.

This time, her grip was punishing. "Just shut up and make me come, Beckham."

I smiled against her flesh, looking up at her. "I want you to come quickly for me, Parker. We have a party to get back to."

She groaned before pulling my head back to where it was. I dragged her nipple back into my mouth, teeth grazing it, before sucking harder than before. I quickened my circles on her clit, reveling in the way her breathing picked up and she had to lean against the railing for support.

God, what I wished I could do to her body right now. But being as anyone could walk out at any minute, I didn't want to risk exposing her further. This would have to be enough—for now.

Her hips moved, riding my hand as I drew her closer and closer to the edge. My tongue flicked against the bud in my mouth before my teeth dug into her skin. Over and over, the cycle repeated until she was panting my name and nearly collapsing.

My arm wrapped around her waist, holding her up as she shook with the waves of her release.

Once I was sure she could stand, I removed my hand from between her legs and straightened. I dipped my fingers into my mouth, licking them clean before I helped fix the top of her dress back into place, finishing by tugging the sleeves of her sweater back up.

She finally caught her breath, each puff coming out in a cloud of white now that the sun had set behind the mountains.

I tugged my handkerchief where it was neatly folded out of my breast pocket. She eyed it, opening her mouth to likely ask what the hell I was doing, but before she could, I dropped to my knees before her.

I tugged her dress up her calves, past her knees, and bunched it around her thighs. With my eyes on hers, and her mouth parted in surprise, my hand with the handkerchief disappeared between her legs. I wiped front to back thoroughly before pulling it away. I let her dress fall back to her ankles, straightening the material before standing. Then I folded the handkerchief and tucked it back in my pocket.

Parker blinked frantically. "Are you just gonna—"

I dipped my head. "Yep."

Her eyes widened. "Oh."

I stared at her while she stared at where the handkerchief was safely tucked away. Maybe she knew I'd use it later when I stroked my cock in my bed. Maybe she thought I was just being nice. But really, she should know me by now. I was obsessed with her.

She swallowed, composing herself before asking, "Is that how you distract other girls if they ask?"

I wrapped an arm around her shoulders—for warmth, I told myself—and led her toward the back door. "Just with you. There are never any other girls."

"I should ask you more often, then," she teased.

The playful lilt to her voice had a smile cracking on my face. "As often as you so wish."

She looked up at me with a closed-lip grin. I slid my arm from around her, opening the door and allowing her to go inside first.

I shut it behind me, only to come to a stop when we found Reed standing in the center of the kitchen, water bottle in hand.

"Everything good?" he asked hesitantly, his skeptical gaze darting between the two of us.

"Everything's great," I confirmed, then sidled up next

to Parker as we crossed to the front door to join the others.

I held the door open for her and shot her a wink as she passed.

Maybe sneaking around with her wasn't so bad after all.

21

BECKHAM

My palms were sweating as I dragged the butter knife through the white frosting. Each swipe turned out worse than before, and by the time I was finished, the cake looked like a lumpy mess. But the entire thing was covered, and that was the most important part.

I didn't have the proper materials for baking a cake, so I'd gone out after finishing up my day at the ranch and bought everything on the list Sage had given me. Everything but some fancy spreading tool that was apparently essential to the entire process.

There wasn't time to fuss over it as the handle on my front door turned, and in popped Parker. She shoved the door shut against the howling, bitter wind before facing me. She paused midstep, eyeing the cake on the counter.

"What is that?" she asked hesitantly.

"A cake."

As if deciding it wouldn't bite, she crossed to it, examining it like some foreign specimen. "Why?"

"Because you never got a gender reveal."

Her entire body seemed to freeze before she slowly turned to look up at me. "But I already know it's a boy…"

I handed her the knife full of frosting. "Yeah, and you're going to find out again."

Her mouth fell open as she carefully wrapped her fingers around the handle. She seemed…stunned?

"Come on, Park. Cut into it." I gestured to the round, two-tier cake, eager to see if my concoction would hold together under the mound of frosting.

She gave me another confused look before finally facing the cake. Hovering the knife over the top, she seemed to contemplate where to cut. Seconds passed, and I decided she needed an extra push.

I wrapped my hand around hers holding the knife. The contact had her darting her gaze up to mine in question. I nudged my head at the cake before lowering our hands toward it. She watched as the knife slid past the inch-thick layer of white, making its way all the way to the bottom. We did the same again, and then used the side of the knife to pull the slice out. Her lips pressed together at the sight of the baby blue frosting in the middle while we set it on the paper plate in front of us.

I took the knife from her, setting it on a paper towel on the counter.

"It's a boy," I murmured, enthusiasm and awe seeping into the words.

When she said nothing, I glanced at the side of her face—and the tear rolling down it.

Instantly, like it was second nature, I wrapped a hand around her arm and turned her to face me. "Park, what's wrong?"

She shook her head, and I couldn't tell if she was frowning or smiling. "Nothing." She waved a hand in front of her face before swiping at a tear. "This was just really sweet."

The corners of my mouth ticked up. "You deserve this." I cupped her cheek as she sniffled. "And I made a promise last week. We're going to make up for everything. You'll have good memories of this pregnancy, okay? No regrets. I won't allow it."

She let out a blubbery laugh, tears still spilling. "Thank you."

"Anything for you, Parker." And I meant it. *Anything.* My heart. My soul. She could have it all. Hell, she already did.

"You want to go change and eat some cake?" I asked.

She nodded. I felt bad that she did this in her work clothes—a gray T-shirt with North State Auto's logo and a zip-up jacket—but I wanted to surprise her as soon as she got home.

Parker disappeared for five minutes before coming back wearing an ivory tank top paired with little shorts that had teddy bears all over them. While she was gone, I'd dished up another slice of cake.

With both plates in my hands, I asked, "Sit or stand?"

"Stand, please. I need a few minutes off my ass. I've been sitting in that office all day."

I frowned, making a mental note to research how that could affect pregnancy before wiping the look off my face.

I set the plates back on the counter and offered her a fork. She took it, but rather than going for her own piece, she reached for mine. Before I could ask what she was doing, she broke off a bite and held it out to me.

"First bite honor goes to you for actually baking a cake," she announced with a smile.

"It wasn't all that hard, really," I mumbled.

She arched a brow. "Sage gave you the recipe, didn't she?"

My eyes narrowed. "Maybe."

She wagged the fork before I reached forward and attempted to take the bite. With her movement, all it succeeded in doing was bumping the cake against my cheek and toppling it to the floor.

Her eyes dipped to my ribs. "Oh shit, I'm sorry." Despite the apology, she couldn't seem to contain her giggles as she reached for a paper towel.

I looked down to find a blue streak down the center of my white T-shirt. "It's alright. I've got probably ten of these lying around."

She began rubbing at the frosting on my shirt, intent on getting it off. "You still buy your shirts in those big bulk packs, huh?"

My eyes narrowed skeptically. "Some. Why? Is there something wrong with that?"

She laughed. A full, belly-aching laugh. "No, it's just so…you."

"They're usually only work shirts," I defended.

"I know—"

"And sometimes I wear them at home. Like when I'm baking."

This only made her laugh harder, her face turning red. "You bake often?"

"Well, no. But on the off chance that I do"—she arched a brow at me—"they come in handy."

Her giggles slowly ceased before she dropped her hand to her side with a huff. "Well, it's stained. Do you have stain remover?"

"Probably?"

She frowned, then gestured to my shirt. "Off."

I cocked my head to the side. "If you wanted me naked, all you had to do was ask. You didn't have to ruin one of my perfectly good, one-of-a-kind T-shirts."

Her eyes turned to slits before she grabbed the hem of my shirt and tugged it upward. Once it hit my pecs, she had a harder time, as I didn't lift my arms.

"Beckham," she groaned.

"Yes, Parker?" The playful lilt to my voice had her rolling her eyes.

"Lift."

I set my hands on her waist, lifting her and plopping her ass on the counter. Right in the slice of cake.

Her mouth popped open with a gasp. "Beckham!"

I shrugged, not even bothering to hide my smile. "You said lift. You didn't specify what."

Her hands fell to her thighs in defeat. "Well, now we're both covered in cake."

"No. *You're* covered in cake. I"—I gestured to the circle of blue on the fabric—"have a stain."

Her glare turned downright murderous before she dug her hand into the cake beside her and grabbed a fistful. I backpedaled, but my efforts were futile as she chucked it at my face.

I scooped chunks of cake and icing off my eyelids before opening my eyes and pointing at her. "That wasn't nice."

She pasted the most innocent look on her face before plopping a frosting-covered finger in her mouth. "Oops."

I quickly crossed back to the counter, her squeal filling the room as I picked up the cake and plopped it right on her head. Her sharp intake of breath echoed through the house. "Beckham Bronson!"

I dug a finger into the mess, scooping a chunk off and slipping it past my lips. "Hmm?"

With revenge clear in her gaze, she reached up and grabbed another handful of cake. She immediately chucked it at my chest, but I caught it before most of it could make contact. I moved closer to her, and she shook her head frantically, hands held up in defense.

"That's not fair!"

I smeared it down her cheek, trailing the remnants down her neck. "You started it."

"On accident!"

My smile was gleaming now, my cheeks starting to hurt from the sheer size of it, and when we paused to take in the mess we'd created, we both burst out laughing. Blue and white decorated not only us, but the counter and the floor, too.

My gaze fell to her ass, where cake was splattered out the side and onto the counter. My eyes slowly moved back to her face, assessing the chaos as they went.

"We should get cleaned up," she said, her voice a bit breathless now.

I nodded, placing my hands on her hips and sliding her off the counter. Her bare feet squelched on the bits of cake littering the floor, so instead of letting her walk, I scooped her into my arms, carrying her bridal style.

"What're you doing?" she asked.

"Carrying you to the bathroom. What else?"

"I can walk."

"Yeah, and then we'd have to mop the whole hallway." I glanced down to find her staring up at me. "Plus, this is way better than walking."

She crossed her arms like she was annoyed by it, but I could tell she secretly loved it. "You sure it's not just an excuse to hold me?"

I stepped into the bathroom, turning the light on with my elbow. "I don't need an excuse for that."

Setting her down on her feet, I glimpsed the blush on her cheeks. I moved past her to turn on the shower, then made my way back to the door. "If you need anything, just let me know. I'm gonna go shower in my bathroom."

She gnawed on her bottom lip, offering no response, so I grabbed the handle and began shutting the door.

"Wait," she started.

I paused, opening it slightly to look at her.

Her teeth seemed to increase pressure before she met my eyes. "Shower with me?"

I blinked, making sure I'd heard her right. Once the realization hit that I wasn't hallucinating, I stepped inside the bathroom and shut the door. "I thought you'd never ask."

She rolled her eyes as I shucked my shirt off. My gray sweats were next, leaving me completely naked.

Her eyes were saucers as she watched me undress with speed. But when her hands didn't move to do the same to herself, I closed the distance and pulled her tank top off for her.

"I can take my clothes off, Beck."

I tugged at the hem of her pants, sliding them down her thighs. "I know. I just do it better."

Her teeth dug into her bottom lip again, and once she was fully naked, I brought my thumb to her mouth, pulling on the abused flesh.

Her lips were puffy as she tilted her head back and stared up at me. I walked her backward until we were both under the spray of the water, eyes never leaving each other, and closed the shower door behind us.

The water turned an odd shade of blue as the frosting and bits of cake quickly washed away. I grabbed the silicone body scrubber from the hook on the wall, squirting a dollop of body wash into the center before lathering it in.

"This is fancy," I commented, grabbing her hand and running it up her arm.

"They don't sell these in packs, I don't think. Makes sense you've never seen one before."

Her comment had a smile tugging at my mouth. "Yeah, I usually just buy the two-pack of loofahs."

Her nose scrunched as I dragged soap over her collarbone. "Those hold so much bacteria."

"So you're saying I should switch?"

"Um, yes. I'll even give you mine and go get a new one."

I shook my head. "I think I like sharing."

Her cheeks turned the shade of freshly bloomed roses. To hide it, she tipped her head back under the water, rinsing her hair. I watched each droplet cascade over the skin I missed so badly. I wanted to taste every inch of it as she watched, worship the air she breathed and the ground she walked on. Hiding my desire for more was damn near impossible, but I'd take what I could get.

When she lifted her head, our noses brushed. A sharp intake of air passed her parted lips and her eyes nearly crossed as she took in how close we now were. I held the body scrubber on her belly before sliding it to her waist. With her bump now brushing my stomach, I froze at the warmth passing between our skin. Flames erupted with the contact, wrapping the two of us in a fire that was destined to never die out. But why—if we both knew we wanted each other—was she forcing us to straddle the edge?

Fuck the rules. I wanted her like before. When I could kiss her any time I wanted. Any place.

I leaned closer, ready to say "fuck it" and break the boundary she'd laid out, because I knew she wanted it too—but before our lips could brush, she dropped to her knees.

I looked down as a delicate hand wrapped around my throbbing cock, and I hissed in a breath.

With her focus solely on my cock, she parted those pink lips and stuck her tongue out, lapping at the tip.

"Parker, you don't have to—" But she silenced me by taking me into her mouth and sucking.

A curse slipped past my lips, and the body scrubber fell to the floor as my hand flung out to brace on the wall. For Parker, I would fall. For Parker, I would break and shatter and end up in a million pieces because *that* was the hold she had over me.

Now, with her mouth on my cock, there was definitely no going back.

What was the difference if our lips were on each other, but we couldn't kiss? She was afraid, but I was a needy fucking asshole who needed her to stomp out the invisible line she'd drawn and *take me*.

She worked my cock with a thoroughness I'd missed —her hand tugging, her mouth sucking, her tongue caressing. The tip hit the back of her throat and she gagged, pulling her lips off to take a breath.

I nearly opened my mouth again to remind her she didn't have to do this, but she was already taking me back in, deeper and deeper with each pass.

My free hand dug into her wet strands, helping her with the pace. "You missed this, didn't you?"

A moan slipped out of her as her big eyes met mine. The look caused me to throw my head back and groan.

"Fuck, Parker."

One palm rested on my thigh, her nails digging into my flesh. Her grip on my cock became firmer as she stroked me, keeping rhythm with her mouth. She quickened her strides, resulting in my balls tightening.

"Parker, I'm going to come." It was a warning—one she seemed to welcome as she went even faster. Her mouth remained around my cock, cheeks hollow, as I spilled onto her tongue. Her mouth popped off, and she swiped at the saliva dribbling down her chin before grabbing the body scrubber off the floor and standing.

"You know, now would be the time I kiss you," I said, hoping to get some sort of change in attitude from her on the whole rules thing.

But instead, she poured extra body wash on the scrubber and started running it in circles over my chest. As if she hadn't just been on her knees for me. As if my cum hadn't slipped down her pretty little throat and she hadn't swallowed every last drop.

"Or you can stop trying to break the rules and let me wash you."

I frowned. "I'd much rather take the kiss."

She paused her movements, sighing. "Beckham, if this is going to work, we have to stick to them."

"I can kiss you and still remember you're making your own choices with your baby."

Something akin to hurt flashed over her eyes. "Yeah, well, I can't."

She didn't have to say anything further for me to know why. I only wished she'd let up on not wanting this baby to be a burden on me. He'd never be. Neither of them would.

But rather than fight her on the matter, I grabbed the scrubber from her and turned her around, running the soap over her shoulder blades and back.

And once I was done, I hung it on the hook and massaged her shoulders, thankful that, at least for now, I could touch her.

22

PARKER

I frowned at my reflection in the mirror as I tugged the waistband of my skirt midway up my stomach for the third time. How was I supposed to style anything nice when all I could comfortably wear were sweats and oversized T-shirts at this point? My ivory sweater was baggy, which I was thankful for, but even then, no matter how I wore the skirt, something looked... off.

A light knock on the bedroom door had me pulling my sweater back down to cover my stomach. Beckham nudged the door open, leaning a shoulder against the jamb. His gaze roamed my body, eyes hungry despite him having been between my legs only an hour ago. We'd been sticking to my no-kissing rule, but that hadn't stopped Beckham from getting his lips on me any way he could over the past several days.

When he made it back to my face, his brows furrowed. "Something is wrong."

I sighed, turning back to the mirror and pinching the fabric of my knit sweater between my fingers. "I just can't figure out how to wear this."

Gentle steps sounded on the floor before he stopped behind me. His arms came around my waist, his hands wrapping around my own and making me drop the material. "It's a sweater, Park. Only one way to wear it."

I scrunched my nose, both at his statement and the way my stomach seemed to pinch slightly. I'd had random nausea all throughout the day, and I was really hoping it'd disappear before dinner tonight. "I mean the skirt."

His eyes dropped, studying it.

"I wanted to tuck the sweater into the top of the skirt so it'd look cute, but the waistband isn't sitting right because of my stomach." I tugged the sweater up slightly, running a hand over my belly. "What am I going to wear in a couple months when I'm even bigger?"

He rested his hand over mine, and a tiny kick met my palm. The sensation of my baby had my shoulders relaxing a fraction. Beckham's presence at my back had my spiraling thoughts nearly dissipating altogether.

"My family won't mind what you wear to Thanksgiving, Parker. Hell, you can show up in sweats and a sweatshirt if you want. We all only want you to be comfortable and happy."

"I am happy," I stated, despite the unknown constantly whirling around in the back of my mind.

He gave me a skeptical look. "And comfortable?"

Saliva pooled in my mouth and my stomach pinched

again. My hand tightened over my belly, fingers gripping the fabric of the skirt before I shoved away from Beckham and beelined for the bathroom.

I threw the lid to the toilet open as I fell to my knees, and despite trying my best to hold it back, I emptied the contents of my stomach.

Mid-heave, a hand gently rested on my back, rubbing slow circles.

I went to grab for a tissue but Beckham beat me to it, holding one out to me.

After wiping my mouth, I mumbled, "Please don't watch this."

"I'm not leaving you."

I heaved a sigh, attempting to calm the roiling of my stomach. "I'm gross."

He continued his soothing circles on my back. "You could never be gross."

I huffed a small laugh, but all it resulted in was another heave into the toilet. After a few minutes, and being sure there was nothing left for me to vomit, he shoved to his feet. "Let's get you out of these clothes."

I rolled my lips together, willing my stomach to relax enough for me to stand without fear of throwing up more. When I reached up to grab the counter beside me, Beckham set a hand on my elbow, the other at my back, and helped lift me to my feet. He disappeared while I washed my hands and brushed my teeth, and reappeared with a pair of sweats and one of his T-shirts.

"I don't want to vomit on your shirt," I said hesitantly.

He shrugged. "I've got a washing machine and twelve more if you need to change. I get the packs, remember?" His wink had a small smile pulling at the corner of my mouth. Despite the shitty situation, he still managed to shine a little light.

He set the clothes on the counter and helped me undress, even unclasping my bra for me. He didn't so much as glance at my breasts as he pulled the shirt over my head, then crouched to help pull the sweats up my legs.

Before I could take a step, he scooped me into his arms and carried me to the bed. With the sheets already pulled back, he set me down and pulled them up to my stomach.

"I'll be right back," he assured me before leaving the room. He was back less than five minutes later with all sorts of things. Water, a bottle of Tylenol, a plastic bowl, and a box of tissues. After neatly arranging them on my nightstand, he rounded the bed and crawled in next to me.

"I don't want to get you sick," I said, voice hoarse from vomiting.

With no hesitation, he looped an arm around my shoulders, pulling me onto his chest where he lay on his back. With a headache blooming and my skin feeling warm, his heartbeat settled whatever protests I was about to weakly deliver.

"Don't worry about me, Park," he murmured into my hair.

My arm draped across his stomach, thigh fitting over his like it used to. "I always worry about you."

When minutes passed and he remained silent, the realization hit me. "Beckham, your family—"

"I already texted them that we weren't coming tonight."

I tried to sit up but he kept me in place. I wanted to tell him he could still go, but if this was contagious, neither of us would want to spread it to them. "But it's Thanksgiving."

"You come before any holiday," he admitted. "We can have dinner with them another time."

"Do they know why?"

I felt him nod. "Callan said Sage insisted you stay as hydrated as possible. And I think we should call your doctor after you take a nap."

"It's Thanksgiving," I reminded him.

"An on-call nurse, then."

The knowledge that Beckham was not only caring for me in this situation, but also my baby, had my heart growing to the size of the moon. Would any other man have stayed for the vomiting? Would they have thought to call a doctor to get advice on how to handle sickness during a pregnancy? And would someone as close with their family as Beckham forfeit a holiday for the smell of puke and a girl with an oncoming fever?

Probably not. Especially not if that baby wasn't theirs.

But here Beckham was, at every turn, showing me that

he cared. Not only by letting me stay in his house for the time being, but with every little thing. Buying granola bars in the flavors he noticed me eating the most. Stocking the fridge with cans of Dr. Pepper, and bringing me an iced one from the gas station on his way home from the ranch.

All these little moments were turning into a load my heart couldn't bear because my head kept telling me to keep this responsibility off his shoulders—to protect him from losing himself because of me.

But I think I was too late for all of that. Beckham had already inserted himself into this baby's life, and I'd been the one to open the door to let him in.

I hadn't realized it before, but he was already adjusting to me and my baby without the pressure of *having* to be a parent. He was doing this willingly.

Would he want to forever, though?

———

I woke to an empty bed.

The door was cracked, letting in a sliver of dim light from somewhere in the house. My hand instinctively went to my stomach, checking for kicks. I'd read once that the side effects of vomiting could induce labor, and the last thing I wanted to do was cause unnecessary stress on my baby. I waited for what felt like minutes before I felt the shift of my boy. A massive sigh of relief passed my lips, and then I rolled over to flick on the bedside lamp.

After my eyes adjusted to the light, I found a sticky note stuck to the side of a water bottle.

Drink me before getting out of bed.

The fact Beckham had written me a note had a smile playing on my lips. Though still slightly queasy, I felt significantly better than when I fell asleep—I blinked at the clock—three hours ago.

Had I really been out that long?

I glanced out the window to find it was dark out now. Uncapping the bottle, I took a small sip, testing how my stomach reacted before swallowing another. When no further nausea came, I slipped out of bed, slid into my fuzzy slippers, and left the room.

My sluggish steps were a clear sign I was trying not to make any sudden movements to upset my stomach again. I hated vomiting, and I was beyond thankful when I'd gotten out of the first trimester with little more than sore breasts and light cramping. Now, I seemed to be paying for it.

I reached the end of the hall, following where the light was emanating from, and found Beckham with his back to me, standing in front of the stove.

The house smelled delicious, and my stomach growled in acknowledgment. Realization hit me then that I didn't feel as warm as when I'd fallen asleep. Maybe it was only something I'd eaten, and not the stomach flu.

I took another small sip of water before making my way to one of the stools.

Beckham turned then, eyes instantly scanning me. "How do you feel?"

I set the bottle on the counter. "Like I just puked my guts out."

His jaw seemed stiff, his brows pulling in slightly.

"Better than earlier, at least," I added, wanting to ease his worries a bit.

"That's good." He turned off the burner while simultaneously opening one of the upper cabinets and pulling out two bowls. "I made chicken noodle soup, if you're up for it. Otherwise, I have bread and butter or crackers."

I offered a small smile. "Soup sounds great. Thank you."

I drank half the bottle while he dished up two bowls and spread butter on two slices of toast. It wasn't garlic or cheesy or anything fancy. He was eating just as bland as I was. On Thanksgiving.

"I'm sorry this isn't a turkey dinner," I said as he set my portion in front of me.

He took the seat beside me. "This is even better."

I twirled the spoon in the soup, guilt gnawing at me. "You don't have to lie to make me feel better."

His hand covered mine, ceasing my fiddling. Our eyes met. "I'm not lying, Parker. A night at home with you sounds a whole lot better than another dinner over there." His thumb stroked my knuckles. "I've had a lifetime of those, but not nearly enough of you."

This time, when my body warmed, I was certain it had nothing to do with a fever and everything to do with the man sitting beside me.

I wanted to say so many things back. That I'd missed him every day. Thought about him constantly. Always wished the few kisses I shared were his lips, not a stranger's. How I woke up every morning wishing my dreams weren't just dreams, but reality.

But when I stayed silent, not sure how to admit any of that without drawing him further into my mess, his touch left my hand and he picked up his own spoon.

"I texted you the nurse's number for when you're up for it," he explained. While anyone else might not have been able to hear how his tone dropped slightly, I did. "I did some googling, which I know they say not to do, but I was worried—" He stopped himself, cleared his throat. "Dehydration is the biggest concern, so between the broth and the water, you should be in the clear, but you should make an appointment just in case."

A noodle slid off the side of my spoon where I moved it up and down in the soup. "I'll call right after I eat." I looked at him, barely catching the glance of his eye as he ate. "Thank you."

He nodded, and we ate the rest of the meal in silence —though my head was anything but a quiet place. Second thoughts rooted themselves in the feelings that had resurfaced the moment I saw Beckham at my father's funeral.

What if my fear of everything between us only resulted in pushing him away?

23
PARKER

I hissed in a breath as the cardboard sliced through the side of my finger. I hated paper cuts. The pesky wounds were small, but they hurt like no other.

I twisted my finger side to side, inspecting the stinging skin. After seeing no more than a thin line of blood, I dabbed a clean tissue on the wound before tossing it in the bin and going back to breaking down the three boxes that had been delivered today. Beckham had taken the parts into the garage a little over an hour ago, and I'd had to practically beg him to leave the cardboard here for me to deal with.

Being an office assistant was pretty straightforward, but that was the problem I was currently facing. I needed something out of my daily routine to break up the spiraling thoughts. Every day, we came closer and closer to my due date, and I didn't even have a nursery set up.

Day by day, I forced positive affirmations into my mind

like the class I'd taken had told me to. Two days after my illness on Thanksgiving, I'd gone to get checked out to be sure everything was okay. When my doctor had suggested I also take a birthing class, I'd jumped at the offer. Beckham had come, of course. He'd gone to all my appointments ever since our conversation—though thankfully there weren't many, as my pregnancy was going as smoothly as it could.

Now, two weeks later, I was finally starting to actually listen to some of the affirmations. Sometimes, even the prospect of Beckham helping when the baby came slipped into my mental list, and it took a load off my shoulders every time.

The blade sliced through the last portion of tape, and I folded the box in on itself until it was small enough to fit in the bin by my desk. Beckham had already told me I wouldn't be walking across the icy back parking lot to get to the dumpster. Instead, he promised to do it himself after our shift, and instructed me to set them in the plastic tub in the meantime.

The tiny bell above the door to the lobby dinged as I folded the pocket knife and set it beside my keyboard to greet whoever was walking in.

As soon as my eyes met the man wearing a deep maroon felt cowboy hat and a growing grin on his face, I knew I was in for it.

I offered a friendly smile. "How can I help you?"

The man sauntered up to the desk, sliding the snow-flecked hat off his head and revealing curly brown hair. "Know of a cute little lady with the prettiest eyes in the west who can call me a tow truck?" He shot me a cheesy wink.

I tried not to roll my eyes, feigning the act like I was looking for a paper in front of me. "We actually have a tow truck here. Did you break down nearby?" A glance at his pants showed stains of water where snow had likely melted on his walk to the shop.

My observation had his mind in the gutter as his grin only widened. "Sure did, ma'am. Bet the cab's still warm, though, if you wanna come take a better look." He hiked his thumb over his shoulder.

My teeth ground together as I moved my focus to the computer screen, hand squeezing the mouse so hard I thought it might burst to pieces.

As if he could sense my discomfort through the wall, the door that connected the shop to the office swung open, and Beckham appeared. His body stiffened as his eyes darted between me and the man.

"Dick," Beckham said stiffly.

My mouth popped open at the sheer audacity for him to act that way, but then the man placed his hat back on his head and approached Beckham with an even bigger smile this time.

"Beckham, my man. I wondered if I was near Bell Buckle." The man—Dick, by the sound of it—held a hand out to Beck, who robotically lifted his own for a shake. "My truck ain't got GPS, and my phone's dead. Hell, I've been using road signs for about fifty miles."

Dick's slap on his back was much firmer than Beckham's awkward pat.

"Yep. You're near it." Beck's voice was so...odd. Like he hated the man but also shared a past with him that warranted niceties.

"My ol' Chevy broke down probably three or so miles away. Think you can tow it?" Dick looked at me, a devious sparkle in his gaze. "Little lady here didn't seem to want to take me up on my offer."

Beck's eyes narrowed on me. "What offer?"

Maybe it was the desire to get Dick out of this office as fast as possible, or the way Beckham seemed to be just as protective of me as he used to be, but I chose blunt honesty. "Dick here offered to let me take a look at him, so long as his cab was still warm."

Beck's fingers flexed, brows tugging together. "You mean his truck?"

I crossed my arms, leaning back in the chair. "Nope. Him."

His gaze turned lethal as he rolled his jaw, aiming his attention back on Dick. "That true?"

The way Beckham took a step toward him had me shoving out of my chair. Maybe I should've sugarcoated Dick's behavior, but what was that protecting? Because it sure as hell wasn't my feelings, and I had no obligation to save this stranger.

But I did have a heart for Beckham, and that included saving him from fighting some worthless flirt.

Dick's eyes widened as they landed on my stomach, which was now in full view. "Jesus, Beckham. You left rodeo because you knocked up some chick?" He gestured to my belly before regarding Beckham again. "I don't get why you would've hid that. I mean, look at the girl. She's *hot*."

Clearly Dick didn't have a speck of common sense, because Beckham was fuming now. Smoke practically billowed from his ears as he clenched his fists and stepped toward the man.

Dick took a step back, finally seeing how his words were pushing Beckham to his limit. I wasn't about to wait around and hear whatever other dumb shit the man had to say, especially because it seemed like everything that passed his lips only resulted in pushing Beckham's buttons. I quickly stepped between the two of them, inching my chin up to look directly at Beckham. But his eyes never wavered on the kill.

"Dick, why don't you go give your keys to the man in the garage and hitch a ride in the tow truck." There was no debate in my tone.

Dick must've noticed it, because he didn't say a word as he slipped out from behind me and disappeared through the door Beckham came in through.

Finally alone, Beckham's eyes slowly lowered to meet mine.

When his jaw ceased to relax and his hands remained fisted, I stepped away and leaned a hip against the desk, crossing my arms.

"Still protective as ever, I see," I teased, though the playful lilt fell a little flat and instead sounded a bit too sassy.

He turned his glare on the door to the shop, listening

to the mumbled conversation on the other side. "For you, always."

"What, because I'm Parker Summerhill, and you'll always step in and save me?"

That tore his attention from the garage. He moved to me, invading my space. His fists finally released, palms flattening on the desk on either side of me. "No."

"No? Then why?"

His thumbs brushed my ass before he slid his hands off the desk and grasped my hips. "Because you're *my* Parker Summerhill, and I'll never let anything happen to you."

I cocked my head to the side. "I broke my arm four years ago."

His body turned to stone, fingers digging into me and tugging me closer, like he hated the idea of anything happening to me when he wasn't around. "How?"

"Fell off a horse."

Beckham snorted, soft and heavy. He wasn't amused. No, I think this whole jealousy bit made him...horny. But I was trying to distract him. We were in public, and we had rules about that.

"I fall off horses all the time."

I tipped my chin up, trying not to stare at his mouth or the way his chain was peeking out from beneath his shirt. "How many bones have you broken since I left?"

"Want me to show you them all? I'd have to take my clothes off."

The idea had my cheeks warming. "No stripping necessary." I held up a hand. "Show me."

He wrapped burning fingers around my wrist, our skin scalding with how hot we both were, and lowered it to the waistband of his jeans. I sucked in a breath when he slipped my fingers beneath the hem of his shirt and slid my palm up his stomach, not stopping until I reached his ribs.

"Six ribs."

"At the same time?" I asked.

"Three different occasions," he clarified, then slid my palm around his side, to his lower back. "Broke my tailbone once."

If it weren't for the way this felt way more sexual than it should, I might've been surprised, but bronc riding was a dangerous sport. Broken bones and brutal injuries came with the territory. My only complaint was that this wasn't working out how I'd wanted it to—by distracting him.

His other hand worked its way down my hip to my thigh, looping around the back. I leaned into his touch, my ass pressing into the edge of the desk. He released my hand, and before I knew it, he slid me onto the desk.

His callused palms caught on the fabric of my jeans as he stroked me, fingers hungry as they squeezed my flesh. His nose brushed my cheek, his breath fanning across my lips. Fuck, I missed the taste of him. "I'm losing my mind, Parker."

So am I. "We can't," I whispered reluctantly.

"Can't we?" he breathed, a plea in his words.

My palms flattened on his hard chest, not to push him away, but because I needed him to hold me steady right now. Around Beckham, I was a sailboat on rocky waters, getting whiplash from the way my emotions threw me around. With Beckham, I led with my heart. Though recently, my mind was agreeing—I wanted to give in, and maybe it wouldn't be so bad if—

"The rules, Beckham," I reminded him, albeit begrudgingly.

My hands slid up his chest, fingers catching in his gold chain. I leaned back to look him in the eye, which was my first mistake. Sheer desperation shone in his eyes, and fuck if it didn't make me want to say *fuck the rules*, too.

With a finger looped in his chain, I pressed my other palm flat to the desk and leaned back slightly. I tugged on the jewelry slightly, urging him nearer but hoping he wouldn't oblige. His lips, puffy and so damn kissable, parted as he inched closer. His eyes were trained on my mouth, and I tilted my chin back, losing all sense of how to breathe.

He gripped my hip bones, holding on like he was trying to keep himself back and utterly failing.

Would I be mad if he closed the distance?

Or more upset if he backed away?

His nose lightly bumped mine, our lips less than an inch apart now. The line we were walking suddenly turned dangerous, something in the way he'd gotten so jealous triggering this response in both of us.

But I was kidding myself. We'd felt this way all along. This incident only brought it to light.

His upper lip brushed my lower with the faintest of touches, and my breath hitched—

My phone buzzing on the desk had me dropping his chain and bracing both hands on the oak.

I'd become breathless without even realizing it, my chest rising and falling with the temptation of him.

"I should get that," I barely managed to get out.

His eyes moved between mine before he slid me off the desk. He hadn't moved back, though, which had our bodies way too close and touching in too many places. My stomach made it hard for our chests to be flush, but fuck—if that wasn't there, there wouldn't be an inch of my body not connected to his right now.

His tongue ran across his lips like he was lapping up any part of me he could get. "You should."

He finally stepped back, allowing me space to move around the desk to grab my phone.

> Lettie: We're going to the Watering Hole tonight if you and Beckham want to come!

"Who is it?" Beckham asked, stuffing his hands in his jeans pockets as he came around the edge of the desk.

"Lettie. She said they're going to Outlaw's Watering Hole tonight." I looked up at him where he stopped beside me. "Wanna go?"

"Who's 'they'?"

I shrugged. "Probably your brothers." But then it hit me. "If you don't want to go because—"

"I'm alright." He sent me a reassuring look. "I might've quit drinking alcohol, but I can still look at it."

"I didn't know." My gaze moved back to the text thread, my shoulders slumping slightly. "I just thought —" I shook my head. "I guess everyone handles it differently."

Gentle fingers gripped my chin, pulling my focus back to him. "It's okay. I'll be okay."

I searched his face for reassurance that he was telling the truth. I didn't know how bad it got with Beckham and his relationship with alcohol, but I didn't want to push him too hard and have him falling back to that again.

"You'll tell me? If it's too much?" I asked.

He nodded, thumb brushing my jawline. "I'll tell you."

One thing I could never see breaking between the two of us was our trust. If he said he'd be okay, I'd believe him.

Me: We'll pop in after work

Lettie: See you two then!

24
PARKER

Walking into Outlaw's Watering Hole was like another homecoming. Nostalgia hit with the moody orange lights casting shadows along the chipped wooden walls and even-worse-for-wear bar. The room looked the same as when I had left, and I was thankful it hadn't turned into some faux western tourist attraction like so many others I'd visited in the west.

Country music drowned out the chatter of the other groups at the bar, but nothing held a candle to the volume at which Lettie shouted, calling us over to them.

Beckham and I crossed the shoe-scuffed floor, boards creaking as we went.

"So, how does it feel? Just like old times?" Lettie asked, looping her arm with mine and pulling me away from Beckham.

I sent him a grin over my shoulder, and he looked like a sad puppy seeing me tugged out of his grasp. I shot him a mopey face back and he chuckled, all woes wiped away as he joined the guys.

It seemed like it was only Oakley and Lettie with their partners tonight.

"Looking at it now, I don't think they should've allowed us in as teens," I said, the scent of spilled whiskey and old beer wafting around me.

Lettie smiled, winking. "Ah, but then we wouldn't remember it like we do."

"Like sneaking sips of your brothers' drinks and them frowning at us the whole time?" Memories of Beckham carrying me out of here had my eyes searching for him. He was at the pool table now, lost in conversation with Bailey and Lennon.

"Exactly," Lettie agreed.

Oakley rested her elbows on the table, leaning in with a grin. Her red hair was half up, half down, the style showing off her sharp jawline and pert nose. Lettie, on the other hand, had her caramel hair loose and wild— much like her personality.

"I would've been thrown in jail if I ever tried to set foot inside a bar in Denver," Oakley said.

"You grew up in Denver?" I asked.

Oakley nodded. "Born and raised. Have you been?"

"I visited a lot of ranches around Colorado. Denver's traffic was always a pain in the ass when I had to pass through, but the scenery made up for it."

Upon seeing the slight look of confusion from her, I clarified, "I traveled a lot for social media."

"Like an influencer?"

"Yeah. I went from ranch to ranch, wanting to learn more about cattle and that lifestyle. I posted about the whole thing and eventually made an income from it."

"Didn't you grow up in that lifestyle, though?" Oakley asked.

A look of something like sympathy passed over Lettie's features.

"No. I got a horse once I saved up enough money, but he stayed at the Bronsons'. He supposedly bucked all his riders off, but I thought if he didn't work out for me, Beckham could train on him. But one very expensive chiropractor visit later, and he was perfect. Never bucked for me once."

"Where's Tex now?" Lettie questioned, a crease in her forehead.

"I sold him after I found out I was pregnant." I looked down at my fingers, picking at a nail. "It wouldn't have been fair to have him sitting. Plus, I was living in my trailer with him. Only exercise he got was when we rode."

"I'm sorry," Lettie offered. I was glad she hadn't taken the route of telling me I should've done something different. Tex was my heart horse, misunderstood and unwanted before I got him. It often hit me that I felt like I failed him after I sold him because he never gave up on me. But I was so lost when I took that test. So clueless on what to do next.

I should've known not to make an impulsive decision when my mind was reeling. But what's done was done. I forced myself not to dwell.

"Speaking of Beckham," I started, giving a much-needed change to the subject, "he's okay to be here, right? With all the alcohol?"

Lettie glanced over her shoulder at the men, a pensive look crossing over her. "Yeah. He's good. It wasn't, like, a long-term thing, if that's what you're worried about."

I shook my head. "He's reassured me that he's fine, but..."

"You care about him. It's okay to be concerned," Oakley said.

"He came home out of the blue, said he didn't want to do rodeo anymore," Lettie explained. "He was... depressed, I guess you could call it. He wouldn't talk to any of us, so Reed would go over to his place every now and then. It wasn't until Beckham socked Reed in the face that he came to his senses."

I sucked on my bottom lip. "He did that because of me."

Oakley held back a smile. "He must love you if he's punching his brother over you."

I choked, eyes watering as I sputtered out a cough.

"Oakley!" Lettie chastised, though she was trying to hold back her laugh.

I didn't have the mental capacity to get into that right now, so instead—after clearing my throat three times—I said, "I was asking because there have been some...things happening on my Instagram that I wanted to tell him about, but the last thing I want to do is make him worry and spiral. We all know how overprotective he is."

Lettie let out an agreeing hum around the straw of her pink drink. "All my brothers are, and that's exactly why I didn't tell them *I've* had weird things happening on my profile, too."

My brows nearly became part of my hairline. "You're getting creepy comments too?"

She nodded, dramatically accentuating the movement.

Oakley leaned in further. "Well, now I'm intrigued." She cocked her head to the side. "And creeped out. What comments?"

"I wanted to talk to you about them tonight, actually," Lettie said, gesturing to me. "Some random accounts have been asking where my favorite hangout spot is or the best places to eat, like they're coming to visit Bell Buckle or something."

That had my hair standing on end. "They said they're visiting?"

Oakley's sharp intake of air had every nerve in my body lifting its head.

Lettie quickly shook her head. "No, no. They never said that. But they *act* like they are. Which is weird, because I don't put my location on my posts. I put my profile on private after the third comment. One came in on the first day, two on the second, and by that night, I was creeped out enough to shut it all down. Blocked the weirdo, too, just to be safe."

I yanked my phone out of my purse so fast, an old receipt toppled to the floor. Worst-case scenarios flew through my head at a pace too chaotic to worry about the paper as I tapped Instagram and scrolled back on my profile. It took at least ten minutes, but I finally made it back to when I was a teenager, still living in Bell Buckle.

Old photos of food, horses, scenery—everything a teenager would deem worthy of posting—rolled by until I found one of me and Lettie smiling at the camera. It was a selfie, and we were standing in front of Tumbleweed Feed, the only feed store in Bell Buckle. If the sign hadn't given away the town, my tagged location of Bell Buckle, Idaho, sure as hell would have.

"Fuck," I muttered.

Lettie grabbed my phone as Oakley squished into her side to get a look. I ran my hands over my face, groaning.

"All the way back to 2014?" Oakley chirped.

I tore my hands through my hair, the heat of the bar making its way down to the marrow of my bones. Yet still chills covered every inch of my skin.

This was bigger than I'd thought.

"It's not a coincidence then," Lettie surmised quietly.

I shook my head. "Doesn't look like it."

"Yeah, but who would be stalking you?" Oakley asked, alarm clear in her voice. Almost like she had a past in that territory.

"I have no idea."

"There's a photo of you and Beckham, too." Lettie turned the phone screen to me. She'd scrolled a bit farther and found ones I hadn't seen yet. As she swiped her thumb, another popped up of me and Beckham, with his arm around my shoulders and his lips on my temple.

"Could it be the guy who got you pregnant?" Oakley asked.

I shook my head. "No. He wouldn't do this." At least, I didn't think he would. He wanted nothing to do with this baby. So why would he care to stalk me now?

I took the phone back from Lettie, quickly archiving the selfies of me and Beckham.

"Okay. That's okay. We'll figure it out," Lettie said, but she didn't sound very sure of herself, despite the courage she was mustering.

I, on the other hand, was about to pass out.

"I need to use the restroom," I announced, shoving out of my chair. I'd deal with the rest of the old posts later.

"We'll go with," Oakley offered as Lettie started to stand.

"No, stay. You two have drinks here, and..." I stared at the ice in Lettie's cup, bubbles sticking to them. "I need a minute."

I offered the smallest flick of a smile before heading for the back hallway. My palms were sweaty, my breaths shallow. Pictures and posters lined the walls, but I barely saw them as I beelined for the women's restroom.

I quickly peed, my shrinking bladder desperately needing a release with the adrenaline pumping through me. I washed my hands three times, splashing water on my cheeks and running my wrists under the faucet in an attempt to cool down. Then I hung my head, breathing deeply.

I was fine. Everything was fine. My baby was fine. Lettie and Beckham were fine. No one was coming to Bell Buckle to kill me.

Right?

Who the fuck would even want to do that?

When I'd started putting my life online and making money off it, I'd feared attracting a stalker could be a possibility one day. Some people took things too person-ally, thinking every post was for them, or believing they were meant to be with you. I never thought I would seri-ously run into this situation, but here I was, and I had no defenses. No safety, all because I hadn't archived posts from my teenage years. I was much more open about my location then, and I should have fucking remembered.

I was an idiot.

But I'd fix this. There was no outcome where I would not get away from this.

With my spiraling thoughts shoved back into the box in my mind, I left the bathroom and headed for the bar to order a water.

As I watched the bartender scoop ice into a plastic cup, a swaying elbow bumped into mine.

I looked up to find none other than Dick staring down at me with a mischievous grin on his face.

"Now, how did I not see you here, little lady?" Dick slurred, looping an arm around my shoulders and tugging me into his side.

I tried to step away, but he held me close. "I'm with friends." It was both an answer and a warning.

His smile cracked the barest amount as he leaned closer, mouth brushing my hair. "One of those friends named Beckham?"

I tried, and failed, to hide my disgust as I grabbed his hand and peeled it off me. His arm was heavy, laden with the weight of a drunk not wanting to be told what to do. "Yes."

For some reason, that made his demeanor shift. Like all of a sudden, he was no longer flirting just to flirt but flirting to win a competition.

"I bet he likes it, doesn't he?" His eyes dipped to my belly before lingering on my breasts.

I crossed my arms in an attempt to cover myself. "Likes what?"

He leaned closer to the point where I had to arch my neck backward so I wouldn't get alcohol poisoning from his breath alone. "How he can come in you whenever he wants?"

I pressed my lips together until pain pinched them and subtly shook my head. "You're disgusting."

He pressed a palm to his chest, feigning hurt as a friend of his came up beside him.

"Who's this?" the redhead asked. He had freckles covering every inch of his face, but they didn't hide the flush of his cheeks one bit. The man was just as drunk as Dick, if not drunker, by the sound of his slur.

"Beckham's lady," Dick answered, a bit of venom lacing the response.

"She's cute," Redhead commented.

Dick's mouth quirked. I'd hate to be a fly on the wall in his head right now.

A glance to the bar showed my water waiting for me. I grabbed it, taking a long sip to rein in my annoyance. I didn't have the patience for them right now.

"It was nice seeing you, Dick." I laid on the sweetest tone I could muster.

I turned to leave, but Dick's rough grip on my elbow had me jerking to a stop.

"In rodeo, we all shared girls."

I wanted to vomit. "It's a good thing this isn't the rodeo then, isn't it?"

"Beckham may have quit, but we still have bro code."

I snorted. "From the looks of it earlier," I said, trying to tug my elbow out of his grasp but failing without my water sloshing everywhere, "you two aren't *bros.*"

Redhead stepped up behind me. His presence was laughable, really. This whole damn thing was. Because the second Beckham saw us—

"Get your hands off her." The command came from my right, and my head swiveled to find Beckham towering over Dick, his eyes incinerating him on the spot.

"Jesus, Beckham. You're always so fucking *serious.* We're just having fun. Aren't we, sweetheart?" Whatever Dick's plan was here, it wouldn't end well. Not for him or his idiot friend.

"You making provocative comments to me isn't fun.

But this is." A furrow marred Dick's brow a split second before I tossed my ice water at him.

A growl ripped from his throat, his fingers digging into my arm harder, but before he could so much as move, Beckham's fist swung.

Dick was tossed back against the bar by the sheer force of Beckham's punch, causing him to release me. My foot fumbled with the force of it and I tripped back a step. My back hit Redhead's chest, but before he could even look at me, Bailey was there, joining the fight.

I took three steps away, careful not to slip on any water that had made it to the ground. From this angle, I could see how bad it was getting. Bailey pinned Redhead up against the wall beside the bar, and Beckham had his hands in Dick's shirt, leaning him over the bar top.

"If you ever so much as look at my girl again, I'll rip your goddamn eyes out and shove them down your fucking throat." He shook him, digging his back harder into the bar. "Do you hear me?"

Dick sniffled once, blood trailing down his lips and chin.

When he didn't answer, Beckham leaned in closer, voice rising. "Do you fucking hear me?"

Dick's tongue lapped out over the blood, eyes shiny from the alcohol. "Loud and clear."

Beckham looked like he was about to punch him again, but one glance at me had him shoving Dick's chest and standing straight. Beck's eyes fell to my elbow where I was unknowingly cradling it. He hadn't hurt me, but between his phantom touch and the comments from earlier, I felt repulsed.

Beckham tried to rein in his anger, but standing in this bar—with all eyes on us and the two beaten men with a death wish—wouldn't calm either of us down.

I turned around and squeezed past Bailey to get to the hallway, and didn't stop until my feet hit the dirt alley out back.

25

BECKHAM

Parker was gone in an instant, cracking my crippling restraint. Seeing Dick's hand on her arm, her skin white and her fingers trembling, had a different sort of predatory desire overtaking all my senses. It wasn't only her I was protecting. It was her baby.

I'd never felt so fucking feral in my life. So ready to annihilate everything that could put them in danger. I could have taken Dick and his worthless friend on my own, but Bailey hadn't hesitated when I split from the group. Wordlessly, we'd chosen our targets.

I was two steps away from slicing Dick's goddamn fingers off for even daring to brush Parker's perfect skin when I forcefully shoved all the rage aside.

With all that done, there was only one thought on my mind.

Parker. Parker. Parker.

Bailey nudged his head in the direction of the hall

when I gave him a reaffirming look. He had this under control. Dick and his little puppet wouldn't do shit.

Once I was out the back door, my eyes landed on Parker.

And fuck, she was breathtaking.

Rage, possessiveness, the urge to get another punch in. It all disappeared into the heavy, lovesick air as I took her in.

She paced, booted feet making imprints in the slightly muddied dirt. Inches of snow piled in odd crevices here or there, but the rest was slowly turning to mush. I wouldn't let her slip, though. Wouldn't stop her from doing what she needed to do, either.

I slid my hands in my pockets, hiding my aching knuckles. She was worked up and didn't need the reminder.

Suddenly, she halted her steps, spinning to face me. "What was that?"

I cocked my head to the side, my eyes twin slits of curiosity. "I punched a guy for touching you."

"Why?" Her bottom lip wobbled slightly, her grip on her emotions dwindling. She could cry, kick, scream. It was all warranted.

"Because *he touched you*." I enunciated each word, as if the issue wasn't clear enough.

"I can take care of myself."

My hands fell to my sides. "Why are you mad?"

Her mouth opened and closed as if there were a million reasons fighting for first place. "Because I can't get used to this." There was disappointment there, but something told me she wasn't being completely honest.

"Why?"

She shook her head, like the question was ridiculous. "He was drunk and trying to flirt with me. He wouldn't have…"

"Wouldn't have what? Hurt you?"

Her glistening eyes lifted to meet mine, but she provided no answer. Even she wasn't sure if he would have. Fuck, he already had.

"Why do you think I don't like him, Parker?"

Her lashes fluttered, throat working. "I don't know. Some drama from when you did rodeo?"

"Because he's forceful with women."

Her eyes widened the slightest bit, her body going eerily still.

"When I saw him do it, I always stepped in and stopped it. But I know I didn't see all of it. So when I saw his hand on you—" Bile clogged my throat. "He's a fuckboy who rides twice as many girls as he does bulls. He has no good intentions with you, or likely any other woman." I swallowed, forcing myself to steady. "Wyatt's working on his truck all damn night to get him the hell out of Bell Buckle."

"I didn't know," Parker admitted quietly.

"You didn't have to." *Because I'll always protect you.*

The battle between laying out every heart-wrenching emotion I felt for her and not putting too much on her shoulders at once was a torturous one. But it was a war

I'd fight every day if it meant she was standing before me.

She shook her head, gaze falling to her muddied boots. "You get jealous," she stated. "You protect me like you used to. You go out of your way to bring me my favorite drink, just the way I like it." Her mouth twisted, a curl sliding out from behind her ear. "Even after all this time apart"—her head lifted, eyes desperate—"you still want me."

I waited for her to go on, but when only silence came and charged energy flitted in the five feet separating us, I knew what she was feeling. She didn't even have to tell me, because *that's* how in tune we were with each other. "You're scared."

Her lashes fluttered once more, blinking away fresh tears pooling there.

I couldn't see her cry. Couldn't feel my heart break with the idea that she might reject me. She had a million reasons to say yes to giving us another chance, but a million more reasons to say no. My mind was too scrambled to come up with pleading words, my adrenaline from the fight waning.

"I'll wait inside so you can have time to think," I forced out quietly while turning like the axis of my world was about to fall off-kilter.

But a barely-there whisper had me pausing, my heart rate spiking like in the last crucial seconds in a race.

"Kiss me."

My head turned, chin nearly touching my shoulder as I wondered if I'd heard her right.

"Kiss me, Beckham. *Please.*"

There was no stopping me as my body swiveled and I raced for her like I couldn't breathe until my next breath was with her lips on mine. Those five steps were the longest, most tantalizing distance a man had ever walked. My feet planted on either side of hers, my hands cupping her cheeks and tilting her head at the perfect angle.

My lips crashed to hers, the universe exploding into a million stars at the sheer force of it.

She tasted like rainy summer nights, winters on the ranch, and home.

My home.

My Parker.

Our mouths worked overtime, trying to make up for the years spent apart. For the weeks spent craving. For the stolen glances and dreaming of each other's taste.

Her hands fisted in my shirt over my chest, tugging me impossibly closer. Our bodies were flush to one another as my hands slid into her hair, trying to memorize every part of her while I had her. The past merged with the present, every stolen kiss from our childhood zipping through me like a live wire as I met her stroke for stroke.

Our tongues danced, teeth clashing and breaths clouding.

I could taste her for a million years and still never be satisfied. With her, I always craved more. With her, I could drown and never wish to come back up for air. With her, I was whole.

Her hands slid up my neck, tiny icicles gliding over the inferno I'd turned into. I sucked in a breath, forcing our lips apart.

My forehead fell to hers as I covered her hands with mine. "Your hands are frozen."

"I don't care," she admitted breathlessly, trying to inch forward and kiss me again.

"I do." I held our hands between our chests as we tried to catch our breath—and maybe our sanity. "We can go inside."

She shook her head like she was afraid that if we did, this dream would cease to exist. But then her hands quickly unwound from my own, and she set them on my ribs.

"Tell me what you're thinking," I pleaded, desperation and a hint of fear coating my words.

"We broke the rules."

I nearly groaned. She and these rules would be the death of me. "We're still doing that?"

She narrowed her eyes on me, and I almost laughed. Parker, clearly worked up and fighting her desires, was adorable when provoked. "Yes, we're still doing that."

"How many more do we have to break?" My tongue lapped out at her puffy lower lip.

Her chin tilted up, a heavy, wanton breath escaping her. "One."

"Which one is that?" I murmured, lips and mustache ghosting over her cheek until my mouth hovered over her earlobe.

"No sex." She barely managed to get the two words out as her eyelids shut.

I nipped her ear, a small moan building in her throat. "I can take care of that."

She shook her head, the movement barely there. "Beck."

"Park."

Goosebumps rose up her neck as I kissed that precious spot beneath her ear.

"You're distracting me," she whined, but it didn't sound like the fact bothered her.

"From?" The one word was a hum as my tongue tasted her sweet skin.

"The fact that you punched a guy and threatened his life over me."

"You're the one who asked me to kiss you," I reminded her, making my way down to the crook of her neck and shoulder. I cupped the back of her head, tugging her hair slightly to give me more access.

She groaned, knowing I was right.

Forcing myself to stop tasting her, I straightened, looking down at her.

"Does this mean we can kiss whenever we want now?"

She frowned, though amusement danced in her eyes. "No public displays of affection, remember?"

I glanced both ways. "Too late. We're kind of in public. And if I remember correctly, we were in public on my parents' porch, too."

Her nose scrunched as she fought the smile trying to bloom. "You're such a rule breaker, Beckham Bronson."

"I'd break every damn one of them if it means I can have you."

She stepped back with a mischievous glint in her eyes. "What a bad boy."

I smirked. My dick twitched. "I can show you bad, Park. Just ask."

She rolled her eyes, and I couldn't help it as my gaze coasted down her body.

"You're a tease, Parker Summerhill."

She clasped her hands behind her back, a picture of pure innocence. But she knew what she was doing. "You always loved a chase."

She gave me her sweetest little smile before she sauntered toward the end of the alley. Once there, she spun on her heel to face me. "Coming?"

She didn't have to ask me twice. I'd follow that woman wherever she pleased.

I joined her, the two of us walking side by side around the building to my truck in the parking lot. It was impossible not to let my fingers brush her as I buckled her in, to keep my hand off her thigh on the way home, and for me not to kiss her goodnight before she disappeared into her bedroom.

And even more impossible not to stroke my cock to the memory of her lips on mine once I was in the privacy of my bedroom.

I was so fucking gone for her.

26

BECKHAM

Fresh snow clung to the soles of our boots, making our step into the boutique store a slippery one. My hand latched onto Parker's arm to steady her while the two of us stomped the packed snow off onto the rug.

Christmas was a few weeks away, and both of us had neglected to do any shopping. I wished I could say it was due to Parker's pregnancy, but really, the negligence was all on us. Partly because we couldn't stop teasing each other until we had no choice but to bring the other to the brink of orgasm. And partly because of Parker's worrying about, well, everything. I got the feeling that Parker thought spending money on furniture for the baby meant she was permanently in my house, and while we hadn't discussed that in depth yet, things between us definitely seemed to be heading that direction. I couldn't complain, though. Having Parker in my house, making my space her own, was a desire I didn't know I had until I saw it with my own two eyes.

We'd driven over an hour away to a town with more choices for shopping. It was decided that we'd shop for the baby first, then get gifts for everyone else after.

"Alright, first order of business," I started, scanning the store. "Furniture."

"Shouldn't we go to a thrift store?" Parker asked for the third time today, likely seeing the immaculate displays and assuming the prices would be too high.

I set a hand on her lower back, steering her in the direction of the bassinets. "C'mon. Let's take a look, and if you don't like anything, we can go somewhere else. Okay?"

She nodded hesitantly, her throat bobbing. "Okay."

While Parker looked at each bassinet and their individual perks, I meandered over to the few dressers they had on display.

"What are you doing?" Parker questioned from her spot.

"Browsing," I said simply.

"We're supposed to be looking at bassinets. Nothing else."

I held up a finger. "Actually, the agreement was bassinets *and* newborn clothes. And where are you going to put his clothes if you don't have a dresser?"

She frowned before moving her attention back to the bassinet in front of her. The look that took over her had me crossing back to her. Her finger trailed along the edge of the bassinet, and I wrapped my arms around her torso, resting my hands on her belly.

"You like this one?"

A breath left her lips, one that had her shoulders loosening and her back pressing against my chest. "I do. It's just so pricey for a bed he'll only sleep in for a few months."

I rested my chin on her shoulder. "But it's the one you want?"

Her hand rested over mine. "It is."

"Then we'll get it."

She eyed me, our faces so close. "I have to penny pinch, Beckham. I can't be making impulsive decisions."

I spread my fingers so hers could fall in between them. "I have some savings."

Her body stiffened before she turned in my arms. Her growing stomach pressed into mine as she looked up at me. "Beck."

The corner of my mouth tilted upward. "Park."

She narrowed her eyes on me. "You're not paying for my baby's stuff."

I arched a brow at the phrasing, only because part of me wanted this baby to be mine. And maybe he wasn't in blood, but—

She crossed her arms, and my brow rose farther. Neither of us would back down from whatever riff was happening between us.

After what felt like minutes, she heaved a sigh, giving in to my stubborn charm.

Her finger jabbing into my chest had my eyes widening. "But I'm helping."

I wrapped a hand around her wrist, pulling her in farther. "Whatever you wish."

The urge to kiss her was almost too strong to resist, and it seemed it was for her, too, as her eyes darted to my lips.

I leaned closer, lips near her ear now. "You're staring."

"You're insufferable."

"Lies," I whispered, pressing a barely-there kiss to the shell of her ear. "You want to kiss me."

"*You* want to kiss *me*," she corrected with a hiss, but it was all false bravado. I could see it in the way her cheeks were the exact shade of a strawberry, and how her lashes fluttered, eyelids heavy, and how her body gravitated toward mine like it knew it couldn't stay away.

I moved until our noses were brushing. "Are you hungry? You're kind of grumpy."

Her mouth fell open, disbelief coating her features.

"I can feed you if you'd like," I went on.

Her lips smacked shut, entire face red now. "We're in a *baby* store, Beckham."

I groaned, brushing a lock of hair behind her ear as an excuse to touch her more. "If only we could make another one here, too."

She choked on a gasp, coughing.

I smiled and glanced across the shop to the brunette

woman at the register, who now had her attention on us as Parker attempted to compose herself.

"We'll take it," I announced.

We were in and out in less than an hour, taking with us a full room's worth of furniture.

———

Deciding to take advantage of the different food choices in this town, we found a little diner that made milkshakes with all kinds of crazy things on top, from cotton candy to ice cream sandwiches to lollipops. Parker saw the photos online and demanded we get them immediately, blaming the need on her pregnancy cravings.

"You decide yet?" I teased as Parker scanned the menu across from me. We were in a hot pink booth surrounded by hanging lights shaped like hearts. Each booth had its own theme, and ours just so happened to be love.

"I don't know if I want the Banana Mudslide or the Strawberry Catastrophe," she mumbled into the laminated menu.

I eyed the photo for each one she named. "Why not both?"

She pinned wide eyes on me. "Calories, Beckham."

I cocked a brow. "Is that really something we cared about when we chose this place?"

She glared at me, knowing damn well I was right.

"You two decide?" Danielle, our waitress, asked as she sidled up to our table.

"I'm in between—" Parker started, but I interrupted with, "We'll have the Banana Mudslide and the Strawberry Catastrophe. And a side of fries."

"And two waters. And an iced Dr. Pepper," Parker tacked on.

Danielle's smile couldn't have been brighter if she tried. "Coming right up."

I could barely stifle my grin. "An *iced* Dr. Pepper, huh? As opposed to what?"

Parker's face flamed, realization dawning on her. She covered her face with her hands. "Oh my God. It's the pregnancy brain, I swear."

I laughed, getting lost in this moment with her. "It's alright. I'm sure she gets it all the time."

She frowned at me, wearing a look that screamed, *You really think that?*

"Well, either way, I had to get a Dr. Pepper. It's the appetizer of drinks, you know."

I laughed, my tongue sliding over my teeth. "Is it now?"

She burst into a fit of laughter right along with me.

The pink from the booth reflected off the apples of her cheeks, her eyes bright and playful. She was beautiful like this—with that weight off her shoulders and that teasing look on her face. Right here, in this diner, it was only me and Parker. The rest of the world was quiet for once.

"You didn't have to order both milkshakes, you know."

I shrugged before leaning back in the booth and

casually slinging my hands behind my head. "We needed them. It's hard work being so good at reading what you want."

She shook her head, smiling. "And what is it you think I want?"

"Well, five seconds ago, it was those milkshakes." I tilted my head. "And a Dr. Pepper. Now I'm guessing it's me."

Her answering giggle had my pulse skyrocketing and my mind racing for what I could say next just to hear it again.

"You know, you can't go around buying everything simply to make me happy," she stated.

My hands dropped to the table, playing with the straw the waitress had laid out. "There's nothing else I'd rather put my money toward."

"What about retirement? Investing?"

I dipped my chin, letting out a huff of a laugh. "I'm smart with my money, Park, but don't think I'm afraid to spend it. Hell, one time, I called up my dad to flag down Bailey and Lettie at a horse auction, all so they could bid on an old horse me and my friend learned to bronc ride on."

Parker leaned forward in her seat, her interest piqued. "What friend?"

Realization at what I'd brought up hit me like a punch to the gut. Just like that, my appetite vanished and my mind shut down. I sat back in the booth, eyes on the table. "One you never got to meet."

She went quiet, dropping the subject. I fucking hated

how the thought of Garrett still did this to me. All I wanted to do was talk about him without it stabbing me in the damn chest.

Parker's movement had me lifting my gaze to find her pulling her phone out of her purse. She didn't seem to be doing it to be rude, but rather to give me a moment. She didn't know the situation, but it was like she could sense it.

A crease marred her forehead as she looked at her phone, and the sight had foghorns blaring through the haze that had clouded my mind.

I sat straighter. "Everything okay?"

She took a deep breath, shaking her head and blinking like she was trying to make sense of what she was looking at. "There are some random accounts that keep going on my social media pages and leaving weird comments."

Instantly, I stiffened. "What kind of comments?"

"Asking about my mental health, commenting on old photos of how I look on a horse. One tried to get my address—"

"Your address?" I repeated, a little too loud.

"I didn't give it to him," she clarified, eyes darting to the table nearest ours like she didn't want anyone overhearing.

"It was a man?"

"I think so. It was a new account, but people use fake profile pictures all the time."

"And you're just now telling me about this?"

"I've been meaning to tell you."

The fact that something had held her back from doing so was a hurt I hadn't expected. "Did you block them?"

"Of course, I did. But there have been multiple accounts now. I don't know if it's the same person on all of them, but I block one and another pops up days later."

"What'd they say today?"

She turned the phone so I could read the screen. A comment under an old photo of Parker smiling with a few girls I'd never seen before read: *Looks like a far way to travel for some fun. Live close?*

A glance at the caption showed she had mentioned a visit to North Dakota.

I grabbed the phone from her, clicking the stranger's profile. No posts, no followers, and no profile photo.

Parker had a fucking stalker, and I had no idea until now.

"I didn't think it would get this bad," Parker admitted, her voice laced with shame.

I set the phone down, sliding it toward her. "Block that account, and make your profile private."

She was an influencer, but with that no longer being her full-time job, making her profile private wouldn't affect anything. If some brand had a problem with it, they could take it up with me. Parker's safety would always come first.

She picked up the device right as our milkshakes, waters, and Dr. Pepper arrived. Two spoons stuck out the top of each monstrosity, but I didn't spare the rest a glance as I thanked Danielle and kept my eyes on Parker, watching her thumb move over the screen.

"Done." She dropped the phone in her purse, meeting my gaze.

I studied her, hating the fact that her life had been broadcasted online for years and creepy men like that probably viewed her content daily. It made my fists burn with the urge to beat each one to a bloody fucking pulp.

"Are you okay?"

She nodded, but that glint in her eye told me she wasn't being completely honest. Whoever was doing this had unsettled her, and I hated that I hadn't known sooner. I didn't want her going through that alone.

"Why didn't you tell me before?" I asked, forcing a calm I didn't feel into my tone.

She swallowed, the sight of regret burning into me.

Then it hit me.

"Because of my drinking?"

She nodded, a barely-there movement.

I reached across the table, grabbing her hand and stroking my thumb over her skin. "Parker, it wasn't as bad as you're thinking."

"I know that now," she said. "I talked to Lettie."

While I wished she'd talked to me about it, I was glad my sister was a person of comfort for her. Someone she could go to that wasn't me. Parker needed that sense of family, people she could trust.

Guilt at the fact that I had yet to tell her about Garrett nudged its way into my mind. How was it fair to want her to be open about everything with me when I wasn't doing the same?

Parker grabbed one of the milkshakes—the one with a spear of strawberries sticking out the top of a massive brownie that was laid atop the glass. Her lips wrapped around the pink and white straw, shoulders instantly sagging as she sipped.

Maybe our troubles wouldn't be completely laid out between the two of us tonight, but at least we had this.

27
PARKER

Beckham had proven he'd never lost his ability to make me smile, even if my mind was threatening to spiral. Throughout our dinner of massive milkshakes, salty fries, and greasy burgers, we reminisced on the best memories. Beckham had a lot more friends than I ever did in high school, but he always promised I was his favorite one. If *friend* was even the right term to describe us back then.

Out of all the acquaintances he made while doing FFA (Future Farmers of America) as a child, to making lifelong connections in the IHSRA (Idaho High School Rodeo Association), I was always his top priority. And he was mine. But when I found the path I wanted to adventure on, and his didn't match, we had no choice but to part. It hurt, but I tried to believe the universe was sending us on our own journeys in order to find what we really wanted.

Ending up back here, living in his double-wide, was proof enough that fate was real.

Beckham's hand rested on the center console between us, open and waiting. But one look at the bulging vein in his forearm, then at the tattoo on the other, and I realized holding hands wasn't on my mind tonight.

Without allowing myself to think twice, I grabbed his wrist and dragged it down to my legging-clad leg. He did a double take, zoning in on where his hand was now draped over my thigh. Our gazes quickly met before he focused back on the road in front of us. We were forty minutes into our drive back home, the truck bed and the back seat full of baby items and Christmas gifts.

His fingers dug into my flesh, either with restraint or need, I wasn't sure—but fuck, I wanted him to move his hand higher. It'd been torture watching him sit across from me for the entirety of dinner. After our discussion of his brief past with overindulging in alcohol, the conversation had turned lighter once again. For that hour, there was no stalker, no baby on the way, and no worrying about a relapse that would never happen.

I couldn't help the fact that everything—the smiles he flashed my way, the full-body laughs he erupted into at my cheesy jokes, the flashes of his gold chain in the pink lights—had my mind in the gutter. After our kiss the other night, I was scooting closer and closer to the idea of throwing our rules off a cliff.

I shifted forward slightly, keeping my focus out the

window at the dark fields. The dusting of snow over the land was faintly glowing under the moon, much like the emergency light in my brain was blaring at the fact that I was way too fucking horny to be sitting in this truck with Beckham right now.

But he wanted to take care of me, right? He wanted us to be more than whatever this I-want-you-but-with-rules thing was. Fuck, since the moment I stepped foot back in Bell Buckle, he'd shown me that was exactly what he wanted. I'd been too scared to see it then, but now I did, and I was so fucking tired of holding back.

I cupped my hand over his, moving it higher until his fingers brushed the inside of my thigh, only inches from where I wanted him most.

My breathing became heavier as I slid another inch forward.

Please, Beckham. Please give me what we both want.

His lips rolled together, his touch moving between my legs. I sighed blissfully, head rolling back against the chair.

"Is this considered public if it's in my truck?" he asked, somewhat teasingly, though I heard the heavy need that was overtaking him too.

"Fuck the rules," I breathed, my voice sounding so damn desperate. But I didn't care. I was about to fucking implode from all this damn tension. Dodging around what we both wanted wasn't doing him or me any favors.

His entire body seemed to freeze, but not a second

passed before he moved again. His fingers slid inside the waistband of my leggings, not stopping until he cupped my pussy with no restraint.

I moaned, *needing* this. Needing him to touch me like we were more than just friends after spending a day pretending.

But was it pretending if we were baby shopping for my son? Was it pretending if we got dinner after and acted as if it wasn't a date?

Lines were blurred, and I didn't have the energy to give a damn.

Beckham was all I wanted, and I was tired of pretending that wasn't the case.

Two fingers slid inside me, and the breath I sucked in should've been embarrassing, but I was so wound up, I didn't have a care in the world for anything but him touching me like this.

"Jesus, Parker," Beckham hissed.

I peeked to be sure his eyes were still on the road.

They were.

He'd never put me in danger.

"How long have you been hiding this?" he asked, sliding in and out at a painfully slow pace.

For years, I thought.

"All day," I lied.

I'd been soaked since even before I saw him slide into his Carhartt jacket this morning. Watching the way his biceps flexed as he put it on in one swift movement should be forbidden for everyone but me. Last night, I'd thought about the way he'd completely ravished me on the porch at his parents' ranch, my hand disappearing between the covers multiple times. I'd been restless knowing that today I'd get Beckham all to myself. No Wyatt to interrupt us. No checking fences or sliding beneath a truck for an oil change or getting distracted by dinner or cleaning the house. Today was all me and Beckham, and that knowledge had the floodgates opening.

His fingers slid dangerously deep inside me, his right hand curving at an awkward angle as he kept a steady left hand on the wheel.

"Pull over," I whimpered. "Please."

He wasted no time jerking the truck off the road and a safe distance into the bordering field. The vehicle lurched as he shifted into park and yanked off his seat belt. Needy hands did the same to mine, then hefted me up and onto his lap. His fingers were back where they belonged in seconds, thrusting in and out of me as I straddled his lap.

Breath fanned out of me like I'd run miles to get to this point with him, my hair cascading around us in an umbrella of heat and lust and pure, utter need. Even the size of my stomach couldn't keep us from each other, so why had I tried in the first place?

My necklace dangled between us as I rocked into his hand. The charm bounced off his chin, grazing his cheeks and bumping his nose. His lips parted, snagging the jewelry in his teeth.

I nearly came apart at the sight.

"Beck," I moaned, though it was barely audible over

our panting breaths and the sounds coming from where he was pumping in and out of me.

Beckham's other hand tore into my hair, pulling my face down to his. My necklace popped off the edge of his tongue before our mouths crashed together.

With his lips on mine and my heart in his grasp, I realized now that the rules I'd conjured up were not to save either of us. They weren't to protect him from the burden of raising my child, or because messing around was foolish. I'd forced them onto us like a lock and key because I knew his kisses would pull me back into an orbit I'd long ago lost. His eyes as he gazed down at me, thrusting his cock inside me, would ruin all chances of us staying on our separate paths.

But I didn't want those chances anymore. I didn't want to forfeit another second of his mouth glued to mine.

The only chance I wanted was giving in to my love for him again.

His thumb brushed my clit, my hips rocking into him as my skin grew so hot, I had no idea how we didn't burst into flames.

"I missed this. Missed *you*," he declared. Because even he knew there was something different in this moment.

"I missed you too," I said against swollen lips.

As if the spoken words had been the final countdown on a bomb, I detonated. My core clenched around his hand, and despite the tightness, he powered through, pumping me faster and harder.

My thighs shook as my gasps came out strangled. Our foreheads pressed together as my eyes squeezed shut and sweat dripped down the back of my neck.

"I've got you," he murmured, movements slowing while his other hand cupped the back of my head. "I've always got you."

My lips pressed to his as I came down from my high. The kiss was soft, a polar opposite to the ravenous hunger that overtook us moments ago. But while our mouths took their time with each other, our hearts beat furiously.

We sat like that, two parts of a whole, for what felt like an hour, kissing slowly, tenderly, so *intimately* it nearly hurt.

"Ready?" Beckham breathed out, though his hold on me told me he wasn't sure of his own answer to that question.

I nodded, our noses brushing. I could stay this close to him forever, live in this truck and be happy.

Once I was back in my seat and buckled, he pulled onto the road. Time was nonexistent as I leaned back against the seat and watched him drive. His hand covered mine on my lap, thumb brushing over my knuckles.

We made it home, and without a single regard for the items in the truck, Beckham opened my passenger door and lifted me into his arms. I wrapped my legs around his waist, and his mouth crashed to mine.

For a while, I'd feared this. This feral need for each

other that overtook us whenever we gave it fuel. But now I knew it wasn't something I should fight.

Life was short, and all I wanted was Beckham Bronson and my baby to be healthy and safe.

Our lips didn't part as Beckham fumbled for the right key, or as we laughed when he dropped them. The man's glutes were stronger than I'd thought as he squatted to grab them, all the while keeping his hold on me.

He kicked the door shut behind us, the windows rattling with the force as he walked us toward the living room. Rather than sit on the couch like I'd expected, he wrapped his hands around my thighs and lowered my feet to the ground. He bent, tugging my pants and under-wear off. As he slid them down, he pressed kisses to my legs. On my knee, my calf, my ankle. Until I was standing in nothing but my T-shirt.

He lowered himself to the ground, sitting with his back to the base of the couch.

"What are you doing?" I asked as he lured me toward him with his hands snaking up the backs of my legs toward my ass.

Those big brown eyes of his looked pleading. "Ride my face, baby."

"Beckham, I'm too heavy—"

He shook his head, reeling me closer until his chin was nearly brushing my pussy. The warmth of his breath sent shivers skating over my spine. "Don't say that about yourself. Parker, I was *made* for you."

I hated that he always knew just what to say. And how I always melted for it, too.

Spreading my legs farther, I moved until my hands were braced against the back of the couch. His fingers gripped my flesh, moving my knees onto the cushions for better support. Then he pressed his mouth to my center, and I *died*.

My teeth dug into my lower lip in a poor attempt to rein myself in. I'd lose it instantly if I didn't breathe, and I wanted to savor this.

The roughness of his mustache against my sensitive skin had electricity shooting up my nerve endings. I rocked into him, relishing in the way it felt. His tongue, his teeth, his breath and lips. All of him had me teetering on the edge.

His hands urged me faster, his head tilting back to devour more of me. He sucked on my clit, tongue flicking across it, and the sound I let out was vulgar.

He moaned into me, the vibrations causing me to settle onto him further as my body lost all ability to stay upright. My fingers dug into the back of the couch so hard, I was surprised it didn't tear.

His blissful tongue moved to my entrance, spearing me. A gasp slipped from me, and I rode his face quicker. Harder. Intent on feeling that sensation over and over and over again.

My core clenched as he moaned again, the sounds and warmth of his breathing too much to take. And when his attention focused on my aching clit, I lost all control. My stomach tightened as pure ecstasy shot through my veins. My eyes squeezed shut, my fingers digging for something to keep me afloat.

Beckham held me steady as I erupted, and when I came back down, he lowered me to his lap. He brushed damp strands of hair off my forehead, his lips pressing to each of my cheeks and my nose before settling on my mouth. My tongue lapped out, tasting myself on him.

The act must've awoken another beast inside of him, because he stood, lifting me with him, and bent me over the couch.

"Tell me we should stop," he gritted out.

The clang of his belt was closely followed by the sound of a zipper.

"We shouldn't," I panted, arching my back so my ass was higher.

A pained breath escaped him, and a heap of clothes fell to the floor. A glance over my shoulder told me he was naked, and—

I choked on my breath.

No matter how many times I'd seen this grown-up version of Beckham since returning to Bell Buckle, it never got old. When we were younger, we'd memorized every inch of each other. I knew every dip of his muscles, every scar, freckle, and tan line. But now... Beckham was all man. Hard and toned and so perfectly him.

I think I was drooling.

"Stopping would be torture," he agreed. "And I'm clean. I was tested—"

"*Please* shut up and fuck me. I trust you."

His hands gripped my hips as he lined himself up. And when he slid inside of me, the world stopped turning. There was nothing outside of the two of us. No day or night, no summer or winter. It was me and Beckham. Living and breathing for each other.

The way it'd always been.

My knees bumped the cushions as he drilled into me again and again, but with his grip on my hips, I wasn't going anywhere. He held me up, helping me even now.

Already, I felt the tension building between my legs. He'd brought me over the edge twice now, and I was feeling the effects of it majorly.

"Come with me," I pleaded.

His pace picked up. "Ask me that every day."

"I will."

"Parker..." He trailed off, but I knew what he was wanting to ask.

"I want you to come inside me."

My demand had his thrusts turning harder, more feral than before. I tried to keep my orgasm at bay, but the effort was futile. My thighs shook as I released, his hold the only thing keeping me upright. Seconds later, when it nearly became too much, he buried himself as deep as he could. He spilled into me, and I whimpered at the sensation.

Our breaths were the only sounds that filled the room as we stayed connected. At some point, one of his hands drifted from my hip to my lower back, his fingers digging into muscles I hadn't realized were sore.

Slowly, he pulled out, and there was no mistaking what dripped out of me as he did.

He'd barely moved before he had a piece of fabric

there, wiping away the mess. With most of it clean, he tossed the rag to the ground.

I straightened, turning to face him, but my eyes caught on what he'd used to clean me.

"Did you use your shirt?"

He shot me a heart-stopping grin. "I've got twenty of them, remember?"

His arms wrapped around my waist, pulling me into him. I rested my cheek on his bare chest, finding his heartbeat instantly.

"I missed this, Park," he admitted, hands running up and down my back.

"I did, too."

We stood like that for a while, the two of us realizing this had been inevitable. We were each other's person. There'd never be any denying that.

His touch moved to my cheeks, tilting my face until we made eye contact. "Give me a second chance."

I arched an inquisitive brow. "Are you asking or demanding?"

"Both." There was no shame in his voice. "*Please.* Don't make me get on my knees, because you know damn well I will."

I trailed a finger over his jawline, moving to his cheekbone. He was entrancing like this, freshly fucked and sated.

"As much as I'd love to see that, we can save it for another time." I paused, my gaze darting between his eyes. What he was asking was genuine. Beckham didn't have a dishonest bone in his body. "I'd give you a million chances, Beck."

Relief sagged his shoulders, a corner of his mouth lifting. "It's a good thing I'll only ever need two."

I tilted my head. "Oh, is that right?"

"Yep." He scooped me up, my legs wrapping around him like they were made to be there, despite my belly getting in the way. "I don't plan on ever letting you go again."

28

BECKHAM

There was no concept of time while I held Parker in my arms. In the bath, in bed, on the couch. Wherever she and I were, if we were connected, the world could end and I'd still be lost in her.

But feeling lost wasn't the way I'd ever describe how she made me feel. Parker was the sense of home I'd missed on the road, and I'd found it wasn't rodeo that made me homesick. It was not being with her that elicited that feeling. After we slept together, I made a vow to never let that happen again.

One week ago today, Parker and I succumbed to the torture of suppressing our feelings and let each other in. A thirty-ton boulder had been lifted from my shoulders, and now all I carried was the weight of loving her. And soon, that'd include the privilege of loving that baby boy, too.

I'd covered every inch of her body in suds that night,

both of us turning to wrinkled prunes while I cherished every second of her.

We continued on with our routines of working, making dinner together most nights, and touching one another every chance we could, but in reality, both of our worlds had changed.

She had an appointment to check on the baby the other day, and everything was as perfect as it could be. But I still worried. I kept an eye on her at the shop. Made sure she wasn't balancing on step stools or lifting heavy boxes. While Parker was sometimes stubborn and demanded to do things on her own—like bear the weight of this child by herself—she was letting me fill the gaps with little to no complaints.

That also might have been in part due to the things I made her promise while my tongue was lapping between her legs.

I emerged from the hallway after taking a long, cold shower, talking myself into leaving her for an afternoon. I did this every other Sunday, so nothing was really different other than the fact that I wanted to cuddle up next to her and binge-watch *Twilight* for the hundredth time.

The sound of my keys clanging together had her neck twisting so she could look over the back of the couch at me.

"I'm going out," I told her. "I'll be back in a few hours if you need anything."

She stared at me, so many thoughts flitting behind

those eyes. When I finally moved to grab my wallet, she spoke up.

"Can I go with?"

The question had me pausing with my hand poised over my wallet. I braced my palms on the counter, staring at an old chip in the laminate countertop. I hadn't expected her to ask, which was stupid of me. Of course, Parker would want to know what I was up to. We were more than roommates with a past now. Titles weren't established, but secrets were secrets, and I wouldn't have them between us.

"Sure."

Less than fifteen minutes later, she was dressed and in the passenger seat of my truck. She'd eyed the casserole dish and the container beside it multiple times, but hadn't asked any questions.

As I drove, the knowledge of her curiosity had my thumbs dragging on the leather of the steering wheel. Finally, I said, "It's shepherd's pie."

Her brows rose in a mannerism mimicking a nod, but still she stayed silent.

"And those are mashed potatoes," I stated, nudging my head in the direction of the Tupperware.

More seconds of silence passed, and it felt like I might crawl out of my skin. It wasn't Parker creating that feeling, though. It was more so my nerves itching at me from the inside out.

Parker's hands were folded neatly on her lap, her entire body barely moving, like she thought I was a foal on the verge of bolting. "And they're for...?"

"A friend." It was all I could say right now without causing further confusion. The sad truth was, I had a lot of sad shit to tell her.

She lowered her chin in a slow, drawn-out nod. "And where are we going?"

"The ranch."

"Is this friend at the ranch?"

"No." My teeth dug into my bottom lip as I imagined her brain flashing warning signals: confusion, no straight answers, ominous. "I promise I'll explain."

She set a comforting hand on my thigh, and the tension physically seeped out of me. "I know."

I took the long way to the ranch, potholes and uneven gravel causing her to steady the casserole dish a time or two. I felt bad, but I needed the time to get my nerves in check. The last thing I needed was to cry on her again.

The ranch was silent as we pulled up, a blessing, given my family knew I visited most Sundays to spend some time in the field. Parker couldn't ride while pregnant, so when I saw Bucky at the gates, relief flooded me. At least I wouldn't be taking her on a few-mile-long hike across the pasture searching for him.

She unbuckled, leaving the casserole and hopping out. I did the same, and before I could even loosen my fist, she weaved her fingers through mine, clasping my hand tight.

She was so in tune with me, it nearly made my heart hurt.

Hand in hand, I led her toward the pasture, opening

the gate to let her through. Like he knew the routine we'd gotten into, Bucky headed over to us, his ears forward, head low, and tail swishing. He let out a long snort, nostrils flaring with the act.

I placed a palm on his forehead as he stopped before us, his eyes closing slightly as I rubbed him. "Hey, Buck."

His head swiveled to Parker, eyes on her. With a small smile, she itched his jaw.

"Up for a walk?" I asked her.

She nodded.

Bucky walked beside us as we went. I typically brought treats with me once I learned he'd do anything for them, but I'd run out on my last visit. He didn't seem disappointed, though, as he sniffed near my pocket and realized they were empty. He simply matched our pace, content to be in our company.

We crested the small hill, the mid-December sunset casting a warm glow over the yellow grass. The sun set so early this time of year, I'd had to start coming before dinner rather than after. But neither of us minded. Bucky loved a good pre-dinner treat.

I tugged off my jacket and laid it over the grass, thankful for my brown thermal keeping in my body heat. With my hand still in hers, I helped Parker to sit on my coat. I took the spot next to her, half of my ass pressed into the dewy grass. On the bright side, at least there wasn't a foot of snow yet.

Bucky knew exactly what to do, grazing on the grass beside us.

"This is Bucky," I started, eyes on him because if I

looked at Parker while I told her this, I'd surely lose it. "He was the horse me and my friend learned to ride broncs on. He was a crazy fucker in his youth, but he always took care not to get out of hand after doing his job, ya know? Once our asses hit the ground, he was done. Calm as can be, like you'd never have expected that he'd just gone haywire moments before."

Parker leaned her head on my shoulder, both her hands wrapping around my own where it was slung between her knees.

"Because of that, he taught a lot of kids. While doing the program, I became really good friends with this one guy. Despite having been acquaintances with a lot of people in high school, I had quite the opposite experience in bronc-riding school. A lot of the guys were dicks, just doing it to get the attention of buckle bunnies, so Garrett and I became really close. We were both there for the same reason: to find ourselves and test our limits." I plucked a few pieces of grass, spinning them between my thumb and forefinger. "I'm taller than your average bronc rider, so I got made fun of a lot. They'd say I wasn't cut out for it, but Garrett believed in me. He did some ranch saddle bronc riding with me to help me feel comfortable. Less like an outcast.

"Fast forward, we stuck together through the whole thing as best we could. Got hotel rooms together, all that stuff. We even bought a camper at one point, thinking it'd be easier to stay in that in between events." I let out a breathy laugh at the memory. "Had to sell it after he broke the damn plumbing, though."

Parker's cheek lifted against my shoulder.

I swallowed, preparing myself for the rest.

"Garrett was too good. He gave up so much for everyone. Bought homeless people burgers on our trips. Hell, he even bought their dogs food when they had 'em. He didn't know it, but he was a big influence on me, and I—" My voice broke and I swallowed again, though this time, it was harder due to the rock forming in my throat. "I owe him so much of me."

Parker remained still, thumbs running over my skin.

"He wanted me to come home with him one weekend to see his mom. She was going to make his favorite. Shepherd's pie."

I paused. Breathed in for eight seconds. Out for many more.

"I told him I would. But right before we were supposed to leave, I got offered to do an event in Billings. I couldn't pass it up, not for the prize money they were offering. I told him I couldn't make it home with him, but that I'd come next time. Garrett being the man that he was, he didn't blink an eye. He wanted so much good for me, and I—"

I choked again, rolling my lips together and blinking away the inevitable tears.

"He left that night. It was a Friday. There was no ice on the roads, no bad weather. He was supposed to make it home." My exhale was shaky. "He never did. A drunk driver hit his truck. Slammed him right into a tree." I tried to swallow again, but my throat was too thick. "He was dead on impact."

Parker's strokes didn't falter, but I felt her melt further into me as my hurt spread from my body to hers.

"There was no salvaging his truck. It was so mutilated, the police guessed the other driver was going at least one twenty, if not more. Somehow, though, that longhorn skull in my living room survived. He'd had them on the grille of his truck, and since the driver hit him from the side, they were barely scratched."

One of Parker's hands slid up my arm to my bicep, squeezing me there. "I'm so sorry, Beckham."

I shook my head. "I should've been there."

"Beck…"

"If I had gone like I'd told him I would, maybe he would have left five minutes later and missed that driver. Maybe he would've been alive today, eating that shepherd's pie with his mother and laughing and reminiscing on all the times he bruised his tailbone."

I shifted to pull out my wallet, opening it and sliding out a worn Polaroid. "This was the two of us, three weeks before his accident. We'd gone out on a lake up in Montana for Memorial Day weekend."

Parker delicately took the photo, her other hand releasing my bicep to swipe at her cheek.

As she studied the last photo of my best friend, I slid out the only other photo I kept in my wallet. When her gaze moved to it, she seemed to stop breathing. It was so worn from years of being stored and touched, the creases had turned into thick strips of white. Still, though, she could tell it was her.

"The night we went to the drive-ins in your truck," she whispered.

"We brought every snack from my mom's pantry."

A wet, heavy rush of breath left her. A sad laugh. "Even your dad's bland unsalted almonds."

"I had to buy him six containers just to make up for the one we threw away."

The memory lightened the mood, but not for long.

Parker looked at me, the orange sun reflecting in the tears clinging to her lash line. "If you focus on what could have been, you'll never heal from what happened."

"I know." But my mind couldn't help but dwell on it. With so much guilt on my conscience, it felt like I owed it to Garrett to imagine that unreachable future for him.

"He's watching over you in little ways. With Bucky. With me." Her hand, holding that memory of Garrett in her fingers, rested on her stomach. "With everything."

With the Polaroid of her in my hand, I placed my palm over hers. "Oh, I know he is. Garrett couldn't let me live without him." He wasn't physically here, but he still showed up in the wind. In the way Bucky never left me alone when I visited. When dawn shone rays of light through my curtained window. When I felt like hope was futile, and blades of grass would brush my skin and reassure me I was alive and well.

I was down for the count when I got the phone call with the news of Garrett's accident. Even worse for wear when I heard about Parker's father's passing. But no matter what, that flicker of hope remained an ember inside of me, never once letting the storms put out its light. I could say that was because of me. That I fought the mental battle of losing my best friend and won. But there was no mistaking that Parker had taught me to persevere, even when all of life was against me.

She'd grown up in a not-so-perfect house with a struggling family, finding salvation on my parents' ranch on the days she felt the most hopeless.

So that's what I did. I sat with Bucky on the days I lost myself to the emptiness of my mind. I talked to him, repeated myself over and over about how it was my fault Garrett passed. That it was my desire to be more than I was that took me away from Parker.

And it all worked out in the end.

I got the girl. And I still have my best friend. Maybe not sitting next to me, cracking jokes and giving me shit. But he lived on in the land. In Bucky, and in me.

In the memories and that longhorn skull in my living room.

In the Polaroid in my wallet.

In my heart.

"I have one more place I want to take you."

Parker looked at me like I hung the moon. Little did she know, she did that all on her own.

"Anywhere."

29
PARKER

The house we were parked in front of told a hundred stories all on its own. From the garden beds surrounding the front porch, their dormant flowers brown and waiting for the spring warmth to once again reach them, to the way the paint on the window shutters looked brand new, despite evidence of old wear layered beneath.

It was a single-story house with an old tire swing hanging off a giant oak tree in the yard. Christmas decorations were spread around the porch: a wreath hanging on the front door, and a snowman holding a Happy Holidays sign beside an aged bench.

It was a home, yet it held so much more than families and beds. The warm light emanating from the sheer-curtained windows boasted of home-cooked meals and laughing with friends. Warm fires and s'mores under the starlight.

It was a picture of everything I dreamed of wanting

as a child. It was everything I hoped to give my own baby.

Beckham stared at the house, a heavy breath lifting his shoulders. I let him have however long he needed. Ten minutes later, he looked over at me with a look in his eyes that spoke a little of his fears, but a lot of his relief.

With a small nod of encouragement, I released his hand and grabbed the casserole dish and Tupperware. Beck eyed the movement, but with the way his nerves seemed to have a chokehold on him at the moment, he seemed to silently agree that the food was better off in my grasp than his.

We both got out of the truck and joined in front of the grille before he led me up the creaky porch steps. Beautiful garlands hung around the banister, tiny fairy lights weaved throughout. From the porch, I could smell sweet vanilla laced with a hint of cinnamon wafting from the house.

Without a knock, Beckham opened the storm door and let us in through the chipped oak main door.

"Ellis?" Beckham's voice floated into the house as the warmth from a crackling fire in the small living room to the right surrounded us in comfort.

"In the library, hon," a soft female voice replied from down a narrow hall.

Beckham took the casserole from me, disappearing for a moment to likely set it in the kitchen before appearing back at my side and weaving his hand in mine. He led me down the hall. Paintings of horses and vast landscapes and herds of cows hung on the wall in rich wooden frames, some with people among the animals and nature, and others more bare.

We turned into a room with a wide entrance and were met with cherry wood shelves full of hundreds of books. The nostalgic smell of aged books hit me, bringing me back to winters in the library when I wanted to snuggle up with a book and not freeze in my parents' house.

With her back to us, a woman with graying hair set a book on a shelf, attempting to squeeze it into a narrow slot between two others. The ends of the strands were a rich brown tinted with hints of red, while her roots grew in silver.

As she tried to shove one of the books to make more space, Beckham dropped my hand and crossed to her, leaning over her small frame to do the hard work for her. With an airy, sweet laugh that sent a wave of peace washing over me, she successfully shelved the book.

Beckham dropped his massive bicep, the muscle looking even bigger next to her, and looked down at who I presumed to be Ellis.

She faced him, brushing her hands on her faded jeans. "Thank you, dear. I think I may have one too many in my collection."

She must've spotted me out of the corner of her eye, because her head swiveled in my direction. As soon as we locked eyes, a heartwarming smile lit her lips. I couldn't help but do the same.

"There are never enough books," I reassured her.

That only made her eyes brighten more.

"Ellis, this is Parker Summerhill. Parker, this is Ellis Swan. Garrett's mother."

A pressure like none I'd ever felt before lit behind my eyes, and I internally forced myself not to cry. The last thing this woman probably wanted was for me to sob at her feet the moment we met. To her, I was a stranger. To me, she was so much more.

With unhurried steps, she crossed to me, a slightly wrinkled hand held out. "Hi, Parker."

I took hers, her skin soft and warm. "Hi, Ms. Swan. It's so nice to meet you."

"Please, call me Ellis. And who might you be to Beckham?" Her eyes darted suggestively to my stomach, her eyebrows waggling with excitement. "He didn't tell me he was having a baby."

Beckham's nervous laugh flitted up from behind her.

"I'm his girlfriend." The title passed my lips with confidence, and it only made her smile widen.

"A girlfriend, huh?" She looked over her shoulder at Beckham. "Is this new?"

"As new as this house, Ell," Beckham said.

She waved a hand in his direction, an incredulous puff of air coming from her. "You weren't even born when this house was built."

But one look at Beckham told me exactly what he was thinking. That he and I were fate. Written in the stars. In the making of the universe. We'd find each other in this lifetime, over and over again, and in every other.

Ellis, still grasping me, turned my hand over and

inspected my fingers. "And is there a reason you haven't put a ring on her finger?"

Beck rubbed at his neck, a sly smile tilting the corner of his mouth. "I'm working on it."

Oh, the things I would do to him in this moment if Ellis wasn't around.

"We brought shepherd's pie," I told her, figuring a change of subject would be appreciated by Beckham. She seemed like another mother to him, one who wouldn't hesitate to grill him on his dating life. It was sweet, really.

She released my hand. A sort of heaviness settled in the air, yet she still kept that playful lilt in her tone. "That boy brings me a casserole every other Sunday. First Sunday of every month, I get Garrett's favorite dish." She cupped her hand on the side of her mouth, leaning closer like she was about to whisper a secret, though she barely quieted her voice. "He just won't leave me alone, you know?"

Beckham's brows rose, a palm plastered to his chest. "Me?"

I inched closer to Ellis. "Oh, trust me. I know the feeling."

Ellis snickered while Beckham's mouth popped open like he was hurt. "Maybe having the two of you meet wasn't the grandest idea."

Ellis looped her elbow with mine, leading me out of the library and to the kitchen where a small four-seater table sat beside a tiny counter. The space wasn't large by any means, but it seemed perfect for her.

She let me go so she could grab plates and utensils, so I scooped up the casserole and Tupperware and brought them over to the table. They nearly filled the space, but she worked around it, putting out three settings. Beckham grabbed glasses of ice water, and then the three of us sat.

Across from me sat an empty chair that spoke louder than any person could. It screamed of memories and love and so many smiles.

It symbolized walking through the pain and never forgetting.

Beckham served all of us, and we began eating.

"You can't bring a pregnant girlfriend into my house and not tell me," Ellis chastised before taking a sip of water. "Are you the father? Or do I need to get my shotgun?"

Beckham's eyes turned to saucers. "Ellis, no."

She shrugged. "I've got to protect *someone*."

She might as well have held the gun and shot it right through my chest, because a crater of hurt dug itself a home right there with her words.

Before, I might not have taken her statement as hard, but with a baby growing inside of me that I'd do anything to keep safe, it hit differently. How could you lose a child and ever go on? He was a part of her, and—

A frail hand covered mine where it was gripping my fork. I looked up, a trail of moisture making its way down my cheek.

But she didn't speak. She didn't tell me it was okay, or that I shouldn't be sorry. She only gave me her eyes.

Proof that she was still living. Still here. Still finding ways to cope and smile when all she felt like doing was suffocating.

I sniffled quickly, swallowing the trace of emotion in my throat. Swiping at my cheek, I said, "He's Beckham's."

This time, Ellis's eyes took on a sheen, but no tears fell. "It's a boy."

I nodded, and her hand slid away from mine to grab her fork again.

"Well, if he's anything like Beckham was after he met Garrett, you've got your hands full," Ellis commented before taking a bite of food.

"Hey. I wasn't *that* bad," Beckham defended.

"Shooting squirrels with BB guns, bursting my water pipes trying to dig a swimming pool in the backyard, snapping my couch in two when Garrett threw you at it during one of your *wrestling matches*." Ellis's shoulders moved from side to side, weighing the severity of each memory. "Nope. Not bad at all." But she cupped her hand around her mouth again, leaning closer to me, and whispered, "Prepare yourself."

Beckham's eyes narrowed playfully. "I heard that."

Ellis feigned innocence, her gaze searching the room. "What? That must be the breeze. Those windows need to be resealed."

"It's on my list," Beckham mumbled before having another forkful.

"List?" I questioned.

Ellis rolled her eyes. "That boy thinks he needs to fix

everything around here. I tell him its charm—he tells me water leaks turn into black mold."

"They do," he grumbled as he brought his glass to his lips.

"The house is old," she said by way of excuse. "You can't get mad at it."

"I can still fix it."

Conversation flowed seamlessly as we finished dinner, stories of Garrett and Beckham coming up now and then. I'd never met Garrett, as he and his mom lived a bit outside of Bell Buckle and I never left that small town, but it seemed that he and Beckham were a rowdy couple of teens when they got together, if her stories were any indication.

Ellis and I did dishes while Beckham did a quick second coat of paint in her guest bathroom. He'd recently taken out some moldy drywall and replaced it. There were only a few finishing touches to go, and it'd be done.

I wasn't sure how I hadn't put the pieces together that he wasn't going to his family's house every other Sunday for dinner. Beckham had never really hid anything from me, though, so I hadn't thought too far into it. For some reason, asking felt like sticking my head where it didn't belong when I already felt like I was intruding on his privacy by living in his double-wide. But I'd have to get over that. We were different now that we were officially together.

The night passed as we sat around the fireplace in Ellis's living room. As the flames died out, she hung on to every word we spoke. I almost didn't want to leave knowing she'd be alone here, but when her eyes grew heavy, I knew we couldn't stay forever.

"We're going to head out, Ellis," Beckham said, noticing the same thing I did. He stood from beside me, holding out a hand to help me off the sunken couch. I wondered if it was the same one they'd broken and she'd just never replaced it. At first, maybe she'd hated it, but some items held memories you could never recreate.

While he helped me to stand, my back stiff and my mind fighting any hint of exhaustion, Ellis got to her feet as well. She folded the wool blanket that had been slung over her legs and draped it over the back of her sitting chair.

"You better bring Parker back," Ellis started, and though her voice sounded tired from hours of talking, her teasing held firm. "I was getting bored just seeing you every visit."

Beckham let out a small chuckle, pulling her in for a hug. "I know you love me."

She patted his back, her arms barely making it around his torso. "I do." She receded a step, setting a palm on his stubbled cheek. "So very much."

Unspoken words passed between them, and I waited until they were done to move in for a hug of my own.

"No more handshakes?" Ellis asked as we squeezed each other.

"I think I like your hugs better," I said.

"Good." She smiled, bright and warm. "I do too."

We said our goodbyes, and Ellis waited in the glow of the porch light while we got in the truck and drove off.

Beckham's large hand wrapped around mine on my lap, and I looked over to find a small, satisfied grin on his face.

"So this is where you've been running off to," I said, stroking a thumb over his own.

He nodded. "Every other Sunday."

"Since he passed?"

This time, his confirmation was a subtle dip of his chin. "I came for dinner on and off before, but without Garrett, Ellis has been lonely. Even though she doesn't want to admit it. She says those books keep her company."

I was sure they did. "Where's his dad?"

"Died when he was young. It had been just the two of them since. And now…"

"Now it's Ellis, you, and me."

His eyes met mine in the dim light emanating from the dashboard, a hint of melancholy reflecting in them.

"You know you can tell me anything, right?"

"I was scared," he admitted.

My brows pinched. "Why?"

His fingers flexed on the steering wheel. "Didn't want you to think I was diving into this with you to cope with Garrett."

My head swung back and forth of its own accord. "I know you're still grieving him, and if I had known, I'm sure that would have crossed my mind. But we have a past, Beckham. A lot of what's going on is new, but *we're* not." I squeezed his hand. "You got me through some hard times. Let me hold you through yours."

"Okay." He squeezed me back. "I will."

"Is he why you quit doing rodeo?" I asked carefully, not wanting to bring up too much after the emotional night.

"He is."

Silence followed, and I let him decide if he wanted to branch out on that or not. He'd finally let me in on the pain he was feeling, and the last thing I wanted to do was push him too far.

"I just couldn't do it anymore without him." His voice cracked on the last word, and I held his hand a little tighter. "Sorry," he whispered.

"Don't be sorry." I wished for nothing more than to climb over the center console and hug him.

I didn't ask any more questions, and when we were almost to his property, he spoke up.

"Thank you for tonight."

"You don't have to thank me. If Ellis is a part of your life, then she's a part of mine too. That's how family works."

The word had him slowing the vehicle as he turned into his driveway, his gaze focusing on me while he let the truck cruise up the gravel, memory taking over as he'd done this a hundred times before.

As he shifted into park, eyes still on me, he wasted no time sliding off his seat belt and leaning over the center console to kiss me.

30

BECKHAM

EIGHTEEN YEARS OLD

My ass grew numb against the heat of the metal pole. The bale of hay beside me was likely a whole pound lighter due to the amount I'd plucked from it, breaking each piece into dozens of tiny slivers only to give my hands something to do.

Parker wasn't late to our final goodbye. I was early.

To avoid acceptance of any hard situation, most people would simply not show up at all. Me? I showed up early, my nerves not allowing me the opportunity of missing our last farewell.

No one was around to ruin this moment—my siblings were either working somewhere on the ranch or at their respective jobs, and my parents were inside the house. They all knew how important Parker was to me, and how badly this would hurt. Hell, it already did. What was I supposed to do without Parker Summerhill in my life? Without her smiling up at me with those big, bright white teeth and those freckles folding into the creases of her scrunched nose? How would I live without her laugh? Or the thought to get her a Dr. Pepper on ice every time I passed that gas station down the road?

What would a gaping black hole look like? Well, this was my answer.

Would there even be a sun without her? Because as far as I was aware, that giant ball of fire only hung in the sky to shine light on her beauty, to deepen the shades of her freckles and sunburn those shoulders I loved so much.

Unable to sit still any longer, I shoved off the fence that led to the pasture and paced the driveway in front of the barn. I did that for thirty minutes until Parker's truck rolled up at exactly two o'clock, just like we'd agreed.

Behind it, she towed a three-horse trailer. She'd found the gooseneck on the side of the road in terrible condition. When she'd asked for my help picking it up, it didn't even have a door. But now, as she swung it around in a large half circle, I saw just how devoted she'd really been to making that thing shine. Her plan was to live in its living quarters while she traveled with Tex, experiencing the country while also learning more about different ranches and their ways of doing things.

She parked the truck and got out, and the forced smile she shot me already had my heart breaking in two.

"You like it?" she asked when she stopped a couple feet from me, glancing at the trailer behind her.

"You sure that's the same one I helped you drag fourteen miles home?"

Her honey-golden eyes landed on me, and I soaked them in a little more than I usually did. If this was the last time I was going to see her, I had to commit it to memory.

"Same exact one. It's crazy what a little help sign at the feed store will get you from the locals."

I chuckled while silently cursing this town and their eagerness to give. But her leaving was inevitable, sparkling trailer or not. At least this way she wasn't couch-hopping or relying on some janky motel.

My hands slid in the front pockets of my jeans, fighting the urge to reach for her. I'd have to get used to not touching Parker whenever I wanted because, well, she simply wouldn't be around.

"I've got Tex in the cross-ties if you're ready for him. Picked his feet and gave him a bath."

"You didn't have to do that," she said, and she almost sounded a little guilty.

I looked down at my boots. "I wanted to." *Because it was the last time I'd ever get to.*

We walked side by side to the barn until we reached Tex. His ears instantly perked when Parker came around the corner, and I almost felt jealous. Of a *horse*. He got to go with her, and I didn't. How the fuck else was I supposed to feel?

"Hey, bud." She ran a hand down his nose before unclipping his halter from the cross-ties.

Tex was a beautiful sorrel with three white socks. He

and Parker were inseparable. As rough of a past as he'd had, he never let that affect how he treated her. I could only imagine he'd be happy as ever bonding with her on this trip—however long it may be.

I walked a bit ahead of her so I could open the back of the trailer. She led him in with ease, and once he was secure, she triple-checked that everything looked good.

"Did you decide where you're going first?" I asked as she closed the door.

"Montana, I think. I won't really know until I get on the road, though. The whole point of this is no rules, you know? I'm just going to go where the wind takes me." She latched the door, eyes scanning to be sure she hadn't missed a lock.

I nodded, unsure what to say because it was hitting me. I'd known for months what her plan was, the same way she knew mine. Yet it hadn't felt real until now, with her standing before me, minutes away from leaving my life for good.

She turned around, and it was like both our worlds stopped spinning. A curl flew across her forehead, caught in the breeze, but our eyes didn't move from one another's.

Was she feeling the pain I felt now? That achingly gutting feeling digging out the depths of my stomach and replacing it with lead? Could I even stomach a world without Parker Summerhill in it?

"So this is it," I said, battling that urge to touch her again. If we were breaking things off, I couldn't be doing all the things I used to do, like hug her whenever I wanted and lay claim to those pretty pink lips of hers.

"This is it." Her shoulders fell with her released breath. Or maybe it was the weight of this goodbye that sat heavy on her.

I knew it did for me.

There wasn't much else for us to say. We'd already discussed everything. How I'd be leaving to dive more seriously into rodeo. How she'd be in a lot of places without cell reception. How we could talk, but we shouldn't. This was supposed to be a time where we both found ourselves. At least, that's what she'd called it.

I'd already found my place, though. With her.

But this would be good for us. We'd figure out what we wanted in this life, and if fate worked the way we hoped, maybe we'd find each other again.

With her mom having just recently passed, I highly doubted Parker would be coming back to Bell Buckle anytime soon, if ever. There was nothing left for her here. Not without me.

I'd wanted to tell her to wait for me. To assure her that once I was back in Bell Buckle, away from rodeo, I still wanted her. But that wouldn't have been fair for her. I wanted her to be happy and find herself. And, well, if that one day wasn't with me, then I'd have to accept the fact that maybe it wasn't just *right person, wrong time.* That maybe it was all wrong.

Except I refused to believe that was the case for us. Parker and I were endgame. Maybe not in the most conventional way, but I had hope this wasn't the end for us.

Yet that little voice in the back of my head told me this might be the last time.

"I should probably go," Parker said hesitantly, looking almost pained as she spoke.

"Right. You could get a few hours underway before it's dark if you leave now."

"Yeah." She inhaled like she was breathing in my presence for the last time.

"Drive safe, okay? For however long you stay in that thing." I lifted my chin in the direction of the truck and trailer. "And close your curtains at night."

She smiled, but it didn't quite reach her eyes. "You've told me that at least a dozen times."

"I'll tell you a dozen more if you don't get going." What the fuck was I doing? I wanted more of her. To soak in this moment a little longer. Yet here I was, shoving her away like her being on this ranch was wasting my time.

I had to think it was some inner part of me telling me that if she didn't go now, I'd never let her go at all.

She opened her mouth a few times like she didn't know how to say the words. Then she cooled her features and landed on, "Goodbye, Beck."

"Goodbye, Park."

We stared at each other a few seconds longer, neither of us knowing what the right thing to do was. Did we hug? Shake hands? Give a whole speech? No one taught us how to say goodbye to the love of our lives at eighteen.

She turned, rounding the end of the trailer to head toward the driver's side of her truck. She barely made it five steps before my feet started moving.

She must've heard my boots crunch the gravel, because she stopped and spun. "Beck, what are you—"

I swallowed the last part of her sentence with my kiss. One hand wrapped around her elbow while my other snaked into her blonde curls. I breathed in her vanilla scent, basking in that hint of almond I loved. I'd snuck a peek at her body wash and bought my own bottle—not to use, but to smell when I missed her. Maybe that was weird, but there was no hiding how obsessed I was with her.

Her mouth moved with mine like it had so many times before. Our tongues bounced against each other before diving deeper into the kiss. My hand slid from her elbow to her waist, tugging her closer until her stomach was flush with mine. She arched her back, wrapping her arm around the back of my neck while her other hand fisted in my shirt.

We were a cacophony of heavy breathing, hungry kisses, and pained thoughts. I didn't want to let her go— not now, not ever. But when we finally stopped, we both refused to open our eyes. Our foreheads pressed together, our noses brushing like they had so many times before.

"Now I can say goodbye," I murmured, utterly breathless.

Our chests rose and fell, bumping against one another's. The realization that this would be the last time I'd feel her heart beat against mine was like a bullet passing straight through me.

I shoved away the pain of her leaving, forcing myself to release her. I took one step back, then another. Her lips were puffy, her eyes glassy. Why the fuck were we doing this to ourselves?

"I'll miss you," she whispered.

"Every single day."

With one last look, she got in her truck. I didn't move as she pulled out of the driveway and onto the road. I stood there for hours, unable to walk away from the spot where I'd last touched her.

I told myself missing her wouldn't always be this painful.

That one day, I wouldn't feel the gaping hole in my chest as badly as I did at that moment.

God, was I wrong.

31
PARKER

Growing up, Christmas was rarely special with my parents. In the corner of our living room, my mom would set up the twelve-inch plastic tree she found in a donation box on the side of the road. Maybe it was considered stealing for her to have taken it from in front of a stranger's house, but at twelve years old, I'd never felt more excited than when she walked in the door holding it.

The lights on it no longer worked—not that they would have plugged it in anyway—but it helped us feel a little more cheerful during the dreary months of winter.

On my fourteenth Christmas, Beckham noticed our house was dark, as always, when he came by to give me a present—a wooden horse he'd carved from a fallen branch near the pond on their property. He'd returned the next night with a small generator in the bed of his truck and dozens of strings of lights. He'd spent hours looping them around scratchy branches, and when he was done, he'd texted my shattered phone to tell me to come outside.

There were many times I'd thought I'd fallen in love with Beckham as a kid. Like the time he punched a boy at school for making fun of my worn clothes. Or when he picked me up and jumped into the pond and didn't let me go, even as I squealed and laughed. Or all the nights I spent in his bed beside him, the ones where we just stared at each other and breathed the same air, enjoying each other's presence.

But the night he lit that tree? My heart never shone brighter.

From that year forward, I went over to the Bronsons' house for Christmas Eve dinner. Sometimes, I'd spend the night and wake up on Christmas morning to find presents with my name on them stuffed under the eight-foot tree.

This year was no different.

We'd shown up to Beckham's parents' house at eight a.m. sharp, per Avery's request. Though there weren't as many gifts now that we were all grown, it was still magical walking into that old farmhouse and seeing the Christmas spirit on full display.

"Ugh, finally!" Avery called out before shoving up from the kitchen table at breakneck speed and sprinting over to the tree.

Sage's mouth popped open as she fought a smile from where she stood at the kitchen counter. "Avery McKinley, that is not polite."

Callan set a hand on Sage's lower back, placing a kiss on her cheek. "She's just excited, baby."

Sage gave him a wide-eyed look that screamed she was well aware.

Avery popped up from where she'd crouched and waved over at me and Beckham, still standing in the entryway. "Hi, Parker. Hi, Beckham." Then she promptly faced her mom, the sassiest look on her face, before plopping back down to the floor in front of the neatly wrapped presents.

The two of us laughed as Beckham helped me out of my coat and hung it on the rack by the door, then did the same with his. The woodsy scent from the Christmas tree and the fire in the fireplace, mixed with whatever casserole dish Charlotte had in the oven, had my stomach growling.

Beckham's brows rose as he eyed my belly. "Sounds like someone's hungry."

"Well, I am eating for two, and it's past my typical breakfast time."

With that knowledge, Beckham set a palm on my belly before leaning in to kiss me. "I'm going to find my mom and see how much longer that food has."

"I'm sure she'll be out here soon," I told him.

He frowned, though his expression was still playful. "My baby mama is starving, and I can't have that."

His words had warmth pooling low in my belly, but before I could say anything, his hand slid off my stomach as he disappeared down the hallway to find Charlotte.

Not a second later, Lettie looped an arm through mine and led me toward the living room.

"Did you talk to Beckham about the comments?" Lettie asked, voice low and close to my ear.

"I did." I glanced down the hallway as we passed it, not wanting Beckham to hear for fear bringing it up would only make him worry and ruin his mood. "He wasn't exactly happy, if you couldn't have guessed."

"Oh, I definitely figured that." She shuffled me onto the couch, my hips sandwiched between her and Brandy. Lettie scooted as far as she could into the arm of the couch to give me and my stomach space.

Travis was in his recliner, glaring at the fire like he'd battled it all morning. Oakley and Lennon sat on the ground, the latter's back to the coffee table and Oakley resting back in his arms. Callan now stood at the edge of the living room having a hushed conversation with Sage, the two of them oblivious to Avery, who was currently digging her fingers into thick wrapping paper, making progress at tearing into a present.

Reed was beside Brandy, hand firm on her thigh, and Bailey was nowhere to be found, presumably outside tending to the animals before breakfast was served.

"I don't know what else to do," I muttered, leaning into Lettie's side. "I blocked the accounts. Put my profile on private. I'm not posting, especially not sharing any personal details. I have no idea who could want information that desperately."

"Any old flings from the ranches you visited?" she asked.

I shook my head. "I didn't really have time for much of that, and if I did, it was never serious. Besides, ya know..." I gestured to my stomach.

"Have there been any more since the night of the bar?"

"Thankfully, no. But that almost unsettles me more. They clearly know I have ties to Bell Buckle, and now to your family. Ask anyone in this town, and they'll know where the Bronsons live. That's not exactly comforting."

"No one would tell a stranger where our ranch is," Lettie explained. "You know that."

I gnawed on my bottom lip, tearing at skin that was dry from the cold. "I know. But all it takes is one slip-up, like the one on my account."

She set a comforting hand on my own. "Nothing will happen to you, or to us. We're safe."

"Internet stalkers... They can get obsessive."

She squeezed me. "Did Beckham say he was going to do anything?"

"If he has a plan, he didn't tell me. But there's not much we can do when we don't know who the person is."

"True." She forced a reassuring smile, but all it did was prove she was just as lost on what to do about this as I was. "Just keep an eye out. Don't go anywhere alone. And don't overthink."

I snorted. "Overthinking is what I do best with my baby months away from being born."

This time, her grin was a bit more confident. "So

focus on that. Don't let this weirdo ruin one of the best times of your life."

"The back pain and waddling beg to differ on that."

"This doesn't fit me!" Avery yelled out, pulling everyone's attention to her—and the gold ring with a sparkly diamond that was dangling from her petite finger.

Collective gasps sounded around the living room, and from behind the couch, the biggest inhale of all signaled Charlotte's entrance. I peeked over the back to find Beckham at her side, a confused look on his face.

When I swiveled back around, Callan was beside Avery, on his knee, facing a surprised Sage. The woman was speechless, eyes round and mouth agape.

"This kind of happened way out of order, but what else is new?" Callan said, and someone chuckled. He slid the ring off Avery's finger, and once she realized what was happening, she screamed.

"Are you marrying Mama *today*?" Avery asked, her voice a high-pitched shriek.

Sage looked between the two of them. "Avery knew about this?"

Callan's mouth twitched with a smile. "I had to ask her permission."

"You kept a secret?" Sage asked her daughter, incredulous.

Pride showed on the little girl's face. "I did. Daddy said he'd buy me another horse if I didn't tell a soul."

Sage frowned at him, but behind her false look of chastisement was so much love and adoration for Callan.

Callan shrugged. "It was a necessary bribe."

Lennon cleared his throat like he was reminding his brother what he was there to do, and Callan shot him a quick glare before focusing all his attention back on Sage.

"Will you be my wife, Sage? For a million years and every day past that?"

As if the words had opened the floodgates, tears immediately pooled in her eyes, a few trailing down her cheeks. And she nodded. "Yes. A million times, yes."

She leaned down, pressing her lips to his, and Callan scooped his two girls into his arms in one massive hug.

The room erupted in claps, cheers, hoots, and hollers as Callan slipped the ring on Sage's finger and kissed it. And while the family gathered around them to say their congratulations, I tilted my head back to find Beckham with his hands braced on the back of the couch, his gaze focused on me.

I had no doubt we were both thinking of Ellis's one question that stood out to both of us the most.

32
BECKHAM

The door creaked shut as I walked across the porch that was covered in a thin layer of fresh snow, my sights set on the girl who'd made this Christmas all the more special. I wrapped my arms around her from behind, resting my chin on her shoulder while nuzzling my nose into the warm crook of her neck.

Parker had a thick blanket wrapped tight around her, and tiny snowflakes had begun to accumulate on the fabric and in her hair. She looked out at the barn strung with golden lights, but I couldn't focus on anything but her.

"Your nose is cold," Parker murmured, though she leaned back into me.

My lips grazed the soft skin of her neck. "Warm me up."

"When we get home, I'd love nothing more. But I don't think we'll get so lucky messing around on your parents' porch a second time. Especially on Christmas."

I groaned. "Today has been torture."

"How so?" I could hear the smile in her voice.

"Watching you with my family and not being able to take you back to my old room and ruin this dress." She'd worn a knitted beige sweater dress, each inch hugging her figure in a way that had my cock aching every time I looked at her—which was nonstop.

She slowly turned in my embrace, neck tilting so she could look at me. "You could have. I wouldn't have complained."

"Now you tell me?"

She grinned wider.

"Thank you for today," I said, running my hands up and down her upper arms through the blanket.

She shook her head, eyes landing on my neck where my chain lay, before pinning me with a raw, honest look. "I should be thanking you. I've been so worried about... well, all of it, that I forgot this was the point. The memories, being with family. Having you with me."

"But that last part is the most important, right?" I teased.

She shot me a wry look, but I wiped it away by grabbing her chin and pulling her face to mine. My Christmas was complete with my lips on hers. Parker in my arms was the greatest gift I could have ever asked for. Now I could kiss her whenever I wanted, touch her whenever I pleased, and call her mine.

With my hold still firm on her face, I deepened the kiss, tongue slipping past her sweet lips to taste more of her. Her grip on the blanket fell when she pressed her palms to my chest, and I grabbed the material before it could hit the ground, holding it so she wouldn't get cold.

"Merry Christmas, Parker," I said against her lips, leaning my forehead against hers. Our mingled breaths fanned out in puffs of white, placing us in our own little bubble.

"Merry Christmas, Beckham."

My arms came around her once more, pulling her into my chest, and we stood there watching the snow fall and time slow, cherishing this Christmas together. It'd be our last one alone, but I didn't hate that thought. I wanted nothing more than to see our children running around our own tree, wrapping paper and discarded packaging strewn about our toy-filled living room.

With my chin on the top of her head, I said, "I have something I want to show you."

She pulled back slightly to catch my eye. "Is it another woman you've been going to see?"

A laugh burst out of me. "I promise it's not another woman. I was only hiding the one."

Her smile rivaled the lights strung up around the ranch. "Show me."

After I brought her inside to say our goodbyes to everyone, my mom sent us off with a gallon-sized thermos of hot chocolate. Parker said her thanks about two dozen times, but my mom never made her feel like she was inconveniencing anyone.

Parker was a Bronson, whether there was a ring on her finger yet or not.

The night was quiet as we walked to my truck in the

driveway. When I opened the passenger door for her, I used my boot to kick the snow off the step, then helped her into the seat. With her buckled, I got in behind the wheel and cranked the heater.

"Where are we going?" she asked, rubbing her hands together as the cab warmed.

"Somewhere."

She frowned as I shifted into drive and headed for the road.

"You have my mind spiraling after the last place you took me, if I'm being honest."

"I already said—" But I stopped when I saw her shaking her head in my peripheral.

"There are so many things that happened to the both of us while we were away from one another, and sometimes it feels like I'm meeting a whole new Beckham."

I stayed silent, because sometimes, I felt the same way. We'd had discussions like this, but at times—like right now—the realization would hit a little harder.

"I thought your brothers hated me for showing up pregnant."

"Parker, no." I set a hand on her thigh before looping my fingers with hers. "My family could never hate you."

"I know. I *know* that. But I've felt so out of my element, and for a while, I didn't even feel like myself. The girl that couldn't get enough of you growing up. The one that spent so much time with your family and on their ranch. I felt like a stranger, even to myself. And tonight really helped me realize that it wasn't the pregnancy or any of that making me feel that way." Her hand tightened on mine, and I returned the squeeze. "I tried so hard to fit in while I was traveling, and I lost a little of myself. But not here. In Bell Buckle, with you, I don't question who I am or what I want." She looked at me, and it took all I had not to pull over early and give her every ounce of my attention.

The timing was perfect, because seconds later, after rounding the corner, we came to a stop at a place full of so many bittersweet memories.

"Beckham," she whispered, astonishment in her eyes and thousands of lights reflecting in them. Parker's childhood home stood brightly in the background, a new family residing there and living their own life behind those walls. But it wasn't the home that had her speechless. It was what I'd done.

I got out and rounded to her side, opening the door and helping her down. Her gaze was glued to the lights, and mine was glued to her.

"I talked to the new owners a few weeks ago, and they were more than happy to let me borrow their tree for a night."

She laughed, though the sound was breathy, distracted. "Borrow."

I held her hand as I led her across the few feet of dead grass to the base of the tree.

Her neck craned back to look up the trunk. "How long did this take you?"

"I stopped here on my way home from the ranch for the last two weeks. Lost count of how many I strung up. But in total? Probably ten hours."

Her mouth popped open, wide eyes moving to me. "Why?"

A confused chuckle escaped me. "Why?"

She nodded, dead serious.

"Because I love you, Parker."

Her lashes fluttered as I grabbed both her hands, facing her.

"You did this when we were younger, when you found out I didn't have a tree to light in our house," she stated slowly.

My chin bobbed in confirmation. "Wasn't as grand as it is now, but it did the trick."

"You hooked up the extension cord to a generator you'd stolen from your dad's garage."

I smiled, remembering my dad's frown when I drove home that night and found him waiting for me in the driveway. "I told him why I'd taken it, and every Christmas after, he left it out front of the garage for me."

"You made the holidays magical," she recalled, the lights reflecting brighter off the moisture building in her eyes.

I shrugged. "I think that was you."

She rolled her eyes, and I tugged her closer.

"Parker, I want this. I want lights in the yard and a house full of chaos and pumpkin candles and family dinners. I want these traditions with our son."

A tear slipped past her lash line, sliding down her cheek and dripping onto the back of my hand.

"Our son," she whispered.

"Yes, Parker. Our son."

Her bottom lip quivered before she sniffled and threw herself at me, looping her arms around my neck and pressing her lips to mine. "I love you too, Beckham."

My hands gripped her waist as I kissed her under the lights. My fingers tugged on the fabric of her dress, feeling her under me like it was the first time.

Then I pulled back. "One more thing."

The laugh that tumbled from her was happiness and nerves wrapped in one tiny bundle.

I jogged the short distance to the truck and grabbed the bag from the back seat, then moved back to her. I handed her the present, blue tissue paper clumsily shoved into the top. I'd have to get better at wrapping before the baby came.

"What's this?" she pondered aloud as she plucked the paper out. I held it for her, and when she reached into the bag and pulled out the gift, I took the bag from her as well.

The folded piece of fabric unraveled as she held it up, and she pressed her lips together, holding back the emotions I was sure had swam to the top.

"For our baby," I told her, though the ivory onesie with little horses and lassos on it was explanation enough.

With one last look, she balled it into her fist and hugged me. She pressed her cheek to my chest, right over my heart, and it nearly burst.

"I love it. I love *you*," she mumbled into my jacket.

I held her just as tight, wishing I never had to let her go.

For hours, we sat in my truck, the heater warming our fingers as we sipped hot chocolate and admired the lights. We talked about our future, what traditions we loved and what goals we both had.

It wasn't surprising when our answers were the same.

Nothing was more important to the two of us than being happy. Together.

33
PARKER

The fabric practically spilled through my fingers as I held it in front of me. I'd never owned such a delicate piece of clothing, and because of that, I was almost scared to put it on.

The pink lingerie came with a top that was so transparent I doubted it'd cover a single thing. Tiny pink flowers in all shades accented the bra, but the sheer camisole that was attached was bare of those details, the delicate pink fabric splitting down the middle to show off my bump. The panties matched, flowers spread across the front before turning into thin straps that held the thong together.

I'd had the bright idea to surprise Beckham after all he'd done for me for Christmas, and now I was slowly regretting it. Wearing sexy outfits was not my forte, and I wasn't sure what had come over me to think I'd like it any more while my body was changing the way that it was.

I loved my bump, but my insecurities got the best of me most days.

"Okay," I huffed at my reflection in the mirror, fisting the lingerie at my side. I was wearing Beckham's shirt that hung to my thighs, so all it'd take was removing that one piece of clothing and I'd be naked. "I'm just going to try it on, and if I hate it, I can take it off. No biggie, right?"

I placed the set on the dresser beside me before shucking off the shirt. His clothing made me comfortable, even though I'd had a hard time feeling that way in my skin recently—but I could do this. And even if I hated it, at least I tried.

I slipped on the flimsy lingerie, adjusting my breasts in each of the cups. The camisole fell seamlessly on either side of my bump, and somehow the slight coverage gave me a boost of confidence as my eyes skimmed my body in the mirror.

I had to give the boutique clerk credit—the pink really did complement my skin tone. The stitched flowers gave it a nice touch, drawing some attention away from my nipples on full display under the thin material.

With a heavy breath, I decided to keep it on for a few minutes. Beckham hadn't texted me that he was on his way home from the ranch yet, so I had time to decide if I still wanted to go through with this.

I grabbed Beckham's shirt from where it was puddled on the floor and folded it, setting it on the end of the bed. Then I padded into the bathroom to touch up my lip gloss, dabbing my finger along my lips as if making sure it was set perfectly was important.

After, I washed my hands, taking my time with the soap and rinsing them thoroughly. With a squeak of the handle, I turned the water off and headed back into the room.

"Parker, you in here?"

Beckham's voice had me freezing at the end of the bed.

Shit, shit, shit.

I quickly glanced down at my body, then to the shirt on the bed. I could still—

"Holy shit."

My head snapped up. Beckham was frozen midstep in the doorway, one hand on the doorframe and the other raised slightly, like he really had stopped in his tracks.

My face flamed. I was so exposed, and he was standing there in a dirty white T-shirt, jeans, chaps, scuffed boots, and a cowboy hat. But even with embarrassment coursing through me at a frantic pace, I couldn't deny the heat building between my legs. If I wasn't careful, I'd likely drip straight onto the floor with the amount of thread these panties had.

"Parker, you're—"

"Crazy?"

He shook his head, but not only in answer. He seemed to be in disbelief.

"Fucking beautiful."

My hands clasped together in front of me, my

bump making the position awkward. "I wanted to surprise you. I didn't know you were coming home already. You said you'd text me when you were on the way."

He finally took a step, but the act was forced, like he was learning how to walk for the first time. "I wanted to surprise you, too."

My brows furrowed. "You did? With what?"

His head moved back and forth again, and he came even closer. "That's not real important right now, Park." His gaze moved down my body, slow and hungry. "Fuck, Parker. You're—" His lips formed a thin line before he wiped a hand down his face.

"This is too much, isn't it?"

His head shook more frantically now and he closed the distance between us, clasping my hands in his own. "Not at all. You've just got me a little speechless."

That had a weight lifting off my chest, and I tilted my head back a little more as some of the shyness left me. "Really?"

He let out an incredulous chuckle. "Really."

That ravenous look in his eyes and the way I could feel his hard cock through his jeans, pressing against my bare thigh, had me shoving away all traces of my insecurities. My hands landed on his chest and I lightly shoved him backward until his ass hit the edge of the dresser. His tongue ran over his bottom lip as I gathered his shirt in my fists.

I tugged it upward, his hat falling to the dresser as I pulled his shirt off the rest of the way. With it slung to the floor behind me, I dropped to my knees and began working at his belt.

He started to unclasp the top of his chaps, but I set my hand over his, stopping him. "Leave those on."

He braced his hands on the lip of the dresser behind him, letting me continue.

I unzipped the outer zippers, then got to work. Once I had his boots, socks, jeans, and underwear off, I looked up. He was looming over me in only his chaps while I slowly slid the zipper back up his legs. The tip of his cock was glistening, and I stuck my tongue out, lapping up the precum beading there.

Beckham hissed in a breath, fingers digging into the wood. "Your tongue is going to be my undoing, baby."

"What do you mean?" I feigned innocence, batting my eyelashes before dragging my tongue up the length of his cock.

He tossed his head back, veins bulging in his arms as he worked to restrain himself. "You're going to make me explain?"

"Please do."

His hand moved, tangling in my hair as he met my eyes. "How you lick me." His other hand cupped my chin, thumb moving over my jaw to tug down my bottom lip. I popped open my mouth and he slid it in, pressing down on my tongue. "How you show me I'm yours. How you lap up every last drop of me and are always hungry for more."

His thumb stroked down the length of my tongue until it reached the end. With my hand wrapped around his cock, I lined the tip up beside his hand, resting it on my taste buds. He moved his thumb to the head of his cock, pressing down on it as he slid past my lips. Saliva pooled in my mouth and I opened my lips wider, needing him deeper.

Beckham watched intently as he gripped the base and slid in and out of my mouth. After a few thrusts, I wrapped my lips around him and sucked hard. He sucked in a breath, quickly pulling out and reaching for me.

He hauled me up by my armpits and spun us around so that my ass was planted on the dresser and he was between my legs. I braced my hands behind me, fingers brushing his discarded hat. I grabbed it, placing it back on his head. His hand trailed down my outer thigh until it hooked under my knee, hiking my leg up around his hip. My back arched as he weaved his fingers into the hair at the base of my neck and tilted my head.

He pressed his lips to mine, his tongue slipping into my mouth. He hooked his fingers in the straps of my panties before tugging them off me. They slipped down my ankles, falling to the floor at his feet.

With his hand hooked under my knee again, he tugged me closer to the edge until we were lined up perfectly.

I reached between us, gripping his cock while running the tip along my clit. My moan was earth-shattering in the midst of our heavy breathing.

"You like when my cock rubs your needy little clit, don't you?" Beckham murmured into my mouth.

A whimper was my only response.

He ran his hand down my front until he replaced my hand on his cock with his own. It took no time at all for him to slide inside of me. I nearly fell apart right then, my body wound so tight at the sight of him in only his chaps and hat. I was just as feral for him as he was for me.

He held me steady, both hands hooked behind my knees now as he drilled into me over and over again. With each thrust, his chain bounced against his now-glistening chest.

I kept one hand braced behind me to keep me upright, and the other tangled in his chain before looping around the back of his neck to tug his mouth down to mine.

As we kissed, he plucked his hat off and set it on my head. He tugged me a little closer, the angle making the head of his cock hit that blissful spot inside of me. Our mouths parted as my head tilted back, the way he ravished me taking over my strength. My core tightened as he moved his lips to my neck, sucking and nibbling on the sensitive skin.

"Beckham," I breathed, his name a plea and a curse.

"Let go for me, Parker. Show me how fucking wet I make you." The rasp in his voice had me sucking in a breath.

"Only if you do, too." My hand moved to his hair, pulling on the strands in a desperate need to hold onto something.

A rush of air burst out of him, warming my neck.

"Baby, I've been ready since the moment I walked into this room and saw you wearing this."

My fingernails dug into the wood as I couldn't take it anymore. His thrusts became more frantic, his pace intoxicating. I screamed out as I came, my limbs stiffening before they dissolved into a shivering mess as the force of my orgasm overtook every bone in my body.

My walls clenched around his cock, and he held my legs even tighter as he seated himself deep inside me and came.

As we both came down from our highs and caught our breaths, he peppered kisses all over my neck and collarbone. Then I remembered.

"What was your surprise?"

His cheeks lifted against my skin as he smiled. "You're going to have to put some clothes on to see it."

"Because it's outside, or because you can't see me wearing this without getting worked up?"

He chuckled softly before raising his head to look at me. "Both. But definitely that second part. This lingerie will give me a boner from hell if you keep it on, even if I just made a mess of you."

I pouted. "But it's so cute."

"Park, *cute* doesn't describe how this thing looks on you." He ran the camisole through his fingers. "I might have to lock you up for being this fucking sexy."

The corner of my mouth ticked up at the thought. "I might not be opposed to that."

His cock twitched where it was still seated inside me.

"You're playing a dangerous game if you want to see your surprise."

"Okay, okay. Fine. I'll be good." My palms flattened on his stomach, giving him a light shove. "You need to move so I can get dressed."

He groaned at the idea. I wished we could stay like this forever, too.

After he pulled out of me and cleaned our mess up with a towel from the bathroom, he helped me out of my top and into the shirt I'd been wearing before. I opened a drawer, searching for a pair of pants, and frowned.

"What is it?" Beckham asked as he worked on taking his chaps off and dressing in his clothes.

"All of my pants are dirty aside from my jeans, and I have no hope they'll button with my stomach this big now."

"So don't wear any."

My head spun to look at him. "What's this surprise, exactly?"

He shrugged. "A surprise."

I let out a little *hmph*. "Fine. If you won't tell me, then maybe I'll just not wear any panties, either."

His body froze mid-tug on his boot. "Parker." There was a warning there.

"What?" I asked innocently. "It's not lingerie."

He shoved his foot the rest of the way into the boot, then straightened. "It's nearly worse."

I mimicked his shrug. "Oh, well."

I tugged on my cowgirl boots, opting for no panties

just to see him riled up while he showed me whatever it was he had in store.

"You know, it's not fair you keep surprising me with things," I said, crossing my arms.

He moved until he was standing in front of me, tilting my chin up with a knuckle. "I like to spoil my girl. Gotta make up for the last ten years somehow, don't I?"

I rolled my eyes, which resulted in him giving me a quick peck on the mouth.

"Come on." He wrapped his hand around mine and led me through the house until we were out the front door and crossing to his dad's horse trailer. It was hooked up to the back of Beckham's truck, but with the overcast sky and tree blocking the way, I couldn't see what was in it from here.

"What did you do?" I questioned as he brought me to a stop at the back of the trailer. He unhooked his hand from mine, moving to open the door.

And when the gap widened, my heart stopped.

Tex—the horse I'd sold when I found out I was pregnant—stood at the far end of the trailer with a big blue bow braided into his mane.

"Beckham." My voice was shock in its purest form.

"He's your baby too, Parker. Wasn't a chance in hell I was going to let you two live apart after you told me."

"But I sold him. He was with a new family." My head couldn't wrap around how unbelievable this was.

"I offered 'em something better."

I turned to face Beckham. "What was that?"

"A horse that wasn't already stolen by the heart of a girl who could change worlds and move mountains."

Tears stung at my eyes as I threw myself at Beckham, pressing my cheek to his chest. "Thank you."

He wrapped his arms around me, pressing a kiss to the top of my head. "Anything for you, Park."

I let him go, hopping into the trailer to cross to Tex. He nickered as I approached, ears perked and eyes homed in on me. I ran a hand down his shoulder before circling my arms around his neck in a hug.

"You're home for good, Texxy."

He pawed at the ground, and at the same time, a little foot kicked inside my stomach.

I let out a watery laugh, nuzzling my head harder against Tex's neck.

I'd never felt like I had a good family growing up, but this one was starting to make up for it without a doubt.

34
PARKER

For the next three days, life was nonstop. I had a doctor's appointment the day after Beckham brought Tex home—one of many before the baby's due date in two months. After that, Beckham spent all day reinforcing the fencing around his property to ensure Tex couldn't get out. I spent as much time with Tex as I could in between all the craziness, soaking in these last moments before the baby came.

The next day, we started painting the room that would soon be the nursery. Beckham had somehow found my Pinterest board full of ideas and insisted on doing the intricate accent wall I'd liked the most. I'd have been fine with something simple, but he wanted me to have everything I dreamed of.

But the real dream wasn't the room or the furniture or the planning. It was watching him stress over covering a nail hole so the wall would be perfect. It was the paint on his shirt and the brush he sometimes held between his teeth. Life with Beckham *was* the dream. And here I was, living it. The sense of awe never seemed to leave.

Today was Sunday, another day to visit Ellis. It had been my second time seeing her, and we'd brought over more food than the three of us could eat to celebrate Christmas together. Beckham got her a new thriller novel, and I had no doubt she was curled up on the couch right now with her nose in that book.

When we got home, before I'd even made it out of the truck, Beckham kissed me, pulling me into his arms cradle-style so I had no choice but to hold onto his neck. My growing belly made it hard to do certain things, and him holding me was one of them. I loved being pregnant and having this time with just me and my baby, but I wanted to do so much more than navigate what was comfortable.

He barely kicked the door to the truck, and the telltale sound of it firmly shutting was nowhere to be heard.

"Beck, the door," I whispered, like someone might hear us and clearly see what we were about to go do.

He shook his head, moving quicker and leaving the door ajar. "No time."

"Why is that?" I asked, teasingly.

He shot me an exasperated look, head tilted to the side. "I can't stay away from you for one more fucking second, Park."

I couldn't help my grin. "Is that so?"

"Your boobs are practically spilling out of that top."

I covered them with an arm, noticing one was most

definitely about to pop out. "They're getting bigger. I can't help it."

He frowned at the sight of me hiding them and reached down to nip at my wrist. "Stop that. I love it."

He quickly fumbled with the key, his impatience making it take longer than it should've, and got us inside the house. With another swift kick, the door slammed shut, and he padded down the hall. Snow clung to his boots, leaving a wet path in their wake.

His uncontainable need for me had my thighs clenching together as heat built in my core. I was already wet—hell, most days, I was *always* wet around him— and just as eager as he was.

Once we passed the bedroom threshold, he set me gently on my feet and shucked off his jacket. I arched a brow as he undressed with a speed I didn't think was possible. His shirt, jeans, underwear, boots, socks—they were all off in less than twenty seconds.

His gaze roamed over my body before he moved in front of me and undressed me all the same. I giggled when my shirt got caught in my necklace, but he quickly rectified the tangle and unclasped my bra in a blink.

His hands framing my face, he tilted my chin up so he could kiss me. His breath was fast and hot on my cheek as he walked me backward toward the bed.

"You're so beautiful," he mumbled against my lips.

"So are you," I murmured back.

He lowered my ass to the comforter, then cradled the back of my head as he laid me flat. His hands coasted down my body, over my breasts and stomach, past my hips, until they gripped behind my knees. He tugged me forward, the fabric of the comforter making my skin restless. I needed more. Needed *him*. Inside of me. On me. All over me.

"Beckham," I pleaded, eyes focused on where he stroked his cock and lined the head up with my entrance.

His gaze was so homed in on our bodies about to join that he couldn't tear his focus away. "Yes, baby."

My hands fisted in the comforter, tugging it like it might bring him closer. His eyes flicked to the movement, noticing my fidgeting, and in one swift thrust, he slid into me.

My head fell back, my body relaxing as soon as he was inside of me.

"Shit, Parker," he hissed, moving deeper and deeper until he bent over me and pressed his lips between my breasts. "I could never get tired of this."

A gasp left me as he slid out and back in.

His lips moved to my nipple, tongue circling the bud.

"Neither could I," I agreed breathlessly. My hips twisted, my back arching as I ached for more of him.

"Tell me what you need, baby," he murmured against my skin. His mustache scratched near my nipple, lighting my nerves on fire.

"You. Just you."

With one hand braced beside my head, he reached down to rub my clit, but with my stomach getting in the way, I was growing frustrated. He filled me, and yet I needed more.

Sensing my inability to sit still, he quickly pulled out

and grabbed my hips. He wasted no time flipping me over until I was on my knees, and with both hands grabbing my waist, he tugged me back until his cock was sliding blissfully back inside of me.

I looked over my shoulder at him as he ran his hand up my spine, then pushed on my shoulder blades until my chest lay flat against the bed. He pounded into me over and over again, each thrust absolutely heaven.

My cheek pressed into the comforter while my fingers tangled in the fabric. He ran a hand over my ass, gripping the flesh before his movements became more rigid.

The hand on my ass slid around my stomach until it stopped between my legs and played with my clit. I moaned, falling deeper into the bed as he drew me closer to the edge.

His cock hit deeper, coiling my core until I was a bomb ready to explode.

He must've felt me tightening around him because he kept that pace, fucking me deeper than before.

I screamed out, turning my face into the mattress as my entire body let go and I came around him.

"That's my good girl," he praised as he stroked my clit harder, faster. "How many times can I make you come, Parker?"

I panted into the sheets, my body strung tight, yet I wanted more.

The pressure of his cock disappeared, and I nearly whimpered, but then he flipped me onto my back. His heated eyes and sweat-glistening chest had me aching all over again.

Our gazes held for a heavy moment before he lowered to his knees and spread my legs apart.

I cursed, our eyes still glued to one another as he dragged his tongue up my center. Remnants of my release stuck to his taste buds, and this time, I *did* whimper.

"You taste so fucking good."

My lashes fluttered as his mouth closed and his throat bobbed on a swallow.

He cocked his head. "Do you want to taste?"

I nodded, almost too eagerly. All that did was make him more feral, his pupils dilating. With his fingers gripping the insides of my thighs, he dragged his tongue up my pussy again.

Mouth still open, he crawled up the bed and offered me his tongue. With no hesitation, I wrapped my lips around it, sucking him into my mouth as his dangling chain bounced against my chin. The taste of my cum had me moaning, the sweet flavor making my pussy throb.

He pulled his tongue out and kissed me hard. My head fell back against the bed as he peppered my skin with kisses, down my neck and over my breasts, until he was back between my legs.

Not even a minute passed of him sucking on my clit before I came again. And again.

Until he finally buried himself in my pussy once more and released every last drop of his orgasm into me.

With our energy spent and our breathing rapid, he

lay beside me and pulled me against him. I rested my cheek on his chest, listening to his heart pound. And right when he started to relax, his heart rate shot up and he dragged a hand down his face.

"Shit."

I sat up, worry instantly taking over. "What's wrong?"

He must've seen the concern in my gaze, because he tugged me back down to him and tightened his arm around me. "I forgot the casserole dish at Ellis's house."

Relief seeped out of me like a flood. "Do you want to go get it?" We needed it for Callan and Sage's small engagement celebration tomorrow. We were making a sweet potato casserole to go with the dinner.

He turned his head to look at the clock. "She should still be up. I don't want to make you go out in the cold, though." A smile lit his lovestruck eyes. "You look so perfect like this."

I returned the smile. "I can take a bath while you're gone."

He turned onto his side, wrapping me in a tighter embrace. My head fit perfectly under his chin, and I hummed in contentment.

"Will you wait for me in there?"

"I'd never pass up the opportunity to take a bath with you."

One of his hands slid down my back to grip my ass. "Good. Because I don't think I'm done with you for tonight."

I laughed, nuzzling deeper into his hold. "I don't think I'm done either."

Reluctantly, he climbed out of bed, and I instantly missed his warmth.

He pulled his phone out of his jeans, presumably to text Ellis that he would be stopping by, before dressing himself.

I frowned. "I liked it better when you were naked and in bed with me."

He smiled that dazzling smile that always made me melt and came around the side of the bed to place a kiss on my forehead. "Trust me, I like that way more."

I sat up, wrapping my arms around his neck to pull him down farther, and pressed my lips to his. "Be safe."

"I will. And stay warm."

I didn't force myself out of the cozy bed until I heard the front door click shut. As soon as I was out of the comfortable embrace of the blankets, goosebumps rose on my skin. Starting the bath would take a minute, and I didn't want to walk around naked, so I grabbed one of his sweatshirts out of the closet and went to the room I used to stay in to tug on a pair of fleece leggings.

Nearly every night since we took the leap into being more, I'd slept in his room. Looking at the guest bed, it felt weird to think we were apart before. Sleeping next to him felt as normal as breathing.

In the bathroom, I turned the warm water on, periodically checking to make sure it wasn't getting too hot. I was overly paranoid about baths while carrying this baby, but I loved them too much to give them up.

While watching the water rise, my stomach let out a low rumble. The more pregnant I became, the more hungry I constantly was. It was both nice because I loved food and terrible because I could rarely do anything these days without needing a snack in my pocket.

After another test of the water temperature, I padded down the hallway toward the kitchen to find something easy to eat in the bath.

I rounded the corner, eyes narrowing on my ankles and wondering if they were swelling. That was yet another paranoia of mine. Deciding it was my mind playing tricks on me, I looked up. And came to a dead stop.

There was a man in the kitchen.

And it wasn't Beckham.

35
PARKER

"Hello, Parker."

Every cell in my body was frozen, my fight-or-flight instincts nowhere to be found as even my heart seemed to stop beating. Disbelief washed over me as I did nothing but stare at the man before me.

"H-how are you here?"

The only reason I recognized him was because of the vertical knife tattoo on his neck. I'd seen my uncle in a picture before, one my parents hadn't wanted me to see. I'd been in their closet, sticking my nose where it didn't belong as I tried to find an extra pair of my mom's shoes so I could play dress-up. No luck with the shoes—I came to find she only owned one pair—but instead I stumbled upon an old photo album.

My dad burned the album that night.

From what I'd briefly gathered from my cousin Axel about his father, my dad had been right to.

When I met Axel for the first time, he'd explained that I was the first extended family member his daughter had ever met. She never knew who her grandfather was, and he planned to keep it that way.

My uncle took a step, moving out from behind the counter to expose the gun tucked into the waistband of his jeans. He had a build similar to my father, but it was apparent he was vastly younger than his brother. His brown hair flaring out from under a ball cap was layered with gray, but he had few wrinkles on his face, giving the impression that the man likely didn't smile much.

"It took a lot of trial and error to finally figure it out. But when your life is on social media"—he shrugged—"anyone can find out anything. Plus, we're family." His toothy smile was unsettling. "Why wouldn't you want to meet your uncle?"

"I don't even know your name." My hand slowly felt for my pocket, and I silently cursed myself for not grabbing my phone.

"My brother never told you?" He quirked his head to the side, inspecting me.

I shook my head.

"Or my son?"

"How do you know I talked to—"

"Because I'm not stupid." His smile fell, replaced with a look of disdain. "All that time traveling the country and you expect me to think you didn't try to find any family? Your father kept you and your mother away from us."

"Because you're dangerous."

His laugh could've rattled the windows. "Dangerous?"

"Axel told me you went to prison for murder." My voice had quieted, like that might keep me from setting the man off.

"It was for a good cause." That haughty smile was back, causing my limbs to begin to shake.

I fisted my hands, debating whether it was worth it to try to run to the bedroom to grab my phone and call for help. But he had a gun, and I had nothing to defend myself with, aside from a wooden door—if I made it that far.

"Rob." He moved toward me, and despite the hostility of the situation, he walked with nauseating smoothness. He held out a scarred hand. "Nice to finally meet you, Parker."

The way he said my name sent shivers up my spine.

I stared at the offering, bile rising up my throat. "Why are you here?"

He waited a few seconds longer before dropping his hand to his side with a sigh. "Right to the nitty gritty, huh? Just like your father. Before he kicked me out of his life, that is."

I simply kept staring, scared to trigger him and unwilling to make conversation.

With another sigh, he went on, "I'm here to get that inheritance."

My brows instantly pulled together in confusion. "What inheritance?"

"From your father's passing."

I tried to remember if any money had ever come up, but the assisted living facility he'd been staying in before he passed had sucked his bank account dry. Anything that was left went toward the funeral expenses. "He didn't have anything to give."

Rob scoffed. "Bullshit. The man was loaded."

I shook my head. "He rarely worked. We…" I trailed off, not wanting to tell him even the tiniest bit about my childhood. But it was also too much to explain. "There's no inheritance."

His eyes dropped to my stomach as he took a step forward, and I instinctively moved back a step.

He stopped and held his hands up in mock surrender. "Woah, now. I don't want to hurt you."

For obvious reasons, I failed to believe that. "There's no money here for you. So please leave."

He clucked his tongue, his head cocking to the side eerily. "Parker, Parker, Parker. I'm not a fool. I've been to prison, and you come to learn a lot of tells there." He moved into my space again, and I forced myself not to flinch. "You're lying."

"My boyfriend will be back soon," I blurted, hoping that would scare him off. I feared if I kept denying the money aspect, it'd only make him angry.

"Roads are icy. He'll be gone for a while."

I swallowed the panic building in my stomach. I was alone, pregnant, with no weapon or phone. Rob wasn't just here to grab some money and go. He'd brought a gun for a reason.

My hands covered my stomach, fearing the worst.

But I'd never let anyone hurt my baby, no matter how hard they tried. His motivations might be strong, but my instinct to protect this baby was unsurpassable.

Rob seemed to think hard on something as he narrowed his eyes on me, then he shrugged and spun around, surveying the space. "You'll be coming with me then."

My heart nearly fell to the floor. "What?"

He swiveled back toward me, and this time, when he faced me, he held the gun in his hand. He gestured the tip of the barrel at my bare feet. "Put some shoes on."

"I—" I blinked. Shook my head. "I don't understand."

"If you're claiming there's no inheritance, then I'll just get money from the state for your baby." He made a fake pouty face. "Poor Parker died in childbirth, and her only remaining family has to raise the baby. The state will throw money at me like it's fucking raining."

I didn't bring up the fact that if that were to happen, Beckham would likely raise my son. Or if it really worked in the sense that my child went to family, Axel would get him before any felon did. But I didn't know the logistics, and I wasn't about to waste time trying to figure that out —because it wouldn't be happening.

My head shook back and forth. "No. That will never happen."

His eyes snapped to mine a moment before his gun followed suit. "I said put some shoes on. Otherwise, you're going barefoot, and the snow is about six inches deep right about now. Probably deeper where we're going."

I had to force my breathing to calm as I tried to think of a way out of this. But with the gun, and his adamance...I was stuck.

The longer we stared each other down, the more tempted he looked to pull the trigger and settle for robbing the place.

Finally, I snapped. "Okay." My hands flexed, fingers stiff with anxiety. "Okay. I'll go with you. But my boots are down the hall." I stepped back in that direction, and he followed my movements.

"Don't even think of trying anything," he warned.

I didn't dare turn my back on him as I moved down the hallway. I went into Beckham's room first, pretending to search the floor for my snow boots. But I knew they were in the guest room.

I scanned the ground for my pants, knowing my phone was in the pocket. Rob stood in the doorway, gun still aimed at me. I bent, reaching for my leggings, and quickly swiped the device and slid it in the front pocket of my sweatshirt.

"That's not fucking boots," Rob sneered before something hit me in the back and I went toppling forward.

I rolled to prevent hurting my stomach, but the pain in my back had me sucking in a breath. I looked up to find his foot outstretched. He'd fucking kicked me.

His crazed eyes darted around my figure until he settled on my stomach. Right as he lunged, I screamed, trying to kick at him, but he was stronger, and he shoved between my legs with little less than a fight.

I shoved at him as his hand slid into my pocket and

grabbed my phone, pulling it free. My body froze as he sat back and crouched before me.

He shook the device back and forth in my face, *tsk*ing me. "Calling anyone will only succeed in promising their death. Is that what you want?"

I swallowed, too scared to even scoot back an inch. "No."

As if that answer satisfied him, he stood and pocketed the phone. Despite losing it on my person, the sight of him keeping it and not tossing it aside sent a glimmer of hope flickering to life beneath the fear enveloping me.

Beckham had asked me to turn my location on for him after I'd told him about the comments and messages, and thankfully, I'd done it. Wherever that phone was, he'd find it. Find me.

Rob stood, towering over me with the gun aimed at my forehead. "Last chance to get your fucking shoes or you're losing your goddamn toes to frostbite."

His words hit me with the realization that he didn't want me dead or injured. If he hurt me, I could lose the baby, and that would only result in him getting no money from the state for whatever fucked-up childcare scheme he was conjuring in his head.

He needed me alive.

I could use that to my advantage and possibly get away from him somewhere outside. I had more chances of hiding somewhere out there, in the dark during a snowstorm, than I did in here.

"Okay." I carefully pushed to a stand, using more

effort than usual due to the ache in my back. "I think they're in the other room."

He nudged the gun in the direction of the door, and I moved, making no other pit stops as I went into the guest room and tugged on a pair of wool socks and my snow boots. Once they were laced, he grabbed me by my upper arm and yanked me toward the hall. The water still running in the bath assured me that at least Beckham would know something bad had happened— that I hadn't simply left.

"You're taking your sweet time, aren't you?" Rob gritted out, practically spitting the words in my ear.

I said nothing because he was right.

He grunted like he knew as much. "Try any more stunts and I'll have to put a shiny little bullet right between your boyfriend's eyes."

Bile rose in my throat again, the sick feeling combining with the urge to fight and do everything in my power to prevent that from happening.

Once outside, he led me around the house and out into the field. I was thankful we weren't on the side where Tex's pasture was, and that no harm would come to him.

The frosty bite from the storm had my limbs shaking instantly, my sweatshirt and leggings doing nothing to keep out the cold as snow fell around us in a thick sheet of white, sticking to my hair and exposed skin.

Minutes passed, and I had begun to wonder if his brilliant plan was to walk somewhere when a cluster of metal began taking form a few feet away. Visibility was so poor, I didn't realize it was an ATV until we were basically right on top of it.

Rob searched our surroundings—what little he could see of them—and shoved me toward the vehicle. "Get on."

I covered my hands with the sleeves of my sweatshirt and shoved off the few inches of snow that had accumulated on the seat. Of all the nights to be kidnapped by a crazed uncle, it just had to be during the worst fucking blizzard this season.

Stiff from the cold, I managed to swing my leg over and perch on the very back of the seat. I didn't want to touch this man in any capacity, but I didn't have a choice on this small of an ATV.

He tucked the gun into the waistband of his pants before climbing on in front of me with ease. The silence of the snow was interrupted by the engine and a distant whinny. He took off, heading away from the house.

The tires slid with each turn, and I wondered if he even knew where he was going. But when the pines started getting thicker and closer together, and the snow got progressively deeper, I knew he was heading for the mountains.

"Where are you taking me?" I asked, forcing my voice louder than the engine. I had to squint my eyes against the snow battering my face, and by this point, my clothes were soaked through and freezing me worse than before.

He ignored me, pushing the ATV faster.

"I'll get hypothermia," I shouted, curling in on myself

more, like maybe I could keep my baby warm even if I froze.

"Can't you see I'm busy?" he yelled over his shoulder, going harder on the throttle.

I snapped my mouth shut, not wanting to waste my energy while also not wanting to anger him further for the fear he'd push the vehicle too much and it'd sputter out—or worse, we'd crash.

By the time we finally came to a stop, I was frozen through. I could barely lift my leg to get off the ATV, and my hands were stuck to my elbows in an attempt to hold in any body heat I could. When I moved too slow, Rob grabbed my arm, tugging me behind him.

"Rob, please. I can get you money. I can—"

"Don't try to plead with me now, Parker. Didn't your dad ever teach you that begging only makes you look pathetic?"

We stopped before a wooden door, snow clinging to every surface possible. I arched my neck back, snowflakes falling into my eyes as I realized he'd brought us to a cabin.

He used a key to remove a padlock then moved inside, not looking back to see if I followed. He didn't have to—I had nowhere else to go. The cabin was the only place to get out of the snow, and if I tried to run now, I'd freeze to death.

Hell, even if I didn't run, I'd likely suffer the same fate.

My fingers were completely numb, my lips surely blue, and when I tried to sniffle, it hurt. The only dry spot on the lower half of my body was my feet, thanks to my boots, but even my toes were cold. So long as I could still walk, though, I had to have hope.

"I'm going to get a fire started," Rob muttered, more to himself than to me. He moved a few things around, mumbling under his breath, and then slammed the front door behind him as he presumably went to find firewood.

With the amount of snow outside, his luck was minimal—which meant mine was, too.

I only hoped he'd succumb to the elements before I did.

Or else I'd be truly, utterly fucked. As if I weren't already.

36
BECKHAM

Despite the low visibility and freezing temperatures, I let out a sigh of content as I drove. All I could think about was Parker with her legs spread and her cheeks flushed as I worshipped her body the way she deserved. Driving slower due to the road conditions was torture. Every second away from her had my heart in a vise, the growing distance pressing it tighter and tighter around the beating organ.

I was thankful when I pulled up to Ellis's house and found her bundled in a blanket on her porch, the clean casserole dish waiting beside her. She stood as I walked as fast as I could up the steps and met her.

I took the glass dish from her. "Thanks, Ellis. Sorry again. I should probably buy a few more of these."

She waved me off. "Don't worry about it. The book hadn't gotten good yet." She shot me a wink as she held the book up with her other hand before setting it on the little table.

I chuckled. "I hope you mean with the action."

She shrugged, burying her hands in the pockets of her wool cardigan. "Something like that. Are you going to be okay getting home? The storm's getting worse." She looked past my shoulder at the snow falling in a thick white sheet in front of my truck's headlights.

I followed her line of sight, seeing the flakes already piling around my tires. "I'll be alright. I've driven in worse."

She shot me a disapproving look. "Of course you have. Let me know when you get home, alright?"

I dipped my chin. "I will. See you in two weeks." I started moving back toward the stairs when Ellis spoke up.

"Beckham."

I paused, one hand on the railing, and looked over my shoulder at her. "Yeah?"

"Do you love her?"

There was not a second of hesitation when I answered, "I do."

Her shoulders loosened as if my answer was the key to all her problems, and it hit me that she'd never get to see Garrett marry or have children of his own.

A soft smile lifted the corners of her mouth, and she wrapped her arms tight around herself after waving me off again. "Get on home to her then."

Warmth spread throughout my chest. Instead of heading down the steps, I spun around and pulled Ellis to my chest with an arm around her shoulders. I pressed a kiss to the top of her head, eyes squeezing shut. "I'm sorry."

She stood there quietly, but she didn't need to speak for me to know all the thoughts bouncing around in her head. Ones she often didn't want to think, because sometimes it was easier that way.

After a few seconds of holding her, she set a palm on my chest and gently nudged me away. She tried to hide it, but I heard her sniffle.

Without another word passing between us, I carefully navigated the steps before getting back in my truck. I waited until she disappeared inside to pull out of her driveway and head home.

Ellis and I shared a lot of memories of Garrett, and with that, we shared the grief, too. She mourned him in different ways than I did, but I could always tell the days when it got to her the most. A parent should never outlive their child. The hole that was left behind was devastating, but she still smiled. Still spoke about him like he was still around, just in a different space. She likely heard him in the wind, too. Heard his laughter down the halls and felt his presence like I did.

After a slow drive home, I rolled up the driveway, my bigger tires digging through the snow until I came to a stop. I killed the headlights and shut off the engine, grabbing the dish on the passenger seat before getting out and heading up to the house.

I stomped my boots on the mat before turning the handle on the door, but as I did, I froze.

My forehead creased.

I'd locked this door when I left.

I shook my head. Parker had likely unlocked it when she heard my truck coming up the drive.

After I was inside, I slowly closed the door behind me and scanned the room. Something didn't feel right, yet everything looked in place. Even the bath water was running down the hall, which meant Parker was simply waiting for me. Maybe she was refilling it with more warm water after it'd gone cold.

With snow slowly melting and dripping off my boots, I set the casserole dish on the counter and headed down the hall.

"Sorry that took so long," I said as I rounded the corner for the bathroom—but I immediately froze when I stepped in a puddle of water.

The bath was overflowing, and Parker was nowhere to be found.

Without thinking to turn off the faucet, I ran for our room.

Empty.

I checked the guest room, then bolted back for my bathroom. Every damn spot where she might have fallen or been hiding was empty.

"Parker?" I yelled out, and when only the sound of running water responded, I knew for sure she wasn't here. Something was wrong. *Very* wrong. And that fact sat in the pit of my stomach like a five-ton boulder. My hands flexed and unflexed more times than I could count, that inner part of me needing to do something but not knowing where the fuck to start.

"Fuck," I gritted out as I darted into the bathroom, boots splashing in the water pooling on the floor, and shut off the faucet. I had no time to pull the plug on the drain without getting my sleeve wet, and if she wasn't in here, that meant she was somewhere out there.

The idea that she might be cold and lost out in this storm, or worse, taken by some fucking maniac, had panic coursing through me.

I ran out of the bathroom, grabbing my pistol and shotgun from the gun safe in my closet, then beelined outside. I left the front door unlocked in case she came back because, with her truck sitting out front, I doubted she had any keys on her, and I didn't want her stuck out here freezing longer than she had to.

Before getting in my truck, I scanned the snow for prints. In the direction of her car, there were none, but the snow was coming down so fast, if there had been any tracks, they'd likely have disappeared by now—depending on how long she'd been gone. It only made me feel more lost, more helpless, and when it came to Parker, that wasn't a fucking option.

Realization dawned on me, and I tucked my shotgun under my arm and yanked out my phone. I clicked her contact, then navigated to the screen where I could see her location. The few seconds it took to load felt like an eternity as every worst-case scenario flew through my head.

Her profile picture—one I'd snapped at the diner of her laughing and biting down on a cherry—popped up in a small circle just east of me, up in the mountain. I zoomed in, confused as to why she'd be up there and how she'd gotten there so fast. It'd taken me a little under an hour to get to Ellis's and back, and that hike on foot would have taken at least five times that.

That meant I wasn't looking for footprints. I was searching for tire tracks. Or a snowmobile. And with her truck still being here, that meant she wasn't alone. Someone had taken my Parker into the fucking mountains during a snowstorm. Ideas of what I'd do to whoever took her flew through my mind, the possibilities endless. But only one outcome was for certain with all of them: they weren't making it out of this alive.

I did one more quick look around the other side of the house and stopped when I came upon exactly what I was looking for. The distance between the tracks was too narrow to be a car or truck, which meant they were on something like an ATV.

That gave me some sort of idea of what I was looking for, at least.

I sprinted for my truck, tossing the shotgun on the passenger seat, and fired up the engine. Squinting through my windshield and the rapidly moving wipers, I followed the path of the faint tire tracks. With the snow falling fast, the tread imprints were quickly disappearing, so I pressed harder on the gas.

I should've been more careful after Parker told me about the comments and messages. I shouldn't have left her alone. I should have installed cameras, reported it to the police, done everything I didn't do because I was so preoccupied with everything else.

That was my fault, and no one else's. The guilt that churned my stomach would have to wait, because the only thing I had space for in my mind right now was finding my girl and our son.

As the trees became thicker and the hills turned steeper, I had no choice but to get out and continue on foot. I killed the engine and the lights, making sure I had both my guns before exiting the truck. I locked it before navigating the deepening snow, being sure to stick close to the trees in case I came across anyone.

The forest was silent save for the howl of a wolf in the distance. I trekked for what felt like hours, my fingers numb on the shotgun as I walked. I barely felt the bite of cold with the adrenaline pumping through me.

I checked my phone every few minutes to make sure I was still heading in the right direction, and finally, what felt like an hour later, I spotted a cabin in the distance.

A dim light flickered through a tiny, snow-filled window, and a plume of smoke billowed out of the chimney. Another glance at my screen confirmed that at least her phone was in there, but whether she had it or someone else did, I wasn't sure. That was exactly why I hadn't tried to call it, for fear they'd turn it off, and I might lose my only chance of finding her.

I double-checked that my phone was on silent before pocketing it. Approaching the cabin, I made sure to stay out of sight of the window. There was no hope in covering my boot prints—not with snow this deep—so I tried to keep myself out of the flicker of light as best I could.

I pressed my back flat to the side of the house, inhaling a steadying breath. If she was in there, and someone was with her, I had to act fast while being careful not to let her get hurt.

I forced away any nerves that threatened to creep up. Parker would be okay. Our son would be okay.

I'd get them out of this.

Carefully, I crept around to the front of the cabin, ducking my head beneath the window as I passed it. Voices filtered out from the door, and I paused beside it, listening.

"Axel always asked why we never had family." A man was speaking to her. One whose voice I didn't recognize. But I remembered Parker telling me about a cousin by the name of Axel.

Had someone in her family taken her? Was he the one who had been stalking her online?

When the man was met with only silence, he continued, "He always knew it was because of my brother. That Clarence was too scared."

"Maybe because you're a felon," Parker muttered.

My heart ceased beating, my grip tightening on the gun. Parker was talking, which meant she had to be okay.

Please, fuck, let her be okay.

The man ignored her comment and continued. "So imagine my surprise when I found out you hung out with my boy. He hated you growing up. Thought you were too privileged to hang out with trash."

"And who made him think that's what he was?"

A sprinkle of pride filtered through me at her boldness, even in a time of danger. But she needed to be careful. Unless she thought he wouldn't hurt her. But why?

"I don't lie to family."

"No, that much was obvious when you said you wanted to take my baby for money."

Her words only intensified my urge to blow the fucker's head off. He'd never so much as get the chance to touch my family. Not if I had anything to do with it.

"Desperate times call for desperate measures. Isn't that what they say?"

I'd heard enough.

No one threatened my girl and got the privilege of continuing to breathe the same air as her.

37
PARKER

Even with the fire crackling in the corner, my teeth still chattered profusely. From the cold or the fear, I wasn't sure. My fingers were very slowly regaining feeling as the warmth from the fire thawed my bones, but my clothes were still soaked. I didn't have much faith they'd dry anytime soon, but at least for now, I was out of the worst of the storm.

"You're so desperate that you're okay with hurting your own family?" I asked Rob from where I sat on the floor, as close to the fire as I felt comfortable with him tending to it every few minutes.

Rob scoffed. "I barely touched you."

"You didn't have to. I'm going to freeze to death regardless of how you treat me."

He stood from his seat by the door, walking over to the fire and grabbing the poker. He moved a log, causing embers to fly every which way. He'd done this so many times, I lost count. Nerves seemed to be getting the best of him, and he couldn't seem to sit still because of it. "You have a perfectly good fire right here."

"The storm will only get worse, and temperatures will drop even more as night passes. If your genius plan is to hold me here until I deliver my son, you're a fucking idiot. A fire won't do shit once it hits the negatives."

He abandoned the fire poker in the flames, taking two large steps until he was directly in front of me. He grabbed my chin before I could move away, squeezing until pain bloomed.

"You think you can call me an idiot?" he bellowed, spit flying from his lips and spraying my skin.

My stiff fingers wrapped around his wrist, but he was unmovable. Tears welled in my eyes as he only tightened his grip on me. "Rob, you're hurting me."

"Maybe you need to be fucking hurt. Teach you a fucking lesson."

The door to the cabin slammed open right as he finished his sentence. In one swift movement, Rob had my back to his chest and his arm around my neck.

Beckham stood in the doorway, snow swirling around his bulky form, his shotgun aimed at Rob. With the position we were in, I knew he wouldn't take the shot. He'd never risk me.

Which meant we were screwed.

"Let her go," Beckham gritted out, eyes quickly darting to me before refocusing on Rob. The howl of wind behind him had me shivering.

"This your fucking boyfriend?" Rob seethed in my ear.

My frantic breathing puffed clouds of white before me, my limbs a shaking mess. All I wanted was to fall to my knees and sob. My baby didn't deserve any of this stress, yet here I was, in danger and unable to protect him.

I was failing already.

"Beckham, please." My voice broke, tears building so heavily in my eyes that it felt like I was looking through a glass bowl. "I don't want him to hurt you."

He held the gun a little tighter, eyes narrowing on Rob. "Let her go, or I'll put a bullet through your fucking head."

Rob's brusque chuckle had me flinching. "You won't risk it."

Beckham took a step to the left, his gaze darting down my body for a split second. Rob moved in the opposite direction, keeping me tight in his hold.

"You think I won't?" Beckham questioned.

"I *know* you won't."

They both moved a few more feet, rotating us in a circle. But now we were farther from the fire, which meant the cold only became worse with the door wide open.

"Lower your gun and I won't hurt her," Rob instructed, and it was then that I noticed he held a knife to my side.

I hadn't felt the sharp bite of the blade with my focus on Beckham and making sure he wouldn't get hurt, but now I realized why Beckham had briefly looked down.

"He won't hurt me, Beckham. He needs m—"

Rob tightened his arm around my neck, and I arched onto aching toes to force in a breath.

Beckham's entire body went rigid, his jacket looking like it was about to tear from the size of his muscles. He needed to fight, to get me to safety, and he was quickly finding that he might be losing.

A tear rolled down my cheek as I dug my nails into Rob's arm, but it was no use through the thick fabric of his coat.

Beckham noted my struggle, pain etching into the depths of his eyes, and it almost hurt me worse to see the helplessness in his gaze.

He slowly bent at the knees, lowering the shotgun until it was lying on the ground. When he stood, hands clenched at his sides, he toed the gun a few inches away. "Alright. It's down."

Rob subtly bobbed side to side on his feet, swaying me with him as if his nerves were eating him alive now. "Now walk outside, go back to that shitty fucking town, and forget all about her."

Beckham's eyes met mine, a determination there I'd never seen before. "Not happening." He took one more step until his back was to the fire.

Rob shook with his rage. "It's not a fucking option."

"You and I agree, then." Beckham's gaze held mine, and I wanted nothing more than to be in his arms, warm and with all of this behind us. "There's no option when it comes to her safety."

One second, Beckham's hand was moving, and the next, the fire poker was swinging our way.

Rob screamed, his hold on me dropping, and I nearly fell to the floor. I caught myself, tripping across the small space until Beckham grabbed my arms and pulled me behind him.

The moment Beckham's hands were on me and I clutched the jacket covering his back, thousands of pounds of fear physically lifted off my chest.

Shouted curses filled the room as Beckham aimed a second gun at Rob, who was clutching his neck. The fire poker lay on the floor by his feet, something wet stuck on the end. When his hands shifted, I noticed a gruesome burn sliced across his flesh.

"You do this, you're ruining a man's life!" Rob shouted as a last resort to save himself.

"Better you than my family," Beckham ground out.

Rob's glare deepened, his promise of vengeance practically wafting off him like a cologne. Then his gaze fell to the floor, directly where the shotgun lay between us. Panic overtook every sense in my body. If Rob grabbed it—

"Cover your ears," Beckham commanded, his bicep flexing under his jacket as he adjusted his grip on the pistol.

As soon as I did as he said, a shot rang out. My body threatened to curl in on itself, my forehead resting on Beckham's shoulder blade as I squeezed my eyes shut. I was scared to check if he'd killed him, but even more scared that I'd imagined us getting out of this unscathed. What if Rob had shot Beckham and then got his grips back on me?

I jumped when something landed on my waist, but when the comforting warmth and size of Beckham's hand registered, a bit of the tension in my body eased.

His muscles shifted as he tucked the gun into the waistband of his jeans, then he turned and pulled me into his arms, blocking my view of Rob.

"Is he..." I whispered into his chest.

I felt him nod as he held me tighter. He didn't need to explain why he'd chosen to go that far rather than injure him. Rob wouldn't have stopped, and though Beckham might not know his entire history, he could tell as much. No one abducted someone—especially a family member—if they didn't intend to get what they wanted out of it.

Beckham didn't release me as he pulled out his phone and made a call.

My focus narrowed to the crackling of the flames and the embers it spit out. How the fire swallowed the branches and sizzled as the heat met the moisture from the snow that once clung to them. I couldn't see— couldn't hear—anything other than that.

"Parker."

I looked up to find Beckham staring at me with a crease between his brows. He was no longer on the phone.

"Did he hurt you?"

I shook my head, then remembered how Rob had kicked me back at the house. How he'd grabbed my chin and squeezed. My fingers moved on their own accord, brushing against my sore jaw.

Beckham tilted my chin up slightly, angling my head

to the side to get a better look. The lethal look in his eyes only turned more severe. "He touched you."

My hands fisted in the front of his coat and tugged on the material. I opened my mouth to reassure him, but after all I'd endured, I really wasn't sure if I could say I was okay.

A single look at my clothes had him moving. One second, his jacket was zipped. The next, he was shucking it off, wrapping it around my shoulders, and tugging it closed at the front. He held me tighter, inching us closer to the fire.

His gaze moved around the room like he was searching for something, then he briefly let me go to close the door to the cabin.

He peeked out the small window. "Was there anyone with him?"

My arms wrapped around my torso, missing Beckham's warmth. "No."

He turned, eyes looking crazed and worried. He crossed back to me, instantly folding me back into his embrace. "Who was he? I heard you two talking, and he sounded like family, but I thought..."

"He's Axel's father. My uncle. I never met him growing up, and I guess that was for good reason." I forced myself not to glance over at the body lying on the ground mere feet from us. "Axel had briefly told me he wasn't good news, but I never would have expected him to come after me for money."

"Money?"

I explained what Rob had told me he wanted out of

this. "But it was no secret my dad was poor," I added. "Even if they weren't part of each other's lives, they didn't exactly have the best upbringing, and that seemed to carry over into both their adult lives."

"Maybe he thought you got money out of the land." His hands rubbed up and down my back. "He was desperate. But all I know for certain is that he wasn't getting out of this alive."

"I just... I don't—" I shook my head, nuzzling into his chest. The man had never met me, and suddenly he wanted to steal my inheritance? Take my baby? All for some cash? None of it made sense.

"Shh," Beckham hushed. "Don't waste any more energy on him right now, okay? Focus on me."

I hadn't even realized I was shivering until I forced every thought of Rob into a locked box in my mind.

"Feel the fire?" Beckham asked quietly. His strained biceps seemed to be fighting a tremble of their own.

"Your jacket—"

"Keep it, baby. I want you warm."

My lips rolled together in a tight line in an attempt to hold in the choked sob climbing my throat. My adrenaline was waning, and with it came the biting cold and the realization of everything that had happened.

"He wanted our baby, Beckham."

His entire body turned to stone, and I swore I heard his jaw crack over the popping of the fire.

"He was going to hold me here until I delivered." I trailed off, thinking of every worst-case scenario if that had happened. "Is he okay?"

Beckham knew I meant the baby.

"He's okay," he murmured into my hair. "He has to be."

Because it wasn't only me who loved this baby anymore. It was Beckham, his family, Ellis. Even Wyatt. I'd dreamed of having other people caring for him and loving him as much as I did, and now it was true. I just needed him to be okay so he could see it every day of his life.

I nodded against Beckham, repeating his words over and over again in my head.

At some point, he had lowered me to the floor, and I'd shut my eyes in his lap. I wasn't sure how long I was asleep, but the sound of a distant motor had me shooting up, panic slicing through me like a knife.

I gasped for air, my heart a blistering thump in my chest as I blinked my eyes into focus, willing the heavy sleep out of my mind.

Where was he? Would he hurt me this time? Try to take my baby again?

Beckham's hand found mine, and I jumped, swiveling my head to face him.

"Parker, it's me. He can't hurt you. You're okay."

His reassuring tone and the concern in his eyes had me releasing a heavy breath. My head hung while my heart feebly tried to calm itself.

The revving outside turned louder, like whoever it was was getting closer. Beckham stood, bringing me with him, and I stayed behind his back as he crossed to the window to peek out.

"It's the police," he muttered, breath fogging up the glass.

That must've been who he'd called. I hadn't had the right mind to wonder or even ask.

Beckham opened the door, and the gust of frigid air that came with it had me wrapping my free arm around myself. I wasn't ready to be cold again. All I wanted was Beckham's bed and his arms wrapped around me, his sweet kisses and reassuring murmurs lulling me into a deep sleep.

I didn't want to be out here, frozen and scared and unsure what our outcome was.

If I lost my baby—

As if the prospect of help had my strength slipping through my control, I broke. I held Beckham's hand tighter, pressing my forehead to his shoulder blade as a sob wracked through me.

He spun at the sound, his arms wrapping me in a safe cocoon.

"Does something hurt? Is it the baby?" Beckham attempted to calm his frantic tone, but even with all his willpower, the panic at the thought of me or this baby not being okay was too much to contain.

I shook my head because that was all I could do.

Of all the times I thought I could do everything on my own, this wasn't one of them.

Help was here, and I was so damn relieved.

38
BECKHAM

If the ride back to the ambulance had been grueling, this was pure torture.

Search and rescue had scaled the mountain on snowmobiles to find us, and after ensuring Parker was well enough to get her down for medical help, I'd slowly started losing my grip on my ability to stay calm.

Adrenaline seeped out of me like water through a crack in a dam—though all my defenses tried to hold it together, there was no stopping the flood of regret. Guilt. Pain. Heartache.

In the hospital, when Parker was taken back without me, I broke. I sat in the chair in the waiting room, ripping my hair out and watching through watery eyes as each tear puddled on the linoleum floor. My clothes were soaked, I still felt cold, and the racing thoughts were painstakingly grueling.

I'd talked to countless officers, explaining what had

happened multiple times. They checked the story, checked it again. There was no hiding the fact that I'd murdered someone, and the only reason I believed I wasn't behind bars was because I fessed up to it on the initial phone call.

Parker was scared when they forced us apart. She had to take tests to be sure she and the baby were okay, and I had to answer what felt like hundreds of questions. Recounting the events was like being on autopilot at this point.

The fear in Parker's eyes. The gunshot. The blood.

There was so much blood.

I'd dealt with all types of injuries on the ranch and delivered so many foals and calves I lost count—but the blood of a person? Someone I'd killed? It stained my mind more than it did the rug in that cabin.

But I'd do it again.

There were no limits I wouldn't cross to keep Parker and our baby safe.

Safe.

I had to focus on that. We were okay now. We weren't standing in that cabin, the two of us freezing and scared and facing potential death.

We were safe.

But I wouldn't breathe until I knew our son was okay, too.

Parker was so strong, doing her best to keep it together for everyone's sake, but I knew her mind was spinning just as much as mine was.

"Beckham Bronson?"

I was on my feet in a blink, focusing on the nurse in blue scrubs ahead of me.

"That's me."

"You can come back now," she said. I tried to read her features to see if anything was wrong. Did we lose the baby, and that was why she hadn't smiled? Were they both hurt, and she didn't want to get my hopes up?

The walk to Parker's hospital room was longer than that trek up the mountain, and each echo of my boots on the floor had my heart skipping beats and speeding up all at the same time.

The nurse slowed and gestured to a room. I wasted no time slipping past her, not stopping until I was at Parker's side.

The tears in her eyes had me leaning over her sitting form to kiss her forehead, then her hair, and finally her cheek. My hand instinctively rested on her bump, hoping and *needing* to feel our baby kick.

"Are you okay?" I murmured into her hair.

She nodded, and I pulled back enough to look her in the eyes. I tucked her hair behind her ears and cupped her cheeks, swiping a rolling tear away. "We're okay."

Air rushed out of me, and there was no stopping the flood. I wrapped my arms around her shoulders, tugging her to me as I kissed the top of her head over and over and over again.

"You're both okay," I whispered, needing to hear it again.

Her head bobbed and she sniffled into my shirt.

Relief had never been a more blissful feeling than in

this moment. All the guilt, the pain, the *what-ifs*—they melted away until there was nothing but Parker in my arms.

"Beck, baby."

I pulled away just enough to meet her gaze, and when I did, she reached up and gently wiped my cheeks.

"We're okay," she said again.

"I know—" I swallowed, forcing the lump of emotion away. "It killed me, Parker. All of this. You possibly being hurt. When I found you were gone, I—I thought—" I shook my head.

Her hand snaked around my head to the back of my neck, and she pulled me close until we were nose-to-nose. "I was scared, too."

"I know, baby. And I'm so sorry."

"But you found me," she reassured in a whisper, and the faintest smile spread across her lips. It was forced, but it was enough.

"I'll always find you, Parker. Fate works that way for a reason."

"For the two of us, it always will." This time, her smile was genuine. Bigger. Beautiful. "Don't you know we can't be apart?"

I grinned, and every worry melted away with the sight of our love shining in her eyes. "I've been waiting for you to catch up."

Then I kissed her.

Slowly. All-consumingly. And I didn't let her go until the doctor came in to go over the tests with me. Parker already knew all the information aside from a few of the blood tests, but other than them wanting to continue monitoring the baby's heart rate and have us track the baby's kick counts at home, Parker and our baby were in the clear.

We discussed signs to look for in case the baby declined for any reason, and set up a weekly appointment to be on the safe side since Parker's due date was fast approaching. They kept her there until the early hours of the morning, offering multiple times to take a look at me. I'd refused, but Parker finally insisted I at least get my vitals checked.

I was fine, and by the time I was done, we were being discharged.

Parker was wheeled out, and while I walked, I thought of how we'd be doing this same walk not too long from now, but with our son in our arms. That had the emotions hitting all over again, because we should've never been here. We should have been safe at my house, soaking up some quality time as just the two of us.

When we walked through the waiting room on our way out and my family was there waiting for us, neither of us could hold back our tears. We were exhausted, crashing from the night's events, and as always, the Bronsons were there. To hold us when we felt like crumbling, to bring gifts and food and make sure we were okay.

I watched as Lettie, Sage, Brandy, and Oakley wrapped Parker in their embrace, all the girls crying and smiling and squished together, and I'd never felt more full.

Parker had a family now, and it was all I'd ever dreamed of.

A family with me.

———

As exhausted as we were, the second thing Parker and I did when we got home was strip down and take a warm bath together. First, she'd wanted to see Tex, so I let her have her moment with him. The horse offered a sort of comfort no person could provide—not even me.

Now, I ran circles over her belly as her head lay back on my chest, her eyes closed and her body slowly relaxing further with each breath.

The sudden burn of oncoming tears would hit every so often, but I did my best to hold them back. Parker was safe. I had no reason to worry any longer. Her uncle was dead, and with that, the threat on her life was gone. There was no longer the question of who had been stalking her social media.

And still...

"Beck."

My murmured name had me snapping my gaze from the wall down into twin hazel eyes. Ones I dreamed of often.

"You're spacing out, baby." Parker's hand left the water, bubbles sticking to her glistening skin as she cupped my cheek. "Talk to me."

We held each other's stare as I tried to think of words that wouldn't bring her down. The truth was, I was beyond relieved that she was okay. That no serious harm had come to her or our baby. But my guilt still held the pain she endured, layering itself with the fear of losing the love of my life. It was suffocating.

"I just keep thinking to myself, what if I hadn't found you?" My throat was closing, my eyes quickly burning. "What if you were gone forever just like—"

I couldn't say his name. Not in the context of him never coming back.

Parker twisted until she was on her knees between my legs, both hands now pressed to my cheeks. "I know it's hard to love after loss. It's hard to open your heart to the possibility of being hurt again. Losing *anyone* is paralyzing." Her thumbs moved of their own accord, grounding me as they swept across my skin. "My first thought when I found out I was pregnant was that I was scared *I* would die, and my child would grow up without a mom. I know what it's like to mourn, and maybe my version of it is different than yours. I mourned while my parents were very much alive and breathing. I constantly thought, why aren't my parents like Beckham's? Why do they not love me enough to change the environment they brought me into?"

Her eyes turned glassy, but she continued after a heavy breath. "But regardless of the way I was raised, or the fear I hold that I could fail my child, I know I'm strong enough to change the future." Her smile was uplifting, but still masked a heavy sadness. "You changed my life, Beckham. In seventh grade, in letting me experience the world instead of selfishly keeping me in Bell Buckle, in taking me in when you didn't have to, in making the decision to *love* me again." She shook her head, shifting so she was a little closer. "What my tired brain is trying to get at here is... You found me. I am here." Her eyes turned stern, hard. "I will never leave your side. You may think history is going to repeat itself to everyone you hold close since you lost him, but I promise you, there is nothing—*no one*—on this entire goddamn planet that can take me from you."

Every word had my heart pinching and melting at the same time. Right when I thought I couldn't fall any deeper, I found myself plunging off a cliff and utterly speechless at the capacity in which I was in love with Parker Summerhill.

She was right—Garrett might not be here with me, and I might still be trying to find ways to cope day to day, but I saved Parker.

She wasn't going anywhere. Not if I had anything to do about it.

"You're right, Parker. I—"

She shook her head, her thumb tugging on my bottom lip in an attempt to shush me. "Kiss me."

There was no hesitation as I leaned forward and plunged my fingers into her hair, rocking her forward. Water splashed over the sides of the tub, and our lips collided.

Within seconds, I was slipping inside of her, thrusting up into her so she wouldn't have to expel more energy. Her moans drove me insane, tipping me over the edge. I spilled every last drop into her sweet pussy as she came around my cock, and as her forehead hit my shoulder, I made a vow to give her and our baby the best life they could ever dream of.

If I could do one thing in Garrett's honor, one thing to make my own parents proud, and one thing to change Parker's life, it'd be that.

Love may be a word other people throw around in desperate times, meaningless and empty. But that was never the case with Parker. Our love stemmed from crispy Dr. Peppers, cheap Christmas lights, and a warm bed.

Life didn't get much better than this.

39

PARKER

EPILOGUE

I wiped a glob of red paint on my denim overalls after the pesky liquid had dripped all over the white base of the bookshelf. The breath I released sent a stray strand of my hair flying into the air, only for it to come back down and further tickle my nose.

"I'm not good at this," I pouted.

Beckham looked over at me from where he was working on the other side of the unit. "Yes, you are."

I frowned and shot a hand out at the murder-like scene on the shelf. "I can't make this up."

He cocked his head to the side, chewing on his lip like he was hiding a smile.

I was opening my mouth to call him out for having to hold in his laugh when he said, "So we'll wipe it, let it dry, and paint over it with more white. Easy fix." He set his paint brush on the plastic tray and scooted closer to me. After plucking a rag from the pile of many other dirty rags, he swiped away the splotch of red.

"Now it just looks like dried blood," I told him.

"It definitely doesn't." He wrapped an arm around my waist, his hand fitting easily against my ribs with my bump now gone. He kept it high enough that it didn't graze my lower belly where my C-section scar sat, knowing the spot was still sensitive for me. "But that's what makes these memories even better."

I rested my head on his shoulder, finding the courage to smile at my mess-up. Beckham wanted these echoes of our past, whether it involved the holidays or making a handmade bookshelf look like a barn.

"I guess the imperfections make it a little more perfect," I surmised.

"For us, everything is perfect." He pressed a kiss to my hair. "Even if it looks like a murder scene."

My jaw fell with a gasp, and then I grabbed my red-coated paintbrush and smeared it down the side of his face. The streak coated not only the entire left side of his face but also a portion of his mustache and lips. He sat there, frozen, with his mouth pressed into a thin line.

I couldn't help the giggle that left me, a snort following in its wake. The sound had him cracking a smile, but when he quickly turned serious again, it wasn't hard to guess what he was thinking.

I scrambled to my feet, moving faster than ever to make headway before he inevitably caught up to me, but it was no use. Before I could take a single step, his arms wrapped around me and he pressed the white paintbrush down my neck.

"Beckham!" I shrieked. "That's cold!"

He made a shushing noise in my ear. "You're going to wake the baby." Yet he still dragged the brush lower until it hit the top of my overalls.

I warily glanced over at our son where he slept in his bassinet. We brought it out on the porch often, the fresh air the easiest way to calm him when he was fussy. "Nothing's waking that baby."

I spun in Beckham's arms, grinning wide at the sight of his half-red face.

"What's so funny?" he asked, smirking.

My head bobbed back and forth as I reached up to wipe a bit off his mustache. It still felt surreal sometimes to have Beckham in this way. Over the last eleven weeks, we'd grown so much not only as individuals, but also together. Poop explosions and sleepless nights will do that to a couple. "I'm just thinking about how lucky I am."

His tongue darted over his lip, and his expression flashed sour as the taste of paint likely hit him. But his smile was back in a split second. "Well don't think too hard. You might start to come to your senses."

I set a palm on his chest, shaking my head. "All my senses are right here, and they're completely obsessed with you."

"Obsession doesn't even begin to describe the way I feel about you," he murmured, inching his face closer to mine. His eyes turned hungry, his hold on me changing from playful to possessive. "You really think he'll stay asleep?" he whispered in my ear before pressing a kiss right behind it.

I nodded, tilting my chin up ever so slightly to give him more access. "Yes."

His arms fell from around me. "I'll wheel him in. You go get undressed."

He moved so quickly, I couldn't help but laugh at his impatience.

"We have thirty minutes before we need to go," I reminded him.

"I know," he said hurriedly, waving at me to hurry inside.

With our paintbrushes abandoned and the bookshelf drying, we were quiet as could be as we headed inside. Each bump of the bassinet had us bracing for his eyes opening or his body moving, but the one thing I had to give our son credit for was his ability to sleep like the dead.

Then, with him safe in his nursery and the baby monitor on, Beckham showed me all the ways he loved me. He kissed every inch of me, murmured sweet and dirty words into every crevice of my body, and trailed a heart around my healing scar.

Twenty minutes later, we were quickly scrubbing the paint off ourselves before dressing. I fed the baby while Beckham prepped the diaper bag and got everything we needed into the truck. We left late, but that was our new norm.

Thankfully, I didn't think the person we were going to meet would mind.

When we arrived at the Bronsons' ranch, Bucky was tied to the pasture fence like Bailey had promised. There wasn't a person in sight as we climbed out of the vehicle and wrapped the baby in a lightweight swaddle. We made our way over to the fence, slipped past the gate, and came up beside Bucky.

A coo sounded from my arms, and I looked down to find the love of my life with his big eyes on the horse beside us.

He'd been curious about horses since the day he was born, and anytime he was around them, he'd light up like he was the happiest baby in the world.

Beckham slid Bucky's halter off, then wrapped an arm around my shoulders and led us deeper into the field. Bucky followed alongside us, just like he always did —except this time, he glanced over every few steps, intently focused on the bundle in my arms. At one point, he stuck his nose over and sniffed the baby's feet.

We didn't walk far, but from where we eventually came to a stop, the Bronsons' house and barns were a speck in the distance.

We'd been meaning to come out here sooner, but with the colder months and me healing from my C-section, waiting was the best choice for me and our baby. But now, as I watched Beckham's shoulders visibly loosen, and how he turned his head to the sky with his eyes closed, a breeze rustling his growing hair, I regretted not coming weeks ago.

We stayed standing, looking out at the setting sun and the vibrant orange it cast across the moving fields. Rather than grazing like he typically did, Bucky aimed his full attention on our baby. His ears were perked, his nostrils flaring as he inhaled his sweet scent.

Beckham reached into the pocket of his jeans, pulling out the flimsy paper he'd written so many thoughts on. The creases were nearly holes from the number of times he'd folded it, the structure barely holding together after all the time spent in his pocket.

He exhaled, staring at the note in his hand. But instead of unfolding it and reading the unspoken words, he knelt and dug a little hole in the dirt with his fingers. He crumpled the paper into a small ball, then stuffed it inside the hole. He hesitated, gaze stuck on the paper, before lightly covering it with the discarded dirt.

Then he stood, coming back to my side and wrapping an arm around my waist. He looked down at me, and I gave a small nod of encouragement.

With a heavy swallow, he turned his gaze to the setting sun.

"It's me again." Beckham rolled his lips into a thin line, like he was trying to hold it together, and I leaned into him a little more to let him know I was here.

"I have a baby now." His voice cracked on the last word, and he shook his head with a chuckle. "Crazy, right? Who would have thought I'd be a father? 'Cause I sure as hell thought all bets on that were off." He looked down at me, so many emotions floating in his eyes. "But even though you never met her, you always knew she was the one for me." His focus turned back to the horizon. "You always told me the universe worked in funny ways, and that everything happened for a reason. Though you had a hard time backing that up when you snapped your wrist and couldn't ride for months. But that's neither here nor there." His mouth quirked into a small smile.

"I've been hard on myself for a long time. Gone over a million different ways I might have been able to save you. But like you said, things happen for a reason, yeah? I didn't want to think of any positives for who knows how long. But I always kept coming back to that. And I got to thinking, maybe I can hate the process, but your stubborn ass got me here. You led me back to her. I came home because of you. Went to the second funeral in my damn life because of you, and while I wish I could say I still hadn't attended a single one, I can't hate what came out in the end. So..."

Beckham turned to me, and I transferred our son into his arms. I nuzzled into his side, arms wrapped around his torso, as he faced the sunset once more.

"Garrett Swan, meet Garrett Beau Bronson."

Tears slid down my cheeks, the droplets both happy and sad. At the same time, Beckham sniffled, and I knew he was feeling the same.

He confided in me that when his best friend passed, the hardest part was coming to terms with the fact that there would never be new memories. I was adamant that that wouldn't be the case. So I promised him every birthday in this field. Every Christmas, every new baby.

We'd visit here for however long he wanted to tell his best friend about all of it.

Garrett was still a part of every moment in Beckham's life. I saw it in the way the breeze brushed our tearstained cheeks, and in how the singular cloud in the sky touched the sun at that moment.

"I already know he's going to be so much like you and me. Causing havoc and loving every second of it. And your mom loves him." Beckham smiled, and I noticed a tear had stained Garrett's onesie. "She wanted me to tell you that."

Then he looked down at our son, and I looked up at him. He shifted Garrett so he was more comfortable in his other arm, and wrapped his opposite around me.

"It's a good life, Garrett. I can't wait to tell you all about it when I see you again."

40

BECKHAM

BONUS EPILOGUE - FOURTH OF JULY

"When he starts sitting, can he ride a horse?" Avery asked from her seat beside me at the—now extra long—table on my mom's porch. She'd had to buy not only a bigger size but two of them to fit all us Bronsons.

Avery had been asking questions nonstop, but I didn't blame her. If I was her age and had two babies around me, I'd be curious as ever.

"With one of us? Maybe. But it might be a year or two until he's holdin' the reins on his own," I told her. I'd already held Garrett a time or two on the back of Tex, but I wouldn't lie and pretend the thought of anything happening to him hadn't made me nervous.

He was in good hands, though. Especially where he was right now: cradled in the crook of my mom's arm, fast asleep, while she ate her meal. My dad sat beside her, arm around her shoulders and a thumb stroking her exposed skin. I'd never seen that man smile as much as he did at the babies in this family, like through his kids and grandkids, he was learning how to be better every day.

Avery stuffed a big helping of mashed potatoes in her mouth. "Can I teach him?"

"Of course. I'm gonna need all the help I can get."

Her eyes lit up, and she hadn't even swallowed her food before she shot off her chair and ran around the table to her mom. Sage was nursing their beautiful three-month-old daughter, Rosemary, while Callan fed her pieces of chicken on his fork. With Avery's arrival, Sage turned her attention to her oldest daughter, listening to every squeal with a huge smile.

Rosemary had the cutest dirty-blonde curls, thanks to Callan, and got her big eyes from her mom. Meanwhile, Garrett got everything courtesy of Parker, as far as I was concerned.

I never got tired of staring at them.

Every morning, while Parker nursed our baby, I'd sit there in awe, unable to comprehend how this was my life.

I got the girl. The baby. Everything else was simply in the background, as my universe revolved around my little family.

A hand rested on my thigh. "Everything okay?"

I nodded at Parker, folding my fingers in with hers and running my thumb over her engagement ring. "Everything's perfect."

She smiled sweetly, her hand still in mine as she

went back to discussing wedding details with Oakley on her other side. Coincidentally, Lennon had proposed to Oakley on the same day I'd proposed to Parker, so the two of them were having a ball planning together.

My other siblings were on their own paths, and I couldn't be happier for them. Bailey and Lettie had disappeared into the barn half an hour ago, like they frequently did. Reed and Brandy had made a mess of the kitchen while shucking and prepping the corn, their teasing having gone a bit too far. But that was what made our family so perfect.

We each had our quirks. Dealt with the things we went through. But we still showed up for each other in the end, whether that be for weekly dinners or when someone had a flat tire on the highway.

Maybe our paths to get here weren't the most ideal, but we got our happily ever afters.

And as we sat on that porch after the sun had gone down and watched Bailey light the craziest fireworks I'd ever laid eyes on, I knew one thing for certain.

I couldn't have asked for anything more.

The End

ACKNOWLEDGMENTS

What do you mean the Bell Buckle series is officially over?! Can you hear me sobbing happy tears?? The feeling is so bittersweet because Bell Buckle really was the series that made me the author I am today. I wouldn't have had the growth and opportunity to reach so many readers without these books. Bell Buckle was the series that showed me where my passion lies. It gave me the confidence to think outside the box and follow my dreams. Not only that, but it proved to me that I can do hard things. This series alone provides more for me and my family than I ever thought imaginable.

Moving on feels scary, but I can't wait to see where the future takes me. I have so many ideas I want to write, so many worlds I want to explore and characters to fall in love with, and I owe so much of that to Bell Buckle. Not only the books themselves, but to the readers who fell in love with them. Who stuck around and binge read them and shouted about them from the rooftops. So often, you pick up a book, and that's all it feels like: flipping the pages. But in doing that, you're changing lives. You're falling in love and getting lost in the words, and that was my main goal for this series. Bell Buckle honestly changed my life, and I know it's only up from here.

I'll stop rambling and get into the other sappy bits. As some of my friends may know, Down for the Count was one of the most challenging books I've written to date (and I've written a whole dang romantasy for crying out loud). I wanted to push myself to explore parts of my characters I haven't had the bravery to explore before. They pushed me and tore me down and built me back up, and I couldn't have gotten through the most difficult parts without my best friend, Bobbi Maclaren. You look at pieces of the puzzle I tend to skip over and are such an important part of my process. I see so many people dream of having a friend like you to bounce stories off of or to tell their crazy ideas to, and I'm so dang thankful I have all of that with you. Not only with the writing aspects, but being able to have you as a friend. Thank you for not letting my failed use of ellipsis and em dashes scare you away in the beginning.

Thank you to my best friend, Kate Crew, for letting me ramble on forever about things that probably don't make sense. For being on board with me potentially wanting to kill a character all because I was spiraling (I'd neverrrr, only simply contemplate it...promise...). You've not only made me feel so loved as an author, but also as a person.

Thank you to my PA for making the best dang marketing plan for this book. You've helped me reach goals I didn't think I'd hit, and helped keep my scattered brain together.

To my family for letting me hide away and write like

my life depends on it, and for my son learning how to independent play so I don't have to write at night anymore (you're the best for that honestly. I'm cranky with no sleep).

Thank you to my content team sticking with me despite the weird lulls I go through when I'm on deadline because I'm so low energy and have a hard time balancing communicating. I love and appreciate you all so much!

To my ARC team for always being so excited for the next release. I promise, if I could send you it all months before release, I would. I'm just as impatient as you!!

To Ali Clemons!!! Ma'am!!! YOU made the face of this series. You gave Bell Buckle its own visual personality, creating the most beautiful covers that catch people's eye. This series will always hold a little piece of you in its heart.

To my editors for being amazing and perfecting all these words. I don't know how you do it, but man am I glad for it!!

To my beta team, you have no idea how much I love all of you! You see all my little mistakes and still say "wow this is so good!!!" (While critiquing of course) so thank you for never failing to boost my confidence in my stories.

And lastly, I want to acknowledge all the people who have had to cut out family for being toxic. Blood or not, we know our worth, and we deserve to be treated well. It can be such a hard transition, and an even harder life to cope with after the fact, but no one and nothing is more important than your mental health. Deciding you can't deal with the behavior any longer is not saying you're weak. It's showing your strength. Know that through every hard holiday or life event, we can get through this.

MORE BOOKS BY KARLEY BRENNA

Bell Buckle series

Spur of the Moment

Beat around the Bush

Scrape the Barrel

Bite the Bullet

Down for the Count

Whiskey Ridge series

Swallow Your Fear

Never Fear

Secrets of Serpentine series

Deadwood

ABOUT THE AUTHOR

Karley Brenna lives in a small town in the middle of nowhere out west with her fiancé, son, and herd of pets. Her hobbies include writing, reading countless books heavy on romance, and listening to country music for hours. If she's not at home, she's either at a bookstore or getting lost in the hills on horseback. To stay up to date with Karley's future projects, follow her on social media @authorkarleybrenna.

9 798988 818496